CURSES OF OLYMPUS

THE OLYMPUS TRILOGY
BOOK TWO

RIVER BENNET

For licensing permissions contact: riverbennetauthor@gmail.com

Developmental Editor: Jodana Thompson - The Untold Story

Edited by: Enchanted Author Co.

Cover by: Shannon Maer

ISBN: 979-8-9891504-7-2

*"I'm getting tired even for a Phoenix
Always risin' from the ashes
Mendin' all her gashes
You might just have dealt
The final blow."*

-Taylor Swift

CONTENT AND TRIGGERS

This book is intended for mature readers, eighteen years and older. It contains the following themes and situations. Please review the them before reading:

Abduction
Anxiety
Assault
Attempted Murder
Attempted Rape
Blood
Death
Emotional Abuse
Fire
Kidnapping
Murder
Physical Abuse
PTSD
Snakes
Spiders
Torture
Violence
War

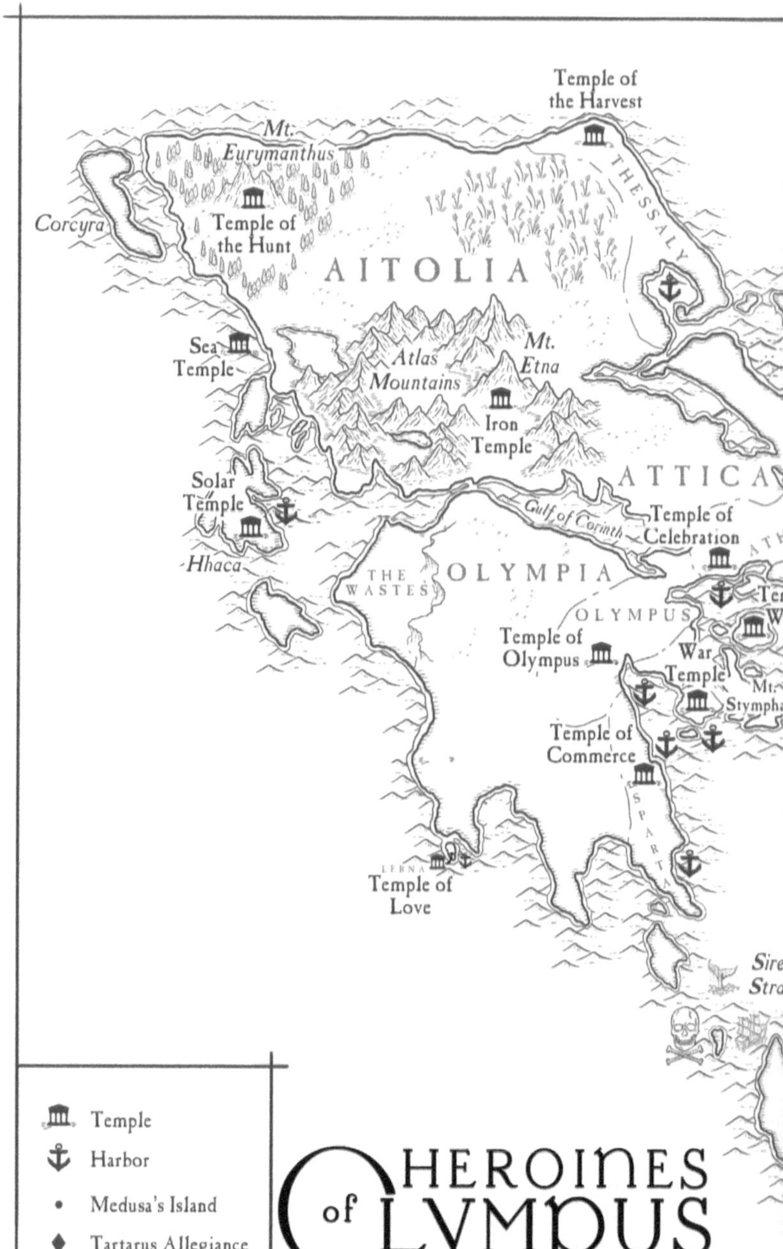

Heroines of Olympus

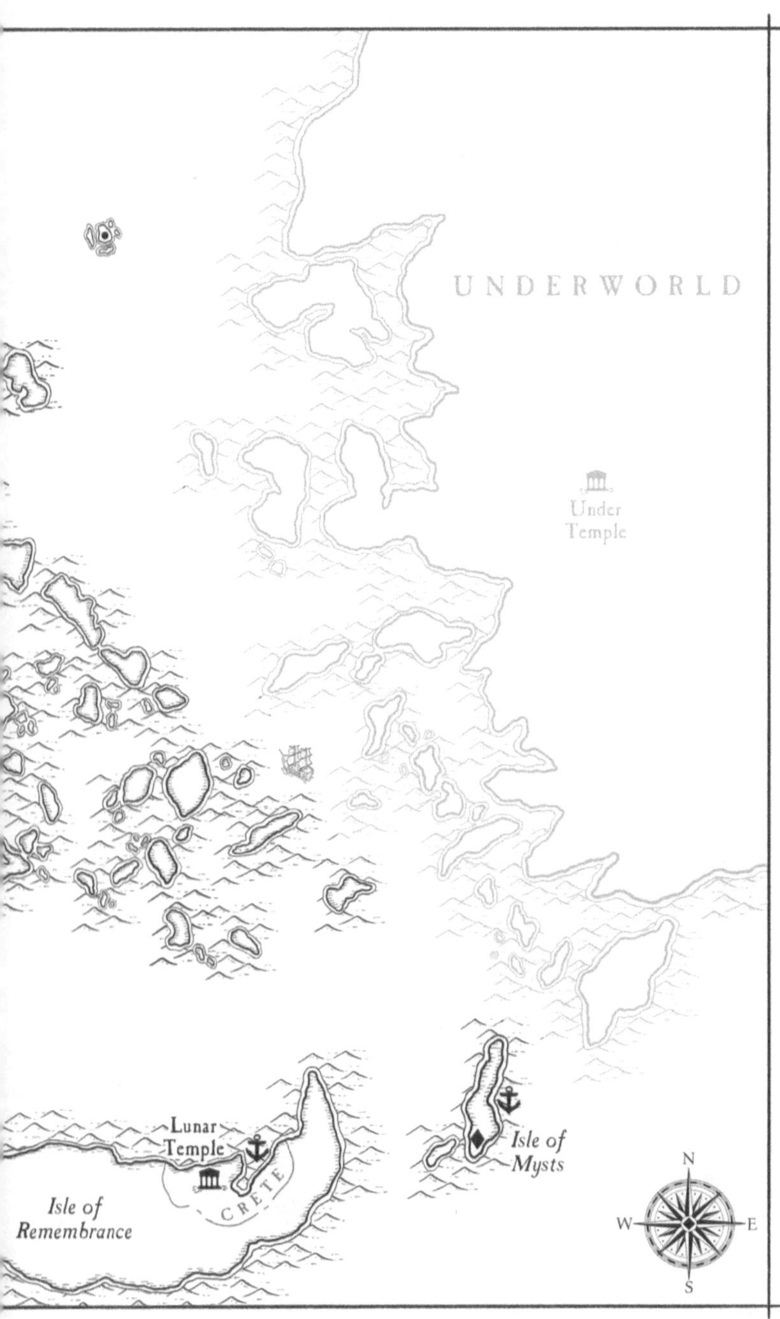

UNDERWORLD
Under Temple
Lunar Temple
CRETE
Isle of Remembrance
Isle of Mysts
N
W   E
S

1

MEDUSA

*M*edusa's hip slams into a pillar, and she lets out a grunt as pain explodes from the impact. She won't cry out. No, she won't give them that, if she can help it.

The more she shows weakness, the more they enjoy it.

The door slams shut, leaving her alone in the confines of this new place. At least her wrists are finally unshackled, and she is free from the cage on Poseidon's ship.

Her serpents slither and hiss in agitation, despite the hood that should be keeping them docile. The connection between them and her emotions is something Medusa hopes she can master eventually... if she ever makes it out of here.

The thick metal door is heavy and doesn't budge no matter how much she pulls and pushes against it. The sconces illuminating the room far above her reach cast an eerie glow from the everflames. There is nothing in the barren space except for a small hot spring, and a stone slab with a mattress on it.

At first glance, one wouldn't think they were in a cell. Perhaps that's the point. To disarm the prisoners, lull them into complacency. That will never happen with her.

This shall not break me.

She rubs the bruise forming on her hip and tries to keep the panic from setting in as it's becoming more and more obvious that the only way out of this room is through that door. Meanwhile, her mind works to commit the twists and turns of the hallways of the Sea Temple to memory, detailing which way to go.

Turn left at the giant painting of Poseidon with enslaved women at his feet. Another left where the hallways intersect with each other. Take an immediate right, then there are marble circular stairs on the right that wind down into the dungeons.

It should be easy enough to backtrack, but will that way be too visible? If her brief time in the temple is any indication, there are Heroes, gods, and nymphs coming and going constantly.

Medusa sags her shoulders as she looks around the small room in despair. The walls of dark blue stone are bare, cold, and uninviting.

The bed isn't horrifically uncomfortable as she lays down, taking a moment to be thankful it is not merely a block of the same material of the walls. The more rested she is, the better she stands a chance of getting through whatever she may have to endure while she is here.

Closing her eyes, Medusa focuses on the mental connection she shares with her serpents. If she can grasp onto their threads of consciousness, maybe it will allow her to be in control of them, as opposed to her emotions.

The door opens about a foot, creaking loudly. Medusa immediately reaches for her hood, ready to end whoever is here to hurt her. An armored hand shoves a frail young woman into the room, a nymph. She holds a tray of food and a pitcher of water, and Medusa releases her grip on her hood.

"If you try anything, Viper, I have strict orders to execute the nymph," a gruff voice calls. His face is still hidden by the door, and his fear of her is palpable in his voice. Good. "Poseidon may not care about her useless life, but he knows you do."

Fates be damned, he has a point. Medusa looks to the nymph who trembles with fear. She drops the tray on the closest stone table, almost spilling its contents, before darting out of the room.

With a sigh, Medusa glances at the tray. The food smells divine, and she desperately needs the water, but she doesn't trust it not to be drugged.

An hour later, the door opens again, and the shaking nymph is once more forced into the cell with Medusa.

"Same thing. Anything funny, she dies." The door slams shut.

Medusa flinches, warily watching the female.

The nymph with pale, bluish green skin looks to the tray and sees it's untouched, and tears begin to well in her wide turquoise eyes.

She says something, but it's so quiet Medusa doesn't catch any of it.

"I'm sorry," Medusa says. "I couldn't hear you. Can you please speak up?"

The nymph sniffles. "He... he said that if you don't eat your food, he will kill me, and my four sisters who also belong to him."

"That's absurd. You don't 'belong' to anyone! Why does he want me to eat this food so badly?" Medusa asks even though she doesn't expect the nymph to have an answer. "What's your name?"

"Echo," the girl mumbles.

"Why do you look so scared of me, Echo?"

"They told me that they probably wouldn't have to kill me because you would beat them to it. They said you are heartless, and a monster."

Medusa nearly scoffs. "And now that you've met me, do I really seem like a monster to you?"

Echo looks up into her eyes, really looks. "No."

"Echo?"

"Yeah?"

"Is the food poisoned?"

Her teal cheeks flush pink, and she drops her gaze. "It won't kill you. It's just to make you sleep for a little while."

A fist bangs against the door, and the same guard from earlier calls, "I'm coming back in there in ten minutes. I sure hope that plate is empty."

Medusa picks up the bread and dips it into the stew. Instinct roars inside her as she braces herself and takes a bite.

It is delicious, but it doesn't mask the taste of poppy. She quickly clears the plate and lies down.

The door opens, and Echo hurries out with the empty tray. Medusa's eyelids grow heavy. Fear claws at her chest. What is she going to wake up to? Her thoughts race between images of people touching her, hurting her, but it's not enough to keep her from being pulled under by the flower's toxins.

Suddenly, her eyes blink open. She's groggy from the drugs and tries to recognize her surroundings. Her senses are dulled, but she can feel sand beneath her fingers. It can't be...

"Medusa?"

She jolts up and turns around. Sitting in the sand, glowing in the soft lights of the Oasis, is Psyche.

"How is this happening?" Medusa asks in surprise. She wants to embrace Psyche but hesitates. Is this a dream? Did the poppy induce vivid hallucinations in her sleep?

Psyche looks at her hands and then to Medusa. "I don't know. I've never had a connection in the Oasis with someone who wasn't present with me," she admits.

"Are you real? I don't think I could bear it if you weren't."

Psyche throws her arms around Medusa. "I'm real. This is real."

Medusa kisses her deeply. The feeling is muted because of the Oasis but even so, it's almost enough to make Medusa forget where she is in reality.

Psyche peppers Medusa's face with small kisses. "Are you alright? Has he hurt you?" she asks, voice tinged with worry.

Medusa tucks a loose strand of Psyche's raven locks behind her ear. "I'm fine, so far. I don't intend to be here long. I'm going to find a way out."

Psyche abruptly pulls back. "No. You're just going to get yourself killed. Please, say you'll wait for us. Cadmus and I are coming for you."

"Cadmus?" Medusa shakes her head. "Why would he care enough to risk coming for me?"

"My love," Psyche says, gently running her hand up and down Medusa's arm, softly caressing it. "Do you really think he doesn't see the universe in your eyes the way I do? Do you think he hasn't been anxiously pacing, breaking things in frustration, missing you?"

"I don't know what to think. I don't know what that means for us."

Psyche opens her mouth to answer, but the Oasis is violently ripped away from Medusa as she comes crashing back to reality. She chokes and sputters from water poured on her as she regains consciousness and realizes she is strapped to a table.

HESTIA

A chill runs across Hestia's skin, leaving goosebumps in its wake as the Allegiance ship sails through the last of the Myst. On this side of the thin veil, the world casts darkness in the absence of the sun, and she can barely make out Isadora and Cassandra to her right. The water below is pitch-black, and the only evidence of its existence is the gentle sound of it lapping against the hull.

In front of them is the soft glow of the dimly lit harbor. On a distant hillside, braziers are lit along a series of stone steps ascending to the Under Temple.

She looks behind her, back the way they came, to the lantern lights on the masts of the other vessels. It took twenty ships to get everyone and their essentials evacuated from the Isle, and Hestia breathes a sigh of relief that they are all safely here.

As they approach the small dock, the other ships hang back and wait. On the ground, people hurriedly move about to prepare for the influx of Allegiance members and refugees. Red hair catches her eye, and she smiles. Hades.

Hestia has always found him to be kind and genuine, and she's grateful to know he is on their side. But will he treat her the same, now that she is a mortal? He does not have a reputation for treating mortals as less-than, but that hardly quells the tide of nervousness rising in her stomach.

Beside him stands Persephone, her petite curvy frame appearing slight compared to his height. Even in the lifeless entryway to the Underworld though, she shines radiantly. Her warmth is visible in her smile as she discusses and delegates. Curls of dark brown hair poke through the golden laurel leaves holding her updo in place. The light from the many braziers on the docks casts her walnut skin in a warm glow. Her fingers are intertwined with Hades's slightly tanned ones and Hestia smiles softly at the easy intimacy between them.

A little ways off in the distance is a small island where a figure in a dark hooded robe stands next to an empty boat. He then steps into the vessel and uses a long pole to slowly take the vessel along the River Styx.

The Allegiance ship docks, and their small group disembarks. Persephone beams, and Hestia can smell the hibiscus flowers adorning her hair from a few feet away. The vibrancy of the flower proves a stark contrast to the muted tones of this space between life and death.

"Did everyone make it here alright?" Persephone's eyebrows furrow.

"They did. We sailed at breakneck speeds, but the entirety of the Allegiance is here." Isadora steps around Hestia, greeting the god and goddess. Her tight black braids along her scalp fall down her back almost to her narrow waist.

"All but one." Cassandra turns to Hades, her long golden robes swirling with the motion as she places a hand on his shoulder. "There is much to discuss, but our first priority must be to recover your sister."

"My sister?" Hades repeats, shaking his head in confusion. "Last time I checked, my family tree was devoid of any sisters."

Cassandra's smile is gentle and her cloud of warm brown hair frames her delicate face. "You wouldn't have known because the Fates only just revealed that fact to me. I'm sure you've heard much about the gorgon, Medusa. What you haven't heard is that she is your half-sister. The Fates have yet to tell me how this was possible, so we're just going to have to go with it."

He blinks, not quite comprehending. "Medusa. My sister."

Persephone interjects, "You'll have to excuse him. He sometimes takes a few minutes to process big news. Come with me and I'll show you the space we've set up for the Allegiance. There's room in the temple for some of you. Please, let's get everyone settled."

Hestia closes her eyes to steady herself for a moment. This will be her fist time entering a temple as a mortal.

Will it feel different? Will everyone be able to tell just by looking at her that her immortality is gone? She knows she should be grateful to still be alive, and to finally get to be with Alec. But it feels like part of her is missing.

By early evening, all Allegiance members and refugees have accommodations. The encampment set up for them is truly impressive.

Where Hestia had been picturing tents, she discovered buildings, each with walls and a roof, with enough space to get the refugee families settled and get their supplies organized. The children were at first frightened of their new surroundings, but Cerberus came bounding through the camp, tail wagging and a trio of tongues ready to slather them with affection. The three-headed canine invigorated their spirits in record time.

Hestia now paces in her chambers. Things haven't been as easy with Alec as she had expected, not for lack of trying on his end. His love has been a welcomed joy, but she can't stop thinking about how that soul is now mortal.

She closes her eyes to think of him, but all she can see is the moon in the sky night, announcing the birth of the new Keeper of Flame.

A knock comes at her door. Her heart jumps for joy, but her stomach drops. She knows it's him before she opens it, but that doesn't stop him from taking her breath away as she takes in the silver of his hair and beard, and his steely gray eyes as they drink her in.

Another hurdle for Hestia has been her chastity. It wasn't a choice, per se. There just always seemed to be much more fascinating things to study and learn. Romance and intimacy beyond friendship never felt like a priority.

Until Alec. The times she spent alone in her library, dreaming of his touch, she never thought he would be touching a mortal body. Does that change anything, really?

Alec reaches out and takes her hand, weaving their fingers together, sealing the gesture with a gentle squeeze. Heat races from the spots where their skin meets, up her arm, igniting a fire in her that she doesn't know whether to stoke or extinguish.

Gods, they haven't even kissed yet. There was so much pain, chaos, and planning after her rescue that they have not had the time to properly dedicate to anything of the sort.

The rush of desire swims inside of her, intermingling with the insecurities over her mortal body. Alec has given no indication that he sees her as any less, but Hestia cannot help but think he *must* feel differently about her.

He fell in love with a goddess, for Fates' sake. How can her mortal body hold up to such a standard?

Despite the vortex of emotions swirling inside her mind, her mortality reminds of her one thing: her days in this world are now numbered, limited. Does she want to waste them by living in a state of uncertainty about everything? Perhaps this is more than enough of a reason to shove her concerns as far down as she possibly can, allowing her to attempt to love Alec without the burden of this noise.

She looks into his eyes, finding the intensity of his gaze a twin to the inferno raging inside of her. It doesn't scare her, though. The heat could never diminish the kindness and patience simmering beneath the surface.

He will wait for her. That knowledge alone is enough to embolden Hestia.

She gently pulls him closer, and his other hand skims along her cheek, sliding behind her neck beneath the nape of her hair. She leans into the touch and sighs.

He bends down slowly, inching closer to her face, giving her every opportunity to tell him to stop until their noses are touching, gently nuzzling.

Hestia almost whimpers when their lips meet. He pulls her even tighter against his body, a low rumble coming from his chest. She runs her fingers through his thick gray hair and his hand encircles her waist as he gently parts her lips with his tongue.

She opens herself fully, and their tongues dance as they cling to each other.

The kiss eventually eases off, and their faces part ever so slightly, still staying within a couple inches of each other.

"Wow," she says, and immediately feels foolish. One would think she is a naïve mortal teenager.

She may not have done any of this before, but she's read books. The never-ending pursuit of knowledge includes the more carnal side of life, of course. And all she could think to say is 'wow.'

Alec has likely kissed many women, and Hestia's heart falls slightly. There is no chance he enjoyed such an inexperienced kiss.

Yet he cups her cheeks with both hands and gazes lovingly into her eyes. "Wow, indeed."

Hestia blushes and drops her gaze, hiding her elation over his response. "Is that why you came by?" she asks.

"Why I came by—what? Oh!" He smacks his forehead with his palm and chuckles. "No. I wanted to tell you I'm leaving for a few days. We have to get Medusa. I can't just sit by and leave her in Poseidon's hands anymore."

Hestia nods her head as she absorbs the situation. "Who is going with you?"

"Psyche and Cadmus. Iris volunteered to be our captain again. We will take a small crew that they've assembled and leave within the hour."

There is some relief in the knowledge that a god is going with him. With her immortality still intact, Psyche bounced back from her time in the god cage in Aphrodite's temple so much faster than Hestia. Speaking of gods, while Alec is away, she can renew her search for Hera. Now that she knows Dionysus is in the Allegiance with her, he can be a more trustworthy asset and ally than she previously anticipated.

As her thoughts of Hera intermingle with those of her first kiss, Hestia briefly wonders what Hera's lips would feel like. Then shame washes over her.

Are these thoughts a betrayal to the man who loves Hestia, who saved her?

3

ICARUS

*I*carus's back hits the solid wall of the stable as her kiss with Aphrodite deepens. The horse in the neighboring stall whinnies in objection to the sudden disturbance, but it doesn't faze them.

They've had to be very crafty these past few days, with neither of them wanting to upset the delicate balance of their worlds by making their relationship known.

Icarus's dreams are within reach. She doesn't want them to slip through her fingers or their validity questioned because of her proximity to such a powerful god. Everyone would assume that nothing she worked so hard for was actually earned.

Is the scratchy hay as nice as the soft sheets of the temples? No, but it's nearly impossible to end up in those sheets without watchful eyes upon them.

Aphrodite's slim fingers deftly release the straps of Icarus's armor when her head jerks back and she lets out a loud sneeze, her pale blonde hair falling over her violet eyes. Followed by another. And another.

Icarus laughs. "I didn't know gods were affected by allergies."

"You think my radiant self is supposed to be around hay of all Fates damned things?" Aphrodite responds through puffy eyes and a red nose. "We have to figure out an alternative. I'll come up with something." She pulls Icarus in at the waist. "In the meantime," she says but is interrupted by another sneezing fit.

Humorously fighting tears, Icarus says, "Go, I'll see you soon."

With another sneeze, Aphrodite nods her head and gives Icarus a brief kiss before slipping out of the paddock door.

Pieces of hay stick out from Icarus's braid, and she meticulously removes them before leaving to return to the barracks. There is a bag of apples by the door, and she decides to grab one and double back to visit her pegasus again.

As if she sensed Icarus coming, Amara is already waiting for her in the stall.

"Hey, girl." She rubs her hand along the alabaster forehead of the steed that chose her. She hasn't gotten to fly on her yet, but she already feels bonded with her.

She holds out the apple, palm open, and Amara gently nibbles at it. Her tail swishes contently, and the bright white strands shine as if the sun or moon shines upon them.

After a few more minutes, and several scratches under Amara's chin, Icarus turns to leave.

Muffled voices carry from one of the small tack rooms in the back. Curious. Should she investigate? It's probably none of her business, right? The decision is taken from her hands and the door swings open.

Lysander walks out, and his cheeks flush when he sees her. His short black hair is tousled as if he just rolled out of bed. "Oh. Icarus. I wasn't expecting you to still be here." He abruptly closes the door, and the *thunk* of someone slamming into it rattles around the stables.

Icarus raises an eyebrow. "I was... spending some time with Amara." She leans around Lysander, peering behind him. "What were you doing here?"

His face reddens even further. The door behind him opens, and he winces as Achilles walks out irritated and disheveled, his dark brown curls that fall to his ears just as mussed as Lysander's. He sees Icarus standing there and straightens, adjusting his silver cloak and shifting his weight between his feet. "Oh, hello."

Icarus doesn't need to guess why they were in the tack room. If the order of events had been slightly altered, it might have been Lysander catching her with Aphrodite.

Silence swells around them, and the uncertainty of who should speak first lingers.

Lysander looks at her, his angular eyes pleading.

"Thanks for hanging out with me in the stables this afternoon, Lysander. I think us taking the time to get to know our steeds was a great idea." She winks, and they both look so relieved they could faint. .

Achilles brushes past them without saying a word. A quick, courteous nod is all the recognition she's to receive for covering for them.

The wool blankets of the barracks are almost as scratchy against Icarus's bare skin as the hay Aphrodite had been pressing her body into earlier that day. She throws them off, welcoming the chill of the night air.

A twinge strikes between her shoulder blades, and the dull itch that's plagued her for days returns. She walks over to one of the walls where the corner protrudes and slides her back across it as the cool stone soothes the irritation.

Are the blankets causing an allergy? Is she allergic to the hay as well?

When her back no longer feels as if it's on fire, Icarus sits on the edge of her bed, tossing the wool blanket onto the floor. She remembers the gift from Aphrodite sitting on her nightstand. It's doubtful she'll be able to return to sleep anytime soon, so it seems like the perfect time to try it out.

The soft petals of the rose slide across her fingertips as she picks it up and sets it beside her. Unfolding the parchment that came with it, Icarus reads the instructions again.

Place three drops from the bottle onto the petals of the flower, then touch its petals anywhere you wish to feel pleasure.

Moonlight shining through the small window reflects off the soft pink stoppered bottle. It's shaped like a heart and has a rose gold filigree cap. The aroma hits Icarus instantaneously after removing the stopper. Notes of rose, chrysanthemum, and orchid caress her senses followed by the subtle undertones of poppy and mandrake. The smell is sensual and enticing. It's almost tempting to bathe in it.

The dropper collects the amber liquid, and Icarus counts the drops around as she delicately lets them fall. "One. Two. Three."

Nothing happens at first, but as Icarus returns the stopper to the bottle, the rose begins to vibrate in her hand.

Icarus's brows furrow in confusion. What is she supposed to do with this?

She brings it up to her neck and the delicate petals tickle at first but when she applies more pressure, she feels her pulse quicken and her breath catches. Oh.

Moving it to her collarbone, and continuing down, she cups her breast with one hand and with the other, brings the pulsating flower to her nipple, sending a jolt of pleasure shooting to her core. Fates be damned, the Goddess of Love really knows how to give a gift.

When her hand travels to her center, she's not surprised to find it already dripping wet, and her fingers slip right in. She slides them in and out, working to a slow rhythm as she brings the rose to the bundle of nerves above her core. She almost cries out at the explosive sensation but remembers that the walls are thin, and the other Heroes will never let her live this down.

She turns her head and moans into the pillow as her fingers

and the rose push her closer and closer to climaxing. In her mind, Aphrodite's hands are her own, and she's using this enchanted flower to bring Icarus to her knees.

She pictures Aphrodite's perfect lips kissing every part of her body as her orgasm explodes and sends shockwaves all the way to her toes.

Her chest heaves, and she can barely catch her breath as her body slowly returns to normal. Wow.

Hopping out of bed, she slides on a loose tunic and soft, flowy pants. A hot bath will be the perfect thing to cap off her night before going back to sleep.

The halls are empty, and Icarus is grateful for it. Everyone has been respectful for the most part, but being one of the few women in the barracks hardly goes unnoticed. It doesn't bother her that they share housing, especially since women have their own rooms, but she wishes there were at least separate bathing chambers.

The baths are empty at this time of night except for one person, Lysander.

She quickly removes her clothes, not shy around her friend, and slips into the warm water.

"Hey." Icarus splashes him gently, pulling him out of his daydream.

He laughs and splashes her back. "Hey, yourself."

"So... Achilles, huh?" She grins.

He gives Icarus a pointed look. "So... Aphrodite, huh?"

Her eyes go wide. "What? How?"

"We had to walk right past the stall you two were in to get to the tack room, genius. Fates damnit, at least we went to a closed room."

Icarus's ears flush, and she averts her gaze to the water. "Whatever. I guess we've both been keeping a pretty big secret. How long have you been with him?"

Lysander shrugs his shoulders. "Just a week or so. We met the day of the pegasus selection."

Icarus had forgotten he was there that day. Now that she thinks about it, she can remember the sea of silver cloaks as Zeus, and his Lightning Legion, came to monitor Selection Day.

But truthfully, she didn't care who was watching that day. Her whole life had been building to that moment, and her dreams were coming true.

"What about you? How long has this thing with Aphrodite been going on?"

Icarus looks at the man in front of her, her best friend. She starts to tell him everything about the night of the gala and her phoenix curse, but something makes her hesitate. She trusts Lysander, but how much does she even know about it?

Wouldn't it make more sense to wait to tell him until she had a better handle on her past? Would he even believe her?

One way to find out.

She tells him everything. She tells him about the gala, sleeping with Aphrodite, learning about her phoenix curse the next morning, everything.

Lysander says nothing, sitting in stunned silence in the water.

"So, yeah. That's what's been going on with me." She shrugs and waits for him to respond.

Finally, he says, "Do you have any powers yet?"

A loud laugh escapes her. "Considering everything I just told you, *that's* your first question?"

"Well, yeah."

After a quick glance around the room to make certain once more that they are still alone, Icarus slides closer to Lysander.

"I haven't been able to do much with it so far." She holds her left hand out of the water, and tiny flames gently flicker from her fingertips for a few seconds before sputtering out.

She sheepishly puts her hand back in the bath.

"That's one of the most amazing things I've ever seen. Don't you tell a single Fates damned person about this. To be honest, what were you even thinking telling me?" Lysander sputters.

"I was thinking, jackass, you're my best friend and I need a support system that doesn't solely consist of my lover," she says flatly.

He side-eyes her. "I get your point. I don't think we'll be able to keep it a secret for too long, but it won't get out because of me."

"Thank you. Oh! Can you please, please, please do me a favor?"

"Maybe?"

Icarus spins around in the water, placing her back in front of him.

"Scratch. Please. Between my shoulder blades."

4

MEDUSA

Shivers rack her body, and the thin shift she has to wear does nothing to protect Medusa from the cold. She is still damp from her last session with the Twins, and she will never doubt the tales of their cruelty again. Their closeness to Poseidon is the only evidence anyone needs to condemn the actions of Castor and Polydeuces, but the brothers are allowed to use Sea Temple prisoners as their own playground.

Medusa's chest tightens as she recalls the way the water felt as it rushed into her airways. She was pretty sure they wouldn't kill her, but when confronted with the reality of the drowning sensation, she wasn't as certain. Her lungs and throat still burn from the sting of the sea water and her desperate gasps for breath.

She rolls over on the stone slab, avoiding the side with the bruised hip, wishing they had not removed the pathetic excuse for a mattress. Anything to make her more miserable, right?

Medusa closes her eyes, clenching them tightly as she tries to imagine the warm pools on her island. She pictures herself sliding into the hot water, inch by inch as it soothes her frozen body. When she opens them again, she feels slightly warmer, and the sharp edge of the glacial pain has dulled.

The door opens, and Echo comes in, but this time, there's no tray of food. She looks terrified. Is Medusa going to have to reassure her all over again? Poseidon steps through behind the nymph. Ah, that's who she's afraid of.

His dark blue cloak swirls at his feet, and the lapis stone walls casts his mahogany skin in an a harsh light.

Medusa sits up, swinging her feet over the side of the concrete slab onto the frigid floor.

This shall not break me.

She locks eyes with his deep brown ones, refusing to appear weak. She will never give him that.

He unclasps his deep blue cloak, and Medusa tenses. He hasn't tried to force himself on her again, not since the garden. He wouldn't do it now, with Echo in the room, would he? Her serpents thrash beneath the hood, their chaotic essence fueled by Medusa's fear. If only they worked on him. Between that, the restraints at times, and their use of Echo as a shield, she doubts she will be able to use this one cursed weapon as a defense.

He reaches out and tries to hand the cloak to her. When she doesn't take it, he leans in and drapes it over her shoulders. The smell of briny seawater and spirits hits her, and she's immediately back in the garden. Her body goes rigid, and she sits still as a stone, as if she too was a victim of her serpents.

After a moment of silence, he says to her, "You know it doesn't have to be this way."

She rasps, "Yes, it does."

"I'm a patient man."

Medusa laughs bitterly in response, and his nostrils flare in a rage.

"But," he continues, "that patience is wearing thin."

"I will never agree to your offer. I would rather die than bed you."

"Then soon, I will have no use for you."

He turns and leaves, dragging Echo by the arm as he departs.

The cloak is warm, but the smell of him makes her stomach

turn. She throws it onto the floor and lays back down, curling up into a ball.

And for the first time since being brought here, she cries.

Tears fall for the rebels, for the nymphs, for the ache in her heart when she thinks about Psyche, and even Cadmus. She cries for her family and what they've been put through, but she also weeps just for herself.

Her emotions are crushing, as if gravity is pulling the weight of the universe down upon her. This world is brutal and oppressive. Would to be so bad if she wasn't in it anymore? Would the souls that were removed from this world at her hand be waiting for her in Tartarus?

Or would she be in Purgatory? Definitely not the Elysian Fields.

She is still lying there, debating the fate of her soul, when Castor and Polydeuces come through the door. Have the Twins arrived to finish the job?

Their short blond hair looks green in this environment and the stony handsomeness of their faces does little to hide the monstrosities lurking within.

Castor motions to Medusa. "Let's go."

He doesn't have to say where. She knows they're going back to *the room*. Fear courses through her veins, but there's no point fighting. It'll just get Echo hurt. Wait, where is Echo?

She leans around Castor but only sees Polydeuces standing at the door. A million thoughts race frantically through her mind.

Should she try and escape? Use her hood?

"I said let's go." Castor walks up and runs his hand along her neck before buckling a collar around it. The long chain of the leash clinks against itself as the cool metal slides across her skin.

He yanks on it to pull her forward, but she doesn't move. She's done with this.

Fed up, Castor grabs her by the throat and forces her back into a wall. She sees stars as her head connects with the solid mass.

Her vision tunnels as his grip chokes her, but she can see Poly-deuces still at the door, smirking and enjoying the show.

Her serpents hiss and slither under her hood. They get restless when she's in danger, but Psyche's magic continues to keep them at bay.

Castor's other hand lands on her hip, and Medusa swats it away with what little strength she has remaining. A blinding pain explodes on the side of her face before she can process that he slapped her.

Through her blurry vision, and lack of oxygen, she remembers Poseidon's last words to her.

Then soon, I will have no use for you.

They might really kill her this time. What's worse? That, or the violation of her body?

Castor's hand is returns to where it was. She tries to stop him but no longer has the strength to raise her arm. Panic and desperation scream at her to move, to do *something* as his touch moves from her waist to her stomach.

When his hand starts to go further down, she croaks out a weak, "No."

He laughs and leans in, his voice a low whisper. "I'd like to see you stop me."

The last of her consciousness is fading, and she frantically tries to see a way out of this. She doesn't have the strength to remove her hood. Maybe if she tries really hard. She musters all her remaining energy but can't move. It's hopeless.

Suddenly, Castor cries out and takes a step back, releasing his grip on her.

Her lungs heave as air floods back in and her vision slowly returns. Castor gapes at his hand in horror and Medusa realizes... it's stone.

One of her serpents slithers back under the hood inconspicu-ously as Medusa realizes what just happened. They saved her.

Castor screams in pain, and Polydeuces runs over to check on him before turning to Medusa in a rage. Without a moment's hesitation, she removes her hood and mirrors the smirk Polydeuces had been wearing at her own pain as he turns into a statue.

She turns to do the same to Castor, but he's stopped crying and is staring at his brother. His twin. She could kill him now. She should. But the door is unguarded and now's her chance. She slips out the door unnoticed as Castor wails and drops to his knees before the statue of his brother.

His cries bounce off the empty walls of the low-lit hallway, carrying his anguish with them.

How does she get out of here? This wasn't well thought out. She doesn't know the layout of the Sea Temple, not to mention how she's going to breathe once she escapes.

A small voice calls from behind a large urn in a narrow alcove. "Psst."

Echo's small face pops out, and she hurriedly waves her over.

Medusa quietly moves in her direction and slips into the nook just as a patrol of guards turns the corner. Castor's screams have stopped, so they continue along their route.

"Thank you. I don't want to put you in danger, but can you help me get out of here?" Medusa whispers.

A flurry of emotions cross Echo's face before a defiant glint sparks in her eyes, and she nods.

Silently, Medusa follows Echo through the labyrinth of hallways that make up the Sea Temple. Echo quickly deviates from the route Medusa spent so much time remembering. Instead of turning left at the top of the steps they go right.

It feels like they are going deeper into the temple, and Medusa has a horrifying thought.

What if Echo is tricking me?

With no option but to trust the nymph, Medusa continues onward. There are so many ostentatious paintings along the way. Each one depicting Poseidon doing something vile.

Echo's eyes flit to one that makes Medusa's stomach turn. Poseidon stands on a hilltop. At his feet are piles of nymph bodies while he holds one in the air by her throat.

How can the Fates allow such evil to exist?

And they call me *a monster.* She shudders.

Medusa is on edge the entire time, anxiously waiting for the temple to go on high alert because of the Twins. Yet it seems Echo knows when every patrol is coming through and exactly where to be to remain out of sight.

Soon, they reach the underwater stables right when the guards are changing shifts, leaving the stalls empty of anyone who might stop her.

As with the hallways, the stable is carved into the same dark blue stone. There are far too many stalls for the surprisingly small space. Medusa leans over the gate of one of them and finds a hippocamp. The lower half of the stall is filled with water, but not enough for the creature to be fully submerged— like they should be.

Echo leads her to a hippocamp named Coral, according to the sign on her stall. Coral is beautiful. Her scales are iridescent blues and greens, and her long tail ends in two elaborate fins, like a siren's.

Medusa pets Coral's horse-shaped head, nuzzling her for a moment before climbing into the saddle. She takes the reins and really hopes it's similar to riding a horse.

Still silent, Echo hands Medusa an air stone pendant and gestures that the stone will allow Medusa to breathe underwater. Medusa is skeptical, but she'd rather die trying to escape than however Poseidon plans to kill her

As Medusa prepares to leave the Sea Temple, she turns to thank Echo and ask the nymph to come with her, but she's already gone.

Glancing around the stable once more Medusa knows she is running out of time, but that does not stop her from going to each stall and lifting the lever that opens the back door of the paddock, freeing every hippocamp from their enclosures.

Returning to Coral, Medusa climbs up into the saddle as shouts ring out in corridor.

Time's up.

Medusa prepares for the sensation of drowning, not confident in the stone's abilities, and clenches with fear as images and feelings from her sessions with the Twins come rushing back.

But the drowning doesn't come, and Medusa's breathing begins to even out once she realizes she is in fact not suffocating.

Which direction should she go? Her brows furrow as she peers around the endless water on either side of her.

"I don't suppose you know how to get me somewhere safe?" she asks Coral, who lets out a whinny that's muffled by the water and takes off.

The musty smell of the catacombs combined with the dim lighting of the everflames makes Aphrodite's head hurt, but she refuses to give up. She's going to find the witch and whatever Athena is hiding. What else does the Goddess of Wisdom whisper about to Zeus?

She should be focusing on Icarus right now. She still can't believe she found her again, but Athena's secrecy has taken over her thoughts. Something is afoot in the Olympic Isles, and she doubts it's solely the rebels that are responsible. It couldn't have worked out better that Icarus ended up being accepted into the Pegasus Legion.

Though they are keeping their relationship under wraps, it's extremely convenient that she's currently living on the same island Aphrodite is searching.

Athena's secrets could be anywhere in the Isles, but Aphrodite feels like Athena is wise enough to keep them close.

The wall is cool as she leans against it to take a break. She rubs her temples and stretches her neck, which is starting to ache. When she turns to the left, she sees a gap in the wall that wasn't there before. She takes a few steps back and looks at the gap head-on, and again, it's not there. It must be an optical illusion.

She grabs an everflame torch from the wall and steps into the space. The narrow path descends gradually, and Aphrodite delves deeper into the island.

When she reaches the end, she finds a large open room. It has a hearth that must be magiked, because she can't imagine where it would vent out. Dried herbs cover the walls, and the surfaces are covered with tools, crystals, and books.

A massive loom sits in one corner, but it looks like it hasn't been touched in ages.

She squints at a dark shadow in the back of the room, trying to get a better look, when two golden eyes come into view and a lioness stalks into the light, a low rumble of warning sounding in her chest.

She finally sees a woman sitting in a chair in the darkness. Her pale skin almost glows in the low light, and her long straight black hair falls past her waist. Golden eyes that match those of the lioness watch Aphrodite intently.

Her cream tunic flows to the floor, only fastened at the shoulders with simple, crude pins. She wears no belt giving her form a shapeless quality.

"Hello, who are you?" Aphrodite asks.

She is met with silence.

Shifting uncomfortably on her feet, she adds, "Will she hurt me?"

Silence, but the lioness stops moving, although she keeps her eyes pinned on Aphrodite.

Alright then... "Are you the witch?" Aphrodite wonders.

The woman's expression doesn't change.

"What are you doing down here? Are you a prisoner?"

Is this pointless, or is she just not asking the right questions?

"Is Athena responsible for you being here?"

At the mention of Athena's name, the briefest flicker of rage flashes across the woman's face but is gone so quickly, Aphrodite isn't even sure she saw it.

A sigh leaves her lips. This isn't going to work.

She turns to leave when the woman suddenly speaks.

"The fates of many may rest in your hands. An object of great power, forgotten by all, will play a role in the days to come. Something you possess, goddess. Can you see it?"

Brow furrowed in confusion, Aphrodite asks, "What do you mean? Is this a prophecy? Tell me, are you Athena's witch?"

The woman's face twists into a sneer. "I belong to no one. Leave me."

Aphrodite takes a step forward to protest, but the lioness moves closer, lips snarling to show sharp teeth.

She backs out of the room, slowly, heading back up the path and into the catacombs. It takes what feels like an eternity, even for an immortal being, before she is once again above the surface and breathing fresh air.

The guest chambers in Athena's Temple spare no luxury, and Aphrodite takes in the rich green curtains, and gold and silver decor as she sits in one of the decadently cushioned chairs next to the small table with her correspondence. How Hermes and his messengers always know where people are never ceases to amaze her.

There are a couple of scrolls from the acolytes in her Temple, filling her in on the goings on while she is away. She's been neglecting her duties, but this island is where she needs to be right now instead of her own.

The last scroll holds her son's seal. If throwing one's babies into the River Styx wasn't strictly forbidden, she wouldn't be having to tolerate him.

She opens it, and the message is short. "I won't be ignored, Mother."

Aphrodite crumbles the rough parchment into a ball and tosses it into the nearest wastebasket with a huff. She desperately wishes she did not have to avoid her son like this, but his behavior leaves her with no choice. Anyone else would do the same.

There's a gentle knock on her door. Aphrodite rolls her eyes and calls, "Come in."

An acolyte for Athena's Temple enters the room and bows to Aphrodite, waiting until she has permission before rising. Good, Athena trains them well here.

She is so pale, she looks like the sun has never touched her skin, but her hair is dark as obsidian. She reminds of her a younger, cleaner version of the mystery woman beneath the catacombs.

"What is it?" Aphrodite asks.

"The wise goddess Athena wishes for you to join her for dinner, if it pleases you, goddess."

"I'll be right there."

"Yes, goddess." She bows once more before leaving the room.

Aphrodite takes a moment to rinse the dirt from her feet from the catacombs and change into a fresh dress.

Her mind turns over the different ways to try and get information from Athena. Should she seduce her? That's regularly worked in the past, but it doesn't feel right now that she's found Icarus? No, this game with Athena works best when she's distracted but that can be achieved without sharing a bed.

She slips on a deep emerald sheer dress that has fabric ivy leaves covering just enough to look modest. She runs a finger through her necklaces before layering three thin gold ones, the longest of which falls between her breasts. This isn't any different from Aphrodite's normal clothing, so it won't stand out as strange, but she knows exactly what to wear from her usual wardrobe to hold Athena's attention.

The dress has a deep slit high up her left hip, and she accentuates it with another gold chain around her upper thigh.

The dining hall's vaulted ceilings still take her breath away. Beams of moonlight stream in through the large skylight, accentuated by the marble Corinthian columns.

When her gaze lands on the gathered group sitting at the table, she wishes she had covered up more. At Athena's side is her right hand, Telegonus. Next to him is Aphrodite's son Oedipus. The short curls of pale blonde hair, so similar in color to her own, is a stark contrast next to the jet black hair of Telegonus.

What is he doing here? Did Athena invite him?

She has never shared her struggles with Oedipus with anyone in the Pantheon. Not only would that show weakness, it would give them something to use against her.

"Athena, darling, you didn't mention that there'd be company." She turns to her son with a forced smile. "My son, how lovely to see you. What brings you here?"

To Aphrodite's surprise, his cloak isn't the generic black one the Heroes wear, but a green one.

"When I heard you've been spending so much time here, I asked for a transfer. The gracious goddess Athena was more than happy to facilitate such a request for family. Why have you been spending so much time here, Mother?" Oedipus drawls.

This isn't how this was supposed to go at all, as Aphrodite is now the one being questioned. Is that why Telegonus is here?

She keeps the smile plastered on. "I just needed a change of scenery. I was actually planning to head back to my island tomorrow. I didn't realize it would ignite an inquiry into my behavior."

"Of course not," Athena chimes in. "I've been happy to have you around lately; I think your son has merely missed you. It's a shame you're leaving just as he got here."

"Yes. Pity," Oedipus says through gritted teeth.

The rest of the meal is awkward, the conversation clunky, and Aphrodite can't be more thrilled when it's finally over.

She returns to the guest chambers and packs the few things she brought with her, before sitting down and writing a quick note for Icarus to let her know where she went. Training for the Pegasus Legion is going to keep her too busy for the next week or so anyway, so it's the perfect time to get some distance from Oedipus and try to figure out what object the mystery woman could have possibly meant.

6

ARACHNE

I cannot believe this is my life. Day in and day out, doing nothing but guarding this stupid goddess.

Dropping down from her perch on one of the grand beams of the abandoned temple, Arachne releases enough web to bring her softly to the ground. Having spent countless years on this island, hidden from the world, it is a miracle she has yet to go mad.

Soft humming carries through the large chamber from one of the back rooms, and Arachne hisses at the sound.

How dare she be happy. How dare she not be just as miserable as I am. Who pissed off Athena more? The goddess imprisoned here, or the beautiful girl turned into a spider and forced to be her jailor?

Every time Arachne lays eyes on Hera, it is a reminder that this is her unfortunate fate. All because she had the audacity to claim she could weave as well as Athena.

I was the absolute best at my craft for a human. Are the gods really so vain that they do not understand hyperbole?

A glimpse of her spider form in one of the broken mirrors along the wall is all the answer she needs.

The humming gets closer to the sanctuary, and Arachne ducks behind a shattered statue of a long-forgotten goddess.

Golden rays beam into the space from open spots in the ceiling, but the effect is more radiant than depressing. Despite the nature of this prison, it is hard to deny its beauty at times. Beauty that seems to grow and thrive in every nook and cranny as if the place possesses its own ancient magic.

Perhaps this is simply how lush and wonderful the world would be if the Pantheon was not running things.

The soft padding of Hera's sandals heralds her arrival into the room, and despite her disdain for the goddess, Arachne pokes her head out slightly to get a glimpse of her.

Hera's satiny brown skin is smooth, and her coral dress clings to her lush curves. Everything about this goddess exudes feminine. The sight stirs longing and anger in Arachne. Looking at Hera's vivacious curls makes Arachne remember her own; a paler brown than the goddess's but much longer.

The two of them have spent countless years on this island, but the time does nothing to dull the memory of being in her human body.

"I know you're there. You can come out, you know?" Hera's voice is soft with a lilt, gentle as if she is coaxing a scared child.

If Arachne were still in her human form, a squeak of shock would have undoubtedly left her. In this spider form, there is nothing but startled silence. She almost skitters angrily out of the room but instead comes to a halt.

I will not run from her presence. She is my prisoner, not the opposite. It might not be by choice, but Fates damnit, I will no longer tiptoe around someone stupid enough to piss off Athena even more than I did.

Arachne's spider steps are silent as she comes out from behind the statue ruins, moving into one of the light beams and letting Hera really see her. This eternity they have spent together has been a separate one, with Arachne always lurking and watching, resenting from afar.

When her reflection catches her eye again, Arachne looks and imagines she is Hera examining this creature for the first time.

What does she see when she looks at me?

The sun rays shine off her opaque white exoskeleton, and it shimmers an iridescent blue and green as the light shifts over it. Arachne's multiple eyes stare at her reflection.

Perhaps I am not so horrific.

Hera takes a step toward Arachne, and it snaps her out of her thoughts.

That single moment of vulnerability makes her feel raw and exposed, like a nerve fraying endlessly. It is disgusting, and Arachne shudders beneath the feeling.

Without caring how it will make Hera feel, Arachne races out of the sanctuary and out to the overgrown abandoned gardens, letting herself get lost in the smells of the wildflowers as they brush against her many legs.

7

MEDUSA

*M*edusa marvels at the large bubble that encases herself and the hippocamp. This is not how she expected the stone to work, but she doesn't care. She's just happy that it *does* work.

It is impossible to be sure where they are heading, but Medusa has developed a calm trust in her steed to take care of her. The most important direction is whichever one carries her away from the Sea Temple.

Who knows how many hours they have been on the move? But she has fallen asleep at least once along the way, that much is certain.

Her stomach rumbles loudly as she tries to ignore the hollow emptiness of hunger. Without knowing how long she and Coral have been traveling it is hard to say when the food situation will become critical. Does she have any other option other than to continue on their current path?

A light-headed fog is teasing at the corners of her mind. She would give almost anything for food, even the drugged food back at the Sea Temple. But Medusa would prefer a slow death from hunger than being back in Poseidon's clutches.

At least he didn't win.

Without warning, the hippocamp makes to ascend, their depth in the water shortening rapidly until Medusa can make out the silhouette of a ship on the surface. Her stomach turns to a ball of hot lead as she imagines who could be aboard. Will this put her right back in the hands of the Pantheon? Is it possibly that her situation is about to go from bad to worse?

Coral seems to have a mind of her own, however, and ignores any attempt to slow their trajectory.

I really hope she knows what she is doing. This shall not break me.

Night air slaps Medusa in the face as she and Coral break the surface of the water, the magic bubble bursting from around her. She gasps as fresh air fills her lungs. She had not realized how artificial the oxygen in the bubble felt until now; she had just been happy to be breathing.

A piercing sound fills the air, and Medusa throws her hands over her ears with a shout before realizing it is Coral's whinny. She has never heard one above water. It is hauntingly beautiful and ear shattering.

Lanterns rush to the front of the ship, and shouts carry across the water, barely audible over the sea waves rocking her and the hippocamp back and forth.

"Get me a dinghy NOW!" a voice bellows, one Medusa would know anywhere. *Cadmus.* His voice has haunted her ever since he was willing to risk his life for her. For Psyche. Since Psyche hinted that he might even care for both of them.

Medusa's heart soars, and tears fill her eyes as she breathes a sigh of relief and waits for Cadmus to reach her through the tumultuous waves.

Coral swims them closer, closing the gap between them, and Cadmus pulls Medusa into the small vessel, clinging her to him in a tight embrace before awkwardly dropping his arms.

Turning back to Coral, Medusa scratches under the hippocamp's chin. "You really did know where to go, huh?" she asks affectionately.

With a gentle bump of her head, Pearl says goodbye and disappears beneath the surface of the water.

The short ride in the boat back to the ship is full of awkward silence. What would she even say?

Strong arms reach over the side of the ship as an Allegiance crew member hoists the dinghy from the water, and Medusa is pulled over the edge into Alec's arms. He sobs openly, and she cannot hold back her own tears that she had yet to realize were even building. Not only does she have a family now, it is one that will *fight* for her.

In the safe embrace of her uncle, everything from the Sea Temple catches up to her. They would have killed her this time. Medusa is certain of it.

"Hey, kiddo, it's alright. We've got you. You're safe now." Alec pats the back of her head to soothe her.

A small tap on Medusa's shoulder startles her, and she turns around expecting to find Cadmus again, but her heart stops and the world tilts off its axis when Medusa sees Psyche. Reaching out and taking Medusa's hands, Psyche laces their fingers together while staring into her eyes.

"You were supposed to wait for us," Psyche says softly. Her tone is lacking the judgement and accusation that Medusa expected, and the relief is so potent it almost brings her to tears again.

"I was going to, but the situation..." Medusa struggles to find the right words. "It escalated. And I needed to get out of there. If I stayed any longer, they would have killed me."

Psyche nods, but her eyes narrow when the moon peeks from behind the clouds and the discolored parts of Medusa's skin become visible. *Bruises, so many bruises.* Her snakes shudder beneath her hood.

"The fucking bastard," Cadmus seethes behind Psyche. "I don't care if he is a god; I am going to rip him apart with my bare hands."

Medusa grits her teeth. "You're going to have to get in line."

Below deck, Medusa could cry in relief when her body meets the soft bed in the ship cabin. She is grateful for the quiet space away from prying eyes while she desperately regains her bearings. She could feel every eye on her, and while none of those gazes held the fear that some once might have, their concern, pity, and curiosity nonetheless crawl across Medusa's skin like insects.

Here, with no one besides Psyche, Medusa can finally breathe. Cadmus will likely join them soon, and she is grateful to have a moment alone with Psyche before she has to confront whatever his feelings are for her... and what hers are for him.

She looks at the goddess who is watching her carefully in the lantern light, and a thought steals her breath away.

My world will never again be complete without this woman.

The notion is terrifying, especially given the state of affairs in Olympus.

What will she do if something were to happen to Psyche? How is Medusa supposed to walk this tightrope of love and terror?

Perhaps Psyche and Cadmus would be safer if Medusa had remained at the Sea Temple. Should she leave them, and the rebels, to keep them safe? Preemptively cleave her heart in two now to avoid a fatal blow later?

As the light bounces off of Psyche's dark lips and disappears into her raven hair, Medusa already knows it is too late for that.

"Promise me something?" Psyche asks, her voice strained with vulnerability.

Medusa takes Psyche's hand and squeezes. "Anything."

"Don't be a martyr again."

Medusa baulks, but Psyche continues.

"I know you think you did it to keep me safe, but you have to know what that was like for me. To not have a single ounce of strength and have to watch the person I love sacrifice themselves. I thought I'd lost you, and it nearly killed me."

Pulling Psyche into a soft embrace, Medusa breathes in the goddess's jasmine scent. "I'm sorry. It was the only way out I could think of to keep you safe. I would rather experience the Sea Temple a hundred times over rather than know you are being harmed. I will always put you first."

The door slowly opens, and Cadmus tentatively pokes his head in. "Can I come in?" he asks softly.

Psyche nods, and his frame fills the small doorway as he steps inside.

He walks over to the chair beside the bed and takes a seat, weighing his words. "I figured the three of us should talk."

Cadmus looks to Medusa, who merely shrugs in response, and he takes that as permission to continue.

"I know you and I didn't get off on the right foot, and I do not place any blame there; it was more than justified. I know you and Psyche are close, but I'd like to think you and I have also become close."

Medusa raises her eyebrows but motions for him to go on.

"Let's put the cards on the table. This is ridiculous—dancing around feelings based on past prejudices and initial interpretations, when what we have here could be beautiful."

All of the air leaves Medusa's body, and she looks to Psyche while her brain tries to scramble over what Cadmus said.

Psyche gently places a hand on Medusa's shoulder. "Like I told you in the Oasis, my darling. That man loves you every bit as much as I do. And if I didn't think you felt the same, I would tell him to fuck off."

They both *love me?*

Medusa picks at the bedspread with her fingers, refusing to look at either of them.

Everyone seems to be making assumptions about how she

feels, not bothering to give her a moment to breathe and figure it out for herself.

Is that true, though? Didn't I know this all along? It was right in front of me, but I was too absorbed into my own world to see it. And can I blame them for bringing this to me now? Life is short, and Allegiance lifespans risk being even shorter.

It never occurred to her that a dynamic could be found for the three of them together. How did she not see it sooner? Committed relationships with multiple partners are not common in Olympus, but they are certainly not unheard of.

Lifting her chin, Medusa looks at Psyche, then Cadmus. If this all comes crashing down around them as a mistake, so be it.

She murmurs, "Falling in love with you, Psyche, was easy. I might have resisted, but it happened so quickly whether I liked it or not." She takes Psyche's hands in hers, and Psyche gives them a gentle squeeze.

Medusa then turns to Cadmus and sinks her gaze into his.

"Cadmus, I don't blame myself for being hesitant to trust you at first, but I do regret not thawing to you sooner," she says. "When Psyche said you could be trusted, that should have been enough for me. I knew I loved you when I saw how far you were willing to go for Psyche. I never imagined that it could be reciprocated."

Psyche reaches for Cadmus's hand. Pride plasters across her face, and she shines more brightly than the moon.

Medusa's heart swells when Cadmus laces his fingers through hers. She pulls at his hand, and he stands up from the chair and climbs into the bed as Psyche situates herself in between them.

Psyche rolls onto her side so she is facing Medusa, and the goddess pulls Medusa's face to her own, drawing her into a deep kiss. Medusa's soul sings in response as her body comes alive.

Running her hand down Psyche's side, Medusa slightly startles when her hand finds Cadmus's hand already on Psyche's hip. She almost flinches at the contact, but he twines their fingers together.

Psyche softly sighs at the kisses he trails across her shoulder. When Cadmus's lips reach her neck, his face is inches away from Medusa's, and they lock eyes.

With only a second of hesitation, Medusa leans toward Cadmus, bringing her mouth to his. She expects his kiss to be much rougher than those she shares with Psyche, aggressive and charged, but it is soft and tenderly full of restraint.

Medusa's pulse races when he lets out a low groan of satisfaction, as if he has been dreaming about kissing her.

Psyche cradles the back of Medusa's neck beneath her hood, and Medusa feels her serpents slither around Psyche's fingers. Cadmus brings a hand to Medusa's hip and the gesture, the feel of his broad extremities on her body, immediately take her back to the Sea Temple.

Bile rises sharply in Medusa's throat, and she fumbles backward on the bed, aggressively rubbing the spot where Cadmus's hand had been, as if she can scrub away his touch. Jagged breaths slice through Medusa as she spirals.

I won't let them touch me. They will have to kill me first.

Psyche takes Medusa's hand, and before Medusa can recoil from the touch, still trapped in her memories, they are in the Oasis.

Medusa blinks rapidly and turns her back to Psyche—and Cadmus—to focus on the horizon and let it ground her. The sky is dark like it has been occasionally, but it isn't because of the time of day in the Oasis. It is stormy, brooding. The kind of sky that will either calm into nothing or escalate into a colossal disaster.

Despite the ominous tone, the Oasis brings Medusa's heart rate back to normal, and the cacophony of thoughts finally dies down. She is safe.

8

HESTIA

"Try harder. There has to be something we're missing." Hestia pinches her brow and sighs. The search for Hera has produced zero results, but she refuses to give up hope.

An equally frustrated Dionysus responds, "Believe me, if I had anything useful to share, I would have found her already."

That's when she really looks closely at her friend. The wine colored cloak over his deep purple tunic complement the honey color of his beard and portly stature, but the low lighting in the sitting room fails to mask the worry lines creased into his forehead. Is it because he doesn't want to be caught helping the rebels? Or does he care much more deeply for Hera than he has ever let on? She's starting to bet it's the latter.

Hestia's reflection in her silver goblet greets her as she raises it to take a sip. It is astounding how quickly her now mortal body is beginning to show signs of aging.

The corners of her eyes show fine lines forming, and her hair is showing hints of grey. How long will it be until Alec no longer finds her beautiful anymore? She has never been particularly vain, but the way her gaze is so often drawn to her reflection now, one would think she is Aphrodite.

Hestia puts her arm around Dionysus's shoulders. "We'll find her. There hasn't been a lotus moon, so she is alive and still in possession of her immortality."

Dionysus rubs his hand across his face. "I guess you're right. I just feel like such an asshole," he mutters. "I'm just sitting here while she could be in danger."

"You seem to care an awful lot about Hera, Dio." Hestia gives him a pointed look, and a blush spreads across his face that sends a pang to her heart.

"The same could be said about you, you know?" He raises an eyebrow, and Hestia bristles as her heart pounds in her ears. She has no idea what she is feeling, certainly not enough to risk what she has with Alec.

"She is my friend, and no one is looking for her. It's not right."

"I agree. But why are you the only one, besides me, who seems to care?" he retorts.

She stiffens. "I don't know what you're trying to imply, Dionysus."

Dionysus gives Hestia an assessing look before getting up from his seat and making to leave. He pauses and puts a hand on Hestia's shoulder as he is walking out of the room.

The silence he leaves in his wake is unbearable. What if he tells Alec about this conversation? Will he reject her because of these feelings that Hestia cannot even be certain exist?

The nerve of him. Hera is my dearest friend. The only person who could pull my attention away from my books—until Alec and the Allegiance.

Hestia jumps out of her seat and paces around the room, retracing her interactions with Hera. Remembering the way she would light up when Hera came into the library. Or how when she found a particularly fascinating tidbit in a book, she immediately wanted to tell Hera.

Have I been mistaking romantic feelings for friendship? Can the two be so intermingled that they are impossible to distinguish?

The fabric of her skirts is smooth beneath Hestia's touch as she worries it between her fingers, itching to do something, desperate to latch onto anything solid as she attempts to rationalize every interaction with Hera.

Deciding the Under Temple Library would be a good start, Hestia begins the long trek toward the one thing she knows will ground her: research.

The rugged, unrefined stone of the Under Temple walls makes the hallways perpetually chilly, and Hestia wishes she had brought a cloak. The cozy hearth fires in the library motivate her to push the cold from her mind, despite her mortal body shivering.

Would a god be cold right now? Does it matter?

Any bitterness over her mortality is allowed into her mind for a single minute when the thoughts arise. A minute where Hestia is free to be devastated, angry, hurt, before she walls it off until the next time she can allow it again.

Perhaps one day it will be easier, and she will no longer care, but until then, her life consists of using all her determination to stay strong waiting for that blessed day. She can't even really talk to Alec about it. He will simply tell her that she is alive, which is all that matters. That's easy for him to say. He hasn't had millennia stolen from his lifespan. Her guilt over her lack of gratefulness threatens to poison any ounce of good that remains in her life.

Hestia almost lets out a cry of relief when she is finally before the hearth in the library. It is only now that her fingers are thawing that she truly realizes how cold she had gotten.

Rows of bookshelves that reach almost to the top of the low ceiling fill the outer perimeter of the room, with a small group of tables and chairs in the center. The smell of parchment and bindings floods her senses and she breathes it in, letting the comfort soak into her soul.

"Hestia!" a voice calls from behind, and she finds Cassandra at a table in a back corner, waving her over.

Taking a seat in front of Cassandra, Hestia glances at the book titles stacked on the table. The ones she recognizes are all about understanding the roots of prophecy and the histories of the oracles.

Cassandra shrugs. "I don't know what I expect to find in these. Answers? It feels foolish now. All of the stories in these books are about typical oracles, and nothing about me is typical."

Hestia lets the oracle's words settle over her. How much does she even know about Cassandra? It is indeed curious that an oracle was born outside of Delphi. What is more intriguing is how she ended up finding the Allegiance. Was it foretold in prophecy?

"It seems most of us have more questions than answers right now," Hestia offers gently. An undeniable truth if there ever was one.

Cassandra nods but then her body goes rigid. Her eyes glow white as she whispers in a low, raspy voice,

"Balances are broken,
and there are many paths ahead.
Prices will be paid,
but your goals can yet be met.
Go now,
if you dare.
What you seek,
is in the spider's lair."

Hestia glances around the table at Cassandra, Isadora, and Iris as they sit in the dining hall of the Under Temple and debate what the prophecy might mean. The wait for Alec's return has been excruciating, and she wishes he, Medusa, Psyche, and Cadmus were sitting with them now.

A large map of the Isles is spread out on the table before them, and Iris has been eyeing it carefully while the others debate. "It has to be Corcyra," they say.

"It is such a small, pitiful excuse for an island. Has anyone even set foot on its shores in hundreds of years?" Isadora asks.

Iris shakes their head. "No, but I think that was intentional. We are operating off what the Pantheon has told us for years, but this is likely a prime example of them skewing the narrative. They're hiding something, and it is there." They point to the island for emphasis. "Think about it. What are mortals told as children? That Corcyra is overrun with spiders. It's our best place to start, and it's far away from any Pantheon temples."

Isadora studies the map, carefully considering Iris's words. "We'll go as soon as the others return." With that, she gets up and walks away without another word.

Hestia has so many questions for the mysterious leader of the Allegiance, but they all fall away when a messenger rushes to their table with news that Alec and the others have returned, and they are all safe.

The moment Hestia is in Alec's arms again, the days of fatigue and uncertainty melt away. Hestia will have to say goodbye to him many more times until this revolution is over, so she intends to cherish every second she can with him, even if that means being courageous in the wake of her fears of intimacy with this mortal body.

Alec has been with mortal women before, and Hestia wonders if they all feel as frail as she does, or is that simply because she is used to a body filled with divine strength?

"What's wrong, my fire?" Alec asks, voice tender with devotion.

Hestia tries to shake the worrisome thoughts from her head. "Nothing. I'm so glad you're back."

The low rumble of his chuckle makes her knees weak. "Did you miss me?"

"You know I did." Hestia's tone is playful, but she adds softly, "It was like all the oxygen left with you."

Taking her hand in his, he brings it to his mouth. The scratch of his beard is rough compared to the softness of his lips as they brush her knuckles. His breath is warm against her fingers as he asks, "Can I show you how much I missed you, too?"

Oh gods. Okay. I can do this. Face my fears. You know this man. If anything doesn't feel right, he will stop.

Alec does not miss her moment of hesitation. He furrows his salt and pepper brows, concern etched across his face, as he takes a step back to give her space. "Please tell me what's wrong."

Hestia chews on her bottom lip. Things were so much simpler when it was just her and her books.

"I..." Hestia searches for the words to say this right. It should be easy, as words are her domain. But alas, nothing seems good enough.

Having never been intimate before, this type of relationship with anyone seemed like a possibility only in a far-off galaxy. Especially with a mortal body. She does not know it herself yet, and he deserves someone who can love him vivaciously.

Is it possible for her heart to beat out of her chest? It sure feels like it. At what point will the confines of her bones and body not be enough to contain this raging torrent of uncertainty?

"Hestia, I never dreamed I would fall in love with anyone. The Allegiance has been my focus, and I could not even fathom considering anyone worthy of being a distraction from that. Until I met you, I thought loving someone would be a liability, but I couldn't have been more wrong. Loving you pushes me even harder to make sure this world is put right. If I have to burn it all down to make it a safe place for you, then so be it."

Warmth floods Hestia's body as his words dance in her soul. And whether it is a mortal one or not, it is his.

Alec steps forward again but does not reach for her. "And as far as intimacy goes, we are on your schedule. I'm in no rush, as long as I can still hold you in my arms and know that you are safe with me."

That should be enough for Hestia to move past all of this, but she is too worried that he will not be satisfied being with someone so hesitant and inexperienced. Plagued by her insecurities, she fakes a yawn. "I am just so tired. I apologize, my love. Can we sleep instead?"

Hestia does not miss the flicker of confusion on his face, but he pulls her into his arms and kisses the top of her head. "Anything for you."

Silent tears run down her cheeks, and she buries her head in his chest to hide them as shame consumes her.

9

ICARUS

Fine tendrils of hair blow around chaotically, slapping Icarus in the face as she soars high over the Olympic Isles on Amara. Ahead, in the front of the formation, fly Athena and her second in command, Telegonus.

A particularly strong gust of wind hits the squadron, and every pegasus manages the turbulence with little disruption, but she laughs when she sees Lysander almost lose his balance on his steed to her right. Her friend is skilled to be sure, but like most other things, riding a pegasus comes more naturally to Icarus, as if the saddle is part of her and exists to get her where she belongs—soaring freely in the air, basking in the warmth of the sun.

The skies are clear today, and the visibility is staggering. Despite the squadron skirting a more isolated outlying region of Attica, Icarus can see almost all of Athens from here. It was a shock to be taken on a training mission so soon after joining the legion, but it makes sense given Icarus's skills. She does wish she had at least asked what they will be doing.

At last, the squadron initiates its descent. The adrenaline thrums in her veins, hungry to come out and play. If only her back did not itch so cursed much. Icarus refuses to see a healer for something so trivial, but it is starting to become a liability.

As they get closer to the ground, a small cluster of tents tucked under a rocky alcove come into view. The encampment would be entirely hidden from anyone looking in from the mainland. Several children run around on the beach as a dog yaps happily at their heels. A few horses are tied to a wagon, their saddles draped haphazardly over the sides of the cart.

Unless there are more inside the tents, Icarus counts twelve adults, three children, and no weapons. In the center of their makeshift campsite, a small fire sends up a plume of gray smoke, counteracting any concealment measures the group took when choosing their location.

They must be civilians. They seem harmless. Are we here to help them? Fates, why does my back itch so badly?

One of the group members, a petite woman with blonde hair, lets out a shriek when she sees the Pegasus Legion making their descent. She yells to the children, telling them to get into the tents.

Not here to help them, then.

A large man steps forward once they land, putting himself between the woman the squadron. The sun reflects brightly off Athena's bronze armor, the wings of her helmet casting the rays in all directions. It has a terrifying effect.

"We have no quarrel with you, goddess," the man says firmly.

Athena laughs but everything about it is cruel as she points to the flag. "Mortal, do not pretend you do not know what flag you fly here. I have flayed men alive for less."

Icarus's breath halts in her chest. She has heard many stories of Athena's cruelty when it comes to her enemies on the battlefield, but these people are defenseless.

Who am I to question Athena? This is what I've worked my whole life for. To be here, protecting the realm. If this is how Athena is behaving toward these people, they must *be a threat.*

The man's face pales, and the woman steps out from behind him. "Don't you touch him! Please, just leave us be."

Athena twists her mouth into a cruel smirk, but her voice is sweet when she says, "I'll just be on my way then. So sorry to have bothered you all."

The woman breathes a relieved sigh as the man pulls her into his arms, watching Athena carefully.

Walking her steed over to Telegonus, Athena's voice is so quiet that Icarus can hardly hear it as Athena orders, "Not a single one is to be left alive. Burn it all down."

Icarus cannot breathe.

Telegonus nods, his smile equally cruel. "Yes, goddess."

A shrill whistle sounds as Athena signals for the group to return to the air. Amara surges into the sky, and Icarus's stomach lurches with the motion as she joins the squadron.

The camp is once again hidden from view behind the rocks when Icarus hears the screaming.

The entire flight back to the Temple of Wisdom, the faces of the humans from before flash in her mind on repeat.

What could have possibly been heinous enough to justify the slaughter of those people? But Athena only has the interest of the realm in mind. I know nothing about them, or what they could have done. Athena is wise and strong. Wouldn't the Fates step in if she was a monster?

The questions still circle when Lysander finds Icarus in the stable brushing Amara.

"You've been eerily quiet today," Lysander says, gently nudging her with his elbow as he comes up from behind.

"Just thinking," Icarus mutters. She knows he is not going to leave it alone.

"You are never quiet, and you know it. Something is up. If you don't tell me, I'll just have to stay glued to your side for emotional support." He crosses his arms.

Icarus rolls her eyes, but a small laugh bubbles to the surface. It dies as soon as the woman's face resurfaces in Icarus's mind. "Hey," she begins tentatively. "Those people today..."

Lysander's smile drops, and he glances around to make sure they are alone. "Rebels."

Icarus's jaw drops. "The rebels? I only heard the occasional mention of a rebellion when I lived on the farm. I certainly never thought there was enough of a presence to warrant Athena hunting them herself. Are they the same ones who attacked the gala?"

Lysander blinks. "I forget just how sheltered you rural hicks are. Yes."

"Hey!" Icarus punches Lysander in the shoulder, and he winces but laughs it off.

"Telegonus is her resident rebel hunter. He is known amongst the Heroes for being ruthless. They call him the Bloodhound because he can sniff out a rebel anywhere."

"I never realized there was such a pressing threat against the Isles," Icarus says softly, but screams still echo in her mind.

Lysander nods. "I've heard some really bad horror stories about the rebels. If you listen to some of the Heroes who have been around for a while, they tell you things that will have you sleeping with a lantern lit."

"But why? The Pantheon takes care of us," Icarus replies earnestly.

"I know." Lysander shrugs. "I think they just don't like that the gods have more power than we do. Some people are threatened by that, jealous of it. They can't see how much we benefit from the benevolence of the gods."

"If Telegonus usually goes after them, why did we go today? They clearly were not armed enough to warrant more than a single Hero."

Lysander sighs. "To train us. Athena wanted to show us how much sympathy she expects us to extend to them. None. Even when they are unarmed. These people want to throw our world into chaos, upheaving our entire way of life. Don't we want to keep that safe?"

Icarus says nothing as she nods and runs her fingers through the flaxen mane of Amara, as a kernel of outrage sparks in her chest.

Shouting carries loudly as Icarus stands outside of the council chamber at the Temple of Olympus. After escorting Athena here this morning, Icarus and Lysander linger in the hallway as the gods debate the rising rebel threat. She was initially thrilled for a change of scenery and to see inside the Temple of Olympus, but now hours later, her armor is heavy, and her undershirt clings to her sweaty skin. The breeze in the air does nothing besides blow the hot air around.

Footsteps thud down the corridor, and Poseidon and one of the Twins round the corner. Fury radiates off the God of the Sea as he rips open the doors of the council chamber and goes inside. The Twin—Icarus has no idea which one—slumps back against the wall. His haunted expression leaves him appearing broken.

He shifts to adjust his cloak, and Icarus freezes when she sees his right hand made entirely of stone.

What kind of monster could cause that?

That pulls him out of his daze, and his eyes snap to Icarus. "That's right. Look at it." He waves it around animatedly. "That gorgon bitch did this."

"Medusa?" Icarus asks incredulously. "How are you not dead?"

The look in his eyes shifts, going from anger to pure hatred. "Apparently that was reserved for my brother. Polydeuces is dead."

The silence is thick, heavier than this cursed humidity.

"Was she being tortured?" Icarus asks, narrowing her eyes.

Castor spits angrily. "Do you think there is any justification for murdering my brother? Are you trying to make an excuse for that treasonous scum?"

Icarus puts her hands up. "Not at all, I was just asking a question. I'm sorry about your brother."

"He didn't deserve this," Castor insists. "Poseidon gave her a room and even offered to give her freedom. She refused him. He tried to tell her she was not a prisoner, and what did she do? She killed my brother and several of the temple nymphs on her way out."

"But they are innocent!" Icarus exclaims.

He scoffs, "What can I say? The gorgon bitch and the rebel scum she associates with have little regard for innocents the way we do."

Indignation burns in Icarus. Her heart shatters for the innocent nymphs trapped in the battle between the rebels and the goodness of the realm. How far will the traitors go to achieve their goal? What if more innocents stand in their way?

"We cannot let this stand," Icarus seethes as the doors of the council room open and Athena walks out with the other gods in tow.

"I'm so glad you feel this way," Athena says with a wide smile. "I'm making you Telegonus's right hand in the hunt. Tell me, golden girl, will you show them mercy?"

"No," Icarus answers through gritted teeth.

"Goddess, are you certain we cannot help you with anything?" The acolyte's voice is timid, and the meekness of it compounds Aphrodite's irritation.

Huffing at the sweaty tendril of hair that continues to cling to her face, Aphrodite snaps, "Get. Out."

She smirks at the sound of eagerly retreating footsteps and looks around the heaping piles once more. In her many years of immortal life, she does not recall a single time that she has stepped foot into the storage rooms of her temple. Piles of junk clutter every surface, and Aphrodite sifts through the ancient linens, dusty furniture, and useless trinkets.

"The fates of many may rest in your hands. An object of great power, forgotten by all, will play a role in the days to come. Something you possess, goddess. Can you see it?"

The words from the woman beneath Athena's temple cycle through Aphrodite's mind on a loop. What could it possibly be?

Coughing as she wipes the dust of the millionth painting away, she squints to make out its subject. Large stones jut out of the earth, with the ground around them peppered with small white flowers that feel so familiar, but she cannot recall why.

The paintings fall back against the wall with a loud *clack*, and she brushes the dust from her hands on her skirts before calling it quits. It has been an entire day since she last saw Icarus, and Aphrodite is eager to return to Athena's temple to see her lover.

When she reaches the top of the steps leading up from the storage room, Aphrodite pauses to check her reflection in the large mirror hanging on the wall. Her eyes skim over the familiar ridges and scales of the dragon that wraps around the circular frame, swallowing its own tail. There is a mirror exactly like this one in every temple, but if they possess any magical qualities, they have yet to be discovered.

Satisfied that her reflection meets her meticulous standards, Aphrodite walks the quiet halls of her temple back to her chambers. The ocean breeze fills the open-air corridors and wraps around the goddess, kissing her skin with salt and sunshine.

Soft rose scents greet Aphrodite when she enters her rooms, along with her curtains flapping happily in the oceanic gusts. A pang of homesickness clamors in her chest. She has spent centuries making her temple feel like home, but there has been very little time lately to spend here. It's all worth it, though. To see *her* again.

Guilt nags at Aphrodite, an unusual emotion for the goddess. This is Icarus's last life cycle. She knows she needs to tell Icarus but cannot bring herself to do so.

It will change everything. It will put too much pressure on Icarus to love me. She deserves to live this life unburdened with the knowledge that it is her last.

Snapping out of her thoughts, Aphrodite collects a few items and calls for an acolyte. A small girl comes running in, eyes wide as she awaits the goddess's instructions.

"Prepare my ship. If it is not ready to make for the Temple of Wisdom by the time I reach the docks, the next vessel this crew sees will be ferrying them across the Styx."

"Yes, goddess." The acolyte nods vigorously and quickly exits her chambers.

The private dock for the gods at the Temple of Wisdom is calm and quiet as Aphrodite's ship pulls into the harbor, sailing past the main marina and its cacophony of sound and activity. The vessel gracefully slides into one of the open spaces, and Aphrodite narrows her eyes when she sees Zeus's vessel alongside Athena's, grumbling under her breath. This will surely further delay her reaching Icarus.

Aphrodite recalls the time when gods could be with whomever they chose, when they were able to be out in the open together. It was during Andromeda's life cycle that the Pantheon's pettiness and ego grew—along with their paranoia.

Leaving the crew to handle the ship, Aphrodite makes for the main temple, walking as quickly as she can without appearing in a hurry.

Mount Stymphalia is visible in the distance behind the top of the Temple of Wisdom poking between the trees.

As she makes her way through the manicured walkways lined with oleander and poplar trees, her mind is a jumble of thoughts and worry. It is likely Zeus is here for an innocuous reason, but Aphrodite will be on edge until she knows what that it is.

Only a few steps into the temple, a low voice greets Aphrodite. "Ah. There she is."

Turning to her right, Aphrodite finds Athena and Zeus walking into the large foyer. "See? I told you we would be better off waiting for her here." Her deep red lips twitch into a smirk as her voluminous curly red hair tumbles over her armored shoulders.

"Aphrodite," Zeus begins, stroking his long grey beard, "what a surprise to find you here... again."

"I did not know my movements were being monitored and restricted," Aphrodite responds evenly.

Zeus laughs, and Aphrodite fights a sneer. "Nonsense. I am just curious. However, your deflection makes me question if the matter does not warrant further scrutiny."

He is suspicious. He will kill Icarus. I cannot lose her again—for the last time.

"Of course not. I just needed a change of scenery." Aphrodite pats Zeus's chest playfully. "Besides, I wouldn't expect you to be complaining about me being closer."

Zeus's eyes darken. "Indeed, I would not be, but this time you are spending here seems to be keeping you from my bed."

"My deepest apologies." Aphrodite paints a demure smile on her face. "I was unaware that our carnal activities were this important to you. I assumed the great Zeus could easily have any maiden in his bed and surely would not notice the absence of a lone goddess." Fluttering her eyelashes, she clings to Zeus's bicep in a way that she knows makes him feel strong and powerful.

"Until I release you from my bed, you are not to make assumptions about what I do or do not want." His tone is icy, his eyes hard as he glares at Aphrodite.

"Of course." Aphrodite nods, bowing slightly, fighting the look of disgust desperately trying to break free.

Athena steps forward. "Shall I have the most beautiful daughters here on my island rounded up and sent to your chambers?" she asks.

Zeus nods at Athena, only turning to leave after letting his stare simmer over Aphrodite for another moment.

11

MEDUSA

$\mathcal{M}$edusa stares at the ceiling in her quarters in the Under Temple as she listens to Psyche's gentle breathing against her chest, not wanting to wake the goddess.

She can hardly believe she is here, gently running her fingers through Psyche's raven locks as she tries not to think of how close she came to death in the Sea Temple. Yet it is a fate she would gladly walk into again, as long as it would keep Psyche safe, Cadmus, too.

Cadmus. She looks to the large empty space in the bed she shares with Psyche and *knows* his body should occupy it, and that she loves him, despite all of her best intentions not to. But she also knows that it is *his* hands that remind her of Poseidon's.

Thoughts of the Hero make Medusa restless, and she delicately places Psyche's head on the pillow before silently getting dressed and slipping out into the halls.

The quiet padding of four paws settles in beside her, and she does not even have to look down as she buries her fingers into the dark hair of Cerberus's fur. As if he can sense her unease, Cerberus has, without fail, found Medusa each time she has wandered the corridors of the Under Temple in the short time she has been here.

They do not walk far before she finds herself stopped in front of a door. It has been days since their ill-fated attempt at relations, but Cadmus was not angry like she expected. His patient and reassuring manner have been unflinching in the face of her rejection. Somehow, his presence is shifting from one Medusa is uncertain around to one she needs, even craves.

She lifts her hand to knock, but then she pauses, knuckles millimeters from his door.

What if he can never touch me? What if Poseidon has fucked me up forever? It isn't fair to do this to him. To string him along when I may never be strong enough for him.

Will Psyche be able to forgive me when I am the reason we can't all be together? Or worse, what if one of my serpents acts on their own like they did with the Twins? I can hardly bear the thought of something happening to him simply because he tried to love me.

Bringing her hand down to her side, she deflates, and fights back tears. She is too damaged for Cadmus.

Medusa turns to leave, but the door to Cadmus's room flies open, startling her.

His hair is wild and his eyes still red from sleep, but his face lights up when he sees her standing there.

"Uh. Hey." Medusa waves awkwardly, as a blush creeps across her cheeks.

A sleepy smile spreads over his lips. "Hey."

"I was just..." Medusa trails off, unsure what to even say. Her serpents are silent beneath her hood, and she prays to the Fates that it is a good indication that they do not see him as a threat, despite the way the thump of her heart drums faster in his presence.

"Come in," he says earnestly. "Please."

Medusa steps into the dark room behind him. A loud clatter and cursing come from the direction she last saw Cadmus, before the faint glow of a lantern fills the small space.

In a few short steps, Cadmus is across the room, the queen-size bed creaking beneath his broad frame as he sits on the edge.

Medusa remains standing, fidgeting with the hem of her tunic. She yearns to sit beside him, to pull his handsome face in her hands and kiss him deeply. To make up for time stolen from them. All three of them.

They were so close to losing it all, and yet the memory of the Sea Temple rises between them like a wall. Of hands on her body ready to take anything they desired, gifting nothing but pain and misery in their wake. This man that she loves is right here in front of her, but he might as well be a million miles away as Poseidon's ruin of her endures.

No. Poseidon will not *claim this part of me.*

Medusa crosses the room to Cadmus, dread and desire twisting together like opposing vines fighting for dominance within.

Standing before him, as he looks up into her eyes, she has never seen Cadmus look this vulnerable. Not even when he was on his deathbed after dragging him from the wreckage. His caramel eyes bore into hers so earnestly as she reaches out, hand shaking, and runs her fingers through his hair. His eyelids flutter closed, and he leans into the touch.

Cadmus raises his hand to caress Medusa's arm, but he halts when he notices her body go rigid in response. Understanding fills his eyes, and he slides back in the bed to lean against the wall.

"I'll follow your lead," Cadmus says softly. "Even if we just sit here and talk."

Medusa pulls her lower lip between her teeth. She is sick of letting her past steer her; she wants to take control. But what if she pushes too far, too fast, and ruins everything with Cadmus irrevocably?

"Don't shut me out. Tell me what you're thinking. You aren't alone anymore, let me in. Please," he pleads.

Medusa's gaze drops to the floor, but she knows he is right. If she wants to work through this, it won't be by internalizing everything. She loves both Psyche and Cadmus, and wouldn't it be so nice to not make every decision alone anymore?

"I don't want to fuck things up any more than I already have." Tears rim Medusa's eyes, but she refuses to let them fall. "What if I am too damaged to be worth waiting for?"

A fire burns in Cadmus's eyes as he responds through gritted teeth, "You are *not* damaged. Your trauma does not define you."

Medusa heaves a sob, and Cadmus continues.

"If you never feel safe enough with me to be intimate in that way, I will remain by your side however you will have me. I love you. I love Psyche. My heart has been cleaved in two, and each of you holds half," he murmurs. "It is done, whether I am in your bed or not."

Medusa wishes the tears running down her face were hidden by the darkness, but in her peripheral the lantern light glints off the silvery tracks as she climbs into the bed, crawling over to Cadmus.

Picking up one of his hands and then the other, Medusa places them on the bed firmly at his sides, and he gives her a knowing nod. Her heart hammers in her chest as she slowly slides one leg on either side of Cadmus, straddling him.

Medusa cups his face in her hands, leaning in for a kiss. Cadmus groans faintly as she parts his lips with her tongue and deepens the kiss. Medusa's caress travels along his shoulders, entwining into his hair. As she caresses his biceps, his muscles strain and ripple as he fights the urge to touch her.

Leaning back in his lap, his hard length beneath her has panic creeping into the edges of her mind. The slithering against her neck makes her freeze.

No. Please don't hurt him.

Sensing the shift in her mood, Cadmus's body language quickly changes from coiled tension to loose and calm. "Do you want to just lay together and talk for a while?"

Relief floods through her as her heart rate evens, and she nods in response.

He situates himself in the bed and then waits silently as

Medusa slides under the blankets and pulls him close to her, snuggling into his arms.

"Are you sure this is okay?" he asks softly.

"Yes." Medusa pulls him tighter. "Tell me about growing up in Lerna."

For the first few minutes, Medusa listens intently as Cadmus tells her about his childhood, but with her head against his chest, the low rumble of his voice lulls her to sleep in his arms.

At some point, Medusa barely stirs enough to register Psyche coming into the room and sliding into the bed on her other side. With the two people she loves most securely embracing her, she slips into the deepest sleep she can ever recall.

12

HESTIA

*H*estia sighs as the group assembled around the large table shout over one another. Debates about who will go on the urgent mission to Corcyra have brought the discussions and planning to a standstill. Most who want to go claim it is because of their loyalty to the Allegiance, but she is certain they are restless and eager to see the long-forgotten island, despite the rumors of massive spiders.

The journey is not a particularly dangerous one, with their path avoiding most of the temples altogether, but they will be skirting the coasts near Demeter and Artemis's temples. The two goddesses have thus far not aligned themselves with the evil underbelly of the Pantheon...

But as far as Hestia is aware, they have not aligned themselves with the Allegiance, either. Seeing Dionysus across the table reminds her she is far from knowledgeable of the Allegiance roster.

Isadora cuts through the cacophony. "We will let Hestia choose her crew."

Hestia's mouth falls. "*My* crew? Shouldn't it be Cassandra leading this mission if it isn't you? Or Alec? Or... anyone else?" she retorts.

A proud smile adorns Isadora's face. "Yes. *Your* crew. This is a knowledge-seeking mission. You will have warriors to protect you, of course, but it is you who must assess what we find and act accordingly. The oracle must remain here. She is too valuable to risk the Pantheon getting their hands on her. If she has any further visions bearing importance on your journey, I assure you it will be communicated through the stones you will bring with you."

The blood drains from Hestia's face. She does not feel even remotely qualified for this, but every member of the Allegiance puts their discomfort aside and gets the job done. She will not be a coward.

Hestia swallows hard and lifts her chin as she says, "If you are certain that it should be me, it would be my honor."

Alec pats her hand as Isadora says, "I am positive. You will have others with you who can assist you and guide you when you need it, but this mission is yours."

Hestia looks around at the gathered faces, all eagerly awaiting her choosing. She hardly knows any of them, so she selects the people she believes she can trust and would like to have on the journey, doing her best to actually choose those with skills to contribute. "Uh. Um. Alec, Dionysus, Medusa, Psyche, and Cadmus."

Isadora nods. "Iris, you will captain their ship. Pick your first mate and a small crew."

As they tell Isadora who they wish to have for their crew, Hestia does her best to hide the panic taking over.

I can't do this. I couldn't do this when I was a god, and now I'm not even that. I'm not strong, I'm not a warrior.

Alec strokes his thumb over the back of Hestia's hand. "There is nothing you can't do, my fire. And I will be with you every step of the way."

Gulping down air, Hestia lets Alec's words settle over her until her breathing evens out. She cannot believe this man knows her so well and can read her even when she is trying to keep her emotions in check.

Does that mean he knows about my thoughts of Hera? Am I so transparent that even my deepest secret is laid bare before him?

The group disperses with orders to be ready to depart in an hour, and Hestia does not say a word as she walks with Alec back to her chambers. He follows behind her when she goes in, as if it are his own room as well.

They might as well be. Every moment spent not attending to Allegiance duties, Alec is with Hestia.

Yet despite the amount of time Alec has already managed to spend between her thighs, they have yet to be fully intimate. As Hestia watches he take off his shirt, a shiver runs across her body as she remembers his lips on her center, fingers plunging into her.

She remembers the way he rescued her in Aphrodite's temple. The way he ferociously defends her peace. As each of his acts of service flash in her mind, the last of Hestia's hesitations melt away and she knows that she wants this man inside of her.

So much has changed since her lonely days in the library. *That* Hestia of the past would never let her dress fall to the floor like this. *That* Hestia would never feel bold enough to stand naked, on full display, for a man. Would never walk over to the bed, spread her legs, and tell him to take her. But *that* Hestia is not *this* Hestia. With a dangerous mission looming over their heads, Hestia feels every ounce of her mortality.

But instead of holding her back, this time it gives her the strength to push past her insecurities so she can fully experience the intimate pleasure that she craves.

Alec stands there, watching her, his gaze traveling over every bare inch of her skin before he takes off his pants. When he walks toward her, his tan muscles ripple like predator about to pounce, but his motions are slow and deliberate.

His hands are rough against her soft skin as they dig into her hips and he leans down to kiss Hestia's stomach, peppering gentle kisses across the delicate rolls of her body. slides his fingers into her already wet core as he stretches up and kisses Hestia deeply.

She moans into his mouth as his fingers torturously work her into a frenzy. Hestia is so close to a climax when Alec pulls his fingers out of her and lines himself up before her center.

Alec hooks Hestia's thighs over his elbows and pulls her closer to him as he stares into her eyes.

"Tell me you want this. I need you to say it," Alec rasps, his voice so low and gruff Hestia can hardly hear him.

I can do this.

"Take me."

"We can stop anytime you need to, my goddess."

She hates to ruin the moment, but she cannot help herself. "Please don't call me that anymore."

Alec cocks his head. "Of course. May I ask why?"

Looking anywhere but at him, Hestia answers, "Keeper of the Flame was my role as a goddess. My place in Olympus. The nickname is a reminder of everything I'm not anymore."

"You will never be anything less than a goddess to me. And if I have to spend every day for the rest of my life worshipping at the altar of *you* to prove it, I will happily martyr myself for that cause."

Alec kisses Hestia's soft belly. "Goddess."

Her inner thigh. "Goddess."

The other thigh. "Goddess."

Shivers cascade through Hestia. Tears stream down her cheeks mixed with whimpers each time his touch grazes her skin. When the word *goddess* leaves his lips, Hestia's mortality seems farther and farther away.

Hestia has read many books on intercourse and is academically familiar with what a woman typically experiences the first time she is penetrated, but now, when faced with the reality of it, she feels wholly unprepared. She never imagined she would have sex, so she hasn't given it too much thought.

But here, with this man who she feels safe with, Hestia is

ready to explore the carnal pleasures on the other side of this brief pain.

Alec trails his kisses up to her lips, centering himself between her legs.

He pauses with his manhood at her entrance.

"I'm ready," she whispers.

Alec buries his face into her shoulder as he slowly thrusts inside of her. His motions are tender and gentle as emotions surge through her. Love, lust, pride—joined quickly after by the now familiar sensation of her body nearing climax.

As her heart rate accelerates and her breathing comes out in soft pants, Alec's thumb finds her clit, and she soars over the cliff of her orgasm, free falling, tumbling across oblivion. Alec groans as his own climax rips through him, spilling into her.

After collapsing onto the bed, Alec pulls Hestia in for another kiss, clinging tightly to her.

After a few moments, Alec disappears into the bathing room.

He reappears shortly after with a washcloth. Hestia is surprised that it is damp and warm when Alec brings it to her thighs and gently cleans the aftermath of their lovemaking from her skin. It is strange how such a small act can be so intimate.

Hestia wishes the rest of the day could be spent lounging together in bed, but alas, an adventure awaits.

MEDUSA

The desert landscape mixes with the purple hues of twilight, and three bright stars shining brightly in the sky. Torches protrude from the sandy ground all around them, casting their group in a warm glow.

Everything about the Oasis is calm and inviting, a welcome change from the doldrum of once again being at sea.

It was Cadmus's idea to work on Medusa's power, but Psyche wants them to practice in the Oasis where Medusa is less likely to have an emotional spike that would result in an injury for Cadmus.

The light from the flames flickers in his amber eyes, and he gives Medusa a reassuring nod. Her hand trembles as she reaches up to pull down her hood, wishing she could close her eyes. Then she stops.

Medusa looks between Psyche and Cadmus. "There has to be another way."

Psyche smiles and puts her hand on Medusa's shoulder. "We have to see if you can learn to control the power of your serpents. Since all curses are tied to the soul, if you work at it, you should be able to master it. I am certain that I can reverse any damage you do to Cadmus in the meantime, especially here in the Oasis."

Medusa prepares to pull back her hood once again. *Please don't hurt him. Please don't hurt him. Snakes, Fates, if any of you can hear me, I do not want to hurt this man. He is not a threat. We are safe.*

Repeating those thoughts on a loop, she slowly lets the fabric fall, and her serpents slither around excitedly. Their emotions surge into her, and she sifts through them, trying to detect any that feel panicked or threatened. Most seem happy to be out from under the hood, a rare occurrence these days, but she senses hints of curiosity in a few of them.

Curiosity that is directed towards the man in her presence—a man who is not a statue.

Psyche sucks in a relieved breath, and Cadmus beams a proud smile.

He didn't turn to stone.

Medusa inhales deeply and closes her eyes.

I did it.

A hand lands on Medusa's shoulder that she was not expecting and she yelps, her eyes flying open as Cadmus cries out. He grips his arm, grimacing in pain, and Medusa yanks the hood back over her head, serpents going quiet once more.

Psyche rushes to help Cadmus. Medusa gets a glimpse at his injured arm, and her heart stutters to a stop. It is now made of stone.

Just like Castor. I hurt Cadmus. What if I killed him like Polydeuces?

Dropping to the sandy ground, Medusa digs her fingers in the sand, wishing she could feel it to help distract her from the thoughts that are threatening to drown her. She wants to check on Cadmus and make sure he is all right, but her thoughts are so far away, below the depths of the ocean's surface, stuck in the Sea Temple once more.

I hurt everyone who gets near me. My presence is a threat to every innocent person in Olympus; either by my serpents directly, or through the wrath of the gods that are so desperate to hunt me. The world was so much safer when I stuck to my island.

In the depths of her despair, a budding kernel of anger in Medusa surges. She just hurt someone she cared about, all because of an involuntary reaction based on trauma gifted to her by the gods.

While said gods sit in their temples and use manufactured benevolence to hide the pain they deliver to those too powerless to stop them.

Poseidon did this to me. I will make him pay if it's the last thing I do. This did not break me.

With her revenge plans slowly forming, Medusa's focus returns to the Oasis.

And Cadmus, oh no.

The sand is thick beneath Medusa's feet as she rushes to him. Dread fills Medusa, but to her surprise, Cadmus is completely fine.

Psyche chuckles at Medusa's shock. "I told you it would be alright."

There is no malice in Cadmus's voice when he adds, "I probably shouldn't have startled you like that. I'm to blame for this accident. Next time, I'll be more careful."

"Next time?" Medusa sputters, taking a harrowing step back. "This wasn't a close enough call for you? You want to risk me killing you instead? You can't possibly ask that of me."

Cadmus steps forward and gently holds Medusa's upper arms. "I think Psyche is right. The serpents are connected to your soul, so if they wanted me dead for panicking you, I would be. Besides, this will help keep you safe. It may not be the most pleasant feeling in the world, but I can tolerate it a million times over with that goal in mind."

The relief with knowing Cadmus is alright does nothing to diminish the ember of rage that is burning deep down. Poseidon will pay for this curse, and every other atrocity he has thrust upon the people of Olympus.

The dark of the ship cabin seems endless as she blinks into the void, unable to sleep. On either side of her lie Psyche and Cadmus, creating a slumbering cocoon of comfort.

How different her life is since the time on her island. There are people who genuinely care about her now. Their safety feels like a liability, a burden, but Medusa is selfishly grateful for them.

Psyche stirs but does not wake, nestling into the crook of Medusa's arm before falling back into the stillness of slumber. Having the goddess beside her after the Sea Temple is something she will never stop thanking the Fates for. She genuinely never thought she would see the goddess again, but every round of torture was that much easier to endure knowing that it prevented Psyche, Cadmus, or Alec from experiencing such hardship.

The thought of Cadmus stirs something in her. This man, despite Medusa's repeated berating, doubts, even an attempt to kill him, has remained by her side, ready to fight for her. He has been willing to risk his safety and life for her repeatedly. Hasn't he proven to her that she is safe with him?

Medusa's eyelids grow heavy as the haziness of sleep finally begins to overtake her, and as she drifts off. Lingering thoughts snag in her mind: the accident in the Oasis today was a fluke, her body is close to being able to show him how safe she feels with him, and the gods will pay for what they have done.

14

ARACHNE

The moss on the overgrown roof of the temple squishes beneath Arachne's spider feet as she skitters across after spending a few hours soaking up the sun. Up here, she can almost forget her curse, the loneliness of this isolating punishment.

The closing door tells her that Hera is awake and wandering about the temple. Arachne produces a small amount of web, wrapping it around one of the wolf statues that adorn the corners of the temple rooftop like gargoyles. The air whooshes as she drops down to the ground floor and wiggles through the broken front entryway.

Following Hera around all day is not part of Arachne's duties, since without a boat of any kind, they are both stuck here, but she likes to keep tabs on the goddess for peace of mind. These days, Arachne finds her grumblings as she follows Hera getting more curious, and less bitter, but perhaps that is simply because maintaining a grudge is exhausting.

Sure, she and Hera have been on this island for countless years, but Arachne would not be stuck here at all if Athena had not needed a jailer. Never mind the likelihood that if Athena had no other use for Arachne, she likely would have just killed her on the spot.

A memory of Arachne as a child pops into her mind, of not speaking to her sister for an entire year because Clea dropped her doll in the mud.

As she does every time she thinks of Clea, Arachne wracks her brain to try and remember her own name. Not Arachne, the cruel moniker given to her by Athena, but the one her mother gave to her when she was born.

It always feels like the name is so close, on the tip of her tongue, but she can never grasp it. Sometimes Arachne wonders if the curse of forgetting her name is worse than being turned into a spider. With one fell swoop, the diabolical goddess ripped all of Arachne's world from beneath her feet.

Arachne stops in the sanctuary when she finds Hera sitting on one of the benches, humming to herself like she always does while braiding wildflowers into her hair.

Ridiculous. Who is she doing that for? There is no one here to even see her.

When Hera sees her lurking, her rosy cheeks widen into a warm smile, and Arachne takes a few startled steps back, still unused to interacting with the goddess.

Hera rolls her eyes. "This is absurd. Please come here."

Arachne pauses before taking a few tentative steps into the sanctuary, creeping up to where Hera sits.

Hera reaches out slowly, and Arachne fights the urge to shy away from the goddess's touch.

A glow emanates from Hera's hand as she places it atop Arachne's head, a tingle washing over Arachne. She jerks back at the sensation and skitters behind a nearby statue.

What was that?

"That was me using what little magic I still have to allow us to communicate with each other. I figured it would be a long eternity otherwise." Her tone is weary with exasperation but more so at the situation than Arachne herself.

Oh.

Hera laughs. "Yes, oh. Now, you know who I am. I would love

to know who you are and how you ended up cursed with your spider form and the task of monitoring me."

Arachne's eight footsteps are silent as she pads out from behind her hiding spot and back over to Hera.

I've never had the opportunity to tell anyone what happened to me. I don't even know if my family knows where I am, or if they are still alive. Is time moving at the same pace here?

"I don't know, but I would be honored to be the first person to learn your story. What is your name?"

Arachne is the only name I know. It used to be something different, but that one was stolen from me as part of the curse.

"Ah. I see someone has a cruel sense of humor. Let me guess, Athena?"

How did you know?

"She was the most likely culprit. That is her brand of cunning cruelty, and since she is the reason I am here with you, it makes sense that she would be responsible for both of our fates."

Why did she trap you here? How has Zeus not intervened?

"I will tell you my story soon enough, little spider. You have waited far too long to tell yours."

Thank you, goddess.

15

ICARUS

"Great work today." Athena's emerald eyes glisten as Icarus dismounts from Amara.

Icarus bows her head slightly. The Pegasus Legion is on their second week of training, and she has proven to be a natural fit for the role.

The incident with the rebels still lingers when she tries to sleep at night, but with no further missions so far of that nature, and how well she is doing in her training, it is easy enough for her to set it aside. But there will be no ignoring it once she becomes Telegonus's right hand in the rebel hunts.

"When you get cleaned up, there is a feast tonight in my temple. It's time for you to begin your ascension through my ranks. I could sense something special in you from the moment you stepped into my arena." Athena hands Icarus a scroll with a deep green wax seal. "I have an eye for warriors, and you, my dear, might just be the greatest of them all. At my side, the world will be at our fingertips, golden girl."

Athena leaves Icarus in a stunned silence, mouth agape, as she rubs her finger over the smooth wax on the scroll.

Icarus is a natural warrior, to be sure, but to receive a hand delivered invitation to a feast from Athena herself? Is this how

Telegonus felt the day the goddess appeared before him and summoned him to her side?

Don't get ahead of yourself. Remember what Mama said about pride. You are a rookie with some potential, do not *start picturing yourself as Telegonus's superior.*

Walking back to the barracks, Icarus unfurls the scroll and reads the delicate script.

You and a guest are invited to the halls of the Mighty Athena to celebrate Pantheon unity and the continued extermination of the rebel threat to our livelihoods.
Please be seated at the table by 7p.m. promptly
(not only will the goddess find tardiness upsetting, but it might be the last mistake you make.)

She rolls her eyes at the threat but is giddy over the idea of the feast. Will Aphrodite be there? Icarus knows without question who she wants to bring as her guest.

The wood of the door is hollow under Icarus's knuckles as she knocks.

It swings open, and Lysander's roommate wipes his eyes sleepily.

Perhaps he was on night watch.

"Yeah?" he asks with a half yawn.

"Where is he?"

"Dunno. It was his day off from training today." He looks back into the room. "Bed is still made, so either he left early or didn't come back last night."

"Thanks." The door closes with a thud.

After confirming that he is not in the stables, bathhouse, or recreational areas of the barracks, Icarus knows where to find him. She did not want to interrupt him with his lover, but she also does not want to attend this feast alone. Besides, this is what he gets for being her only friend.

Besides, it sounds like they've had more than enough time already today.

Behind the temple, past the ruins of an even older temple, a small cave lies tucked behind a grove of willow trees. Even recalling the stories about his favorite secret rendezvous spot, it takes Icarus a moment to find it.

She parts the long, swinging branches hiding the entrance and pauses to listen. Soft laughter fills the air, followed by quietly murmured words and moans that make her grimace.

"Lysander?" She calls into the cave, so she does not walk in on them naked or intimately entangled. "It's Icarus. I need to talk to you."

He stammers from within, "Uhh. Give me a minute?"

Icarus laughs. "I'll go wander, but I don't have all day. This is time sensitive."

"Yeah, yeah. Go away."

Walking back through the grove, Icarus finds a mossy boulder and sits on it, soaking up rays of glorious sunshine. She glances up to the glowing orb in the heavens with a fully open gaze.

The sun does not burn her eyes as it does everyone else. As she has done often, she stares at the glowing orb in the heavens, and it calls to her. She cannot explain why, but the urge to spread wings she does not have and fly higher and higher until she is completely enveloped by the solar warmth and power of the cosmos almost overwhelms her.

As Icarus looks, yearning, for a moment, her reality flashes. The blue sky turns dark and claustrophobic, as if she is suddenly underground. The sun no longer glows the same golden yellow but is now the bluish white of the hottest part of a flame.

Icarus blinks and shakes her head, and when she opens her eyes, the world is normal again. She is once more in the grove of willow trees, sitting on the mossy rock, waiting on her horny best friend.

She scrunches her brows. *That was weird.*

Before she can worry too much about it, Lysander appears from within the cave. His slouchy neckline does nothing to hide the love mark on his collarbone. Icarus crinkles her nose and looks pointedly at the mark.

He sighs dramatically, pulls a cloak out of his satchel, and throws it on, clasping it at the base of his throat. "I've told him to be careful about that, but you know things can get, Miss Likes to Fuck Goddesses."

Icarus jabs her elbow into his side, and he laughs, hooking an arm over her shoulders.

"So, what was so important that you needed to interrupt my day off with that delicious specimen of a man?" Lysander drawls.

"Do you want to go with me?" Icarus asks, waggling her eyebrows and handing him the scroll from Athena.

As he reads it, he quietly mouths the words. When he finishes, his eyes go wide as they meet hers.

"A feast. In the temple. With Pantheon gods. Slap my ass and send me to Tartarus, how did you get this?" he exclaims with a grin.

Icarus shrugs. "Athena gave it to me. She likes how I've been doing in training."

Lysander whistles and runs his hand through his straight black hair. "Damn, Icarus. You really are going to outshine all of us, aren't you?" There is no malice in his tone or expression, only wonder.

Waving him off, Icarus says, "Well, I can at least try to take you with me. So, let's go have dinner with the gods, shall we?" She extends her elbow to him, and Lysander lops his arm through hers.

"Yes, we shall."

When Icarus arrives in her room in the barracks, there is a message waiting for her from Aphrodite.

My love,
While it will be torturous not to touch you tonight, we must remember how important
it is to keep our relationship away from watchful eyes. Even if it were not forbidden, I
have many enemies, and you would instantly become a target. We should not dare to
even make eye contact for longer than three seconds. But in those three seconds, I want
you to remember what my hands feel like on your body, how my lips feel on your breasts,
and know that once this feast is over, you will be my *feast.*

Forever yours.

Icarus carefully folds up the note and tucks it under her mattress with the other notes from Aphrodite. It is foolish sentimentality that has her keeping the letters, but she cannot bear to burn them like her goddess suggested.

Opening her wardrobe, Icarus thumbs through the meager selection within. In the time since the gala, her gown collection has grown slightly, but she is not sure she wants to wear a dress tonight. The silky fabrics slide under her fingertips as she flits between her dresses and armor.

This will be her first time in front of the gods outside of the arena, and initial impressions matter. Does she want to look elegant and sexy? Or should she wear her armor, showing how serious she is about being in the Heroes?

From the stack of pants at the bottom, Icarus pulls out a pair of dark brown leather trousers and slides them on, slipping her feet into knee-high dress boots. The Heroes have two uniforms: a dress uniform and a battle uniform. The dress uniform is less restrictive and worn for official ceremonies. Battle uniforms are their armor.

Deciding against the usual shirt of her dress uniform, she picks the bright blue tunic her mother gave her before she left home. The gold embroidering around the trim gives it a touch of elegance without being over the top. She enjoys putting on a racy dress and fully embracing her femininity, but she also knows that same femininity makes others look down on her, see her as weak. For feasts and non-gala functions, that is not the appearance she would like to present.

Her fingers move deftly as she plaits her golden hair down over her shoulder, weaving a glittering ribbon through the braid.

The reflection that greets Icarus in the mirror is a pleasing one. Satisfied with the way she looks, she plays with the sunstone pendant between her fingers for a moment before turning to go collect Lysander.

I carus and Lysander arrive to the temple early, wanting to have a chance to get situated before the gods show up. All of them are somehow notorious for being late, so they are seated in the dining hall with plenty of time to spare before the first visitors.

Once they find their table, a nymph rushes over quickly, her head down and her eyes careful to avoid Icarus's gaze. She fills their goblets with mead from the pitcher she carries.

"Thank you," Icarus tells the nymph softly.

The nymph lets out a small shriek before quickly disappearing back to the kitchens.

Heat fills Icarus's chest. She'd heard rumors of the gods using the nymphs as servants but assumed there was no accuracy to them. Perhaps some nymphs choose to work in the temples and are compensated?

The gods protect the realm, and I don't know the full situation. Besides, now is not the time to get involved. I just have to get through this dinner without ruining my prospects among the Heroes.

Guests make their way to their seats sporadically, and the hall fills with the echoes of conversation bouncing off the stone walls. Important merchants and diplomats arrive in droves, and the wine and mead are already flowing heavily once the first god arrives.

Hermes glides in, all smiles as he greets the merchants first, shaking hands with familiar faces before taking a seat next to Icarus. His wavy ginger hair curls over the tops of his ears and his light green eyes are jovial when he turns to greet her, extending his golden hand to shake hers.

A breath of relief escapes her. She had not realized how nervous she was about who might be seated next to her besides Lysander. The thought of sitting beside Zeus or Ares is intimidating, and Icarus really wants to enjoy tonight.

Hermes turns to Icarus. "You must be Athena's shining star," he muses.

Not a question, but a statement. He knows exactly who she is. How far has word spread about her talents?

It sounds like Athena has at least been boasting to the other gods. Pride swells in her chest. This is everything she has ever wanted. She can see it so easily. Being at the head of the Heroes, favored by the Pantheon, beloved by the mortals she wants to protect.

A large clamor comes from the entrance of the hall followed by shouting, and Icarus cranes her neck to see what's happening.

"Useless fucking fool!" a gruff voice shouts. Someone down the table moves from their seat, and Icarus can see it belongs to Poseidon. A nymph on her hands and knees scrambles to pick up a tray and its spilled contents.

Castor shifts from behind Poseidon and stalks over to the nymph, kicking her hard in the stomach. She cries out in pain, falling onto her side.

He leans down and grabs her by her hair with the hand that wasn't lost to Medusa, forcing her to look at him. "Worthless piece of filth. Get this picked up and then stand outside of my quarters for the remainder of the evening until I come for you."

A sob escapes the nymph, and Castor jerks her by the hair again.

"Did you hear me? If your ears aren't working, I'd be happy to remove them from your head," he sneers.

The nymph nods profusely, saying, "Yes," over and over as tears stream down her face.

Icarus's blood runs cold, and the people around her laugh—some forced, some genuine. The mead goes sour in her stomach.

Is this what the gods are really like?

"Arrogant bastards," Hermes mutters under his breath, so quietly Icarus almost is not sure she even heard him say it.

After an awkward silence, Poseidon and Castor take their seats, at the opposite end of the table fortunately, and conversation resumes as if the horror show they all just witnessed never happened.

Ares is the next to arrive, running a hand through his sandy blonde hair, followed by Aphrodite. The Goddess of Love looks mouthwatering in the cream satin dress with lace panels showing peeks of her breasts. The effect of her soft sleeves sliding off her shoulders is so intimate that Icarus almost wants to hide Aphrodite from view of the others, keeping that sacred just for herself.

There is also a thrill coursing through Icarus's body knowing everyone in the room wants to end the night in her goddess's bed, but Icarus will be the one claiming that honor.

Let them look. It is my mouth that will be on hers and my body that her hands will be touching.

Hephaestus comes in next, and Icarus has to hide her shock when she sees him. Whispers circulate amongst the citizens of Olympus about the god, claiming the reason he is a hermit is because of his hideous appearance. The god before her however looks absolutely normal. His charcoal hair falls down to the sharp line of his jaw, and his blue eyes dart around the room taking in the people at the table as he unclips his light grey cloak revealing muscular arms from years of metalworking, despite his slender build.

Athena and Zeus are the last to enter the dining hall and Athena signals for the feast to begin as she takes her seat.

Trays of food, carried by mortal servants, come into the hall from the kitchens. Icarus smiles kindly at the mortal who places a tray of candied figs and cheeses on the table in front of her, but the servant quickly rushes away like the nymph before. She cannot blame them if the tempers of the gods can be provoked so easily.

But why is a mortal serving them? The nymphs are enough of a surprise, but as far as Icarus is aware, a feast like this would be served by the acolytes.

Glancing around the table, she is not the only one giving the mortals a curious look.

The clatter of trays eventually quiets, and the servants return to the kitchens or their spots along the wall to monitor for food and drink refills.

Athena stands from her seat at the head of the table closest to Icarus. Her thick red hair is pulled up into golden clips, with loose tendrils falling onto her face and neck giving her a soft romantic appearance that Icarus assumes is designed to be misleading. Opting for a gold dress instead of her usual dark green, Athena looks like she was dipped into a cauldron of molten gold from the heavens.

"Welcome to my home," Athena says, her voice projecting so everyone can hear her. "It is so wonderful when we can gather like this. It is becoming increasingly more apparent that not everyone in the realm thinks the way we do, so it is more important than ever that we continue to meet and ensure that the future of the Isles is shaping up the way *we* want it to."

Pausing for the soft claps that follow, Athena sips from her mead before continuing.

"Disruptors threaten the safety and stability of everything we hold dear. Every day there are new attacks from these so-called rebels. We must not let them succeed."

Heads around the table nod, and Icarus finds herself nodding along as well.

"We must keep our children safe from these terrorists. They have no regard for innocent life. Instead of bringing the attack directly to the Pantheon, they target the vulnerable on the outskirts. Just the other day, I discovered an encampment of mortals of the eastern coast of Attica."

Athena puts her hand to her chest and heaves a sigh. "The rebels burned it to the ground. The people were unarmed. There were children, livestock. Nothing was spared."

Icarus pulse roars in her ears as shocked murmurs break out around the table.

That isn't what happened at all!

Her brow furrows, and she looks to Athena who merely raises an eyebrow as if daring Icarus to challenge her. Looking to Lysander, she finds a more neutral but also confused expression on his face. She opens her mouth to say something, but he squeezes her hand under the table and lightly shakes his head.

"We were able to capture some of the rebels. They are the mortals who have been serving you this evening," Athena proclaims.

More gasps sound around the table, and Athena turns toward the hallway to the kitchens.

Her voice echoes, "Send them out."

A group of people emerge from the hallway, their faces covered in masks of terror. Twenty mortals file into the room, and some of them look like they could be teenagers.

Icarus palms sweat, and she bites the inside of her cheek to keep her shit together.

Walking up and down the line the mortals have formed in front of the serving table, Athena stops before a small woman who looks like she is twenty at most and crooks her finger for her to step forward. Athena takes the woman's hand and walks her to head of the table and stands her there facing the dinner guests.

Athena plucks a sharp knife off the table, a devious smile twisting on her lips. Meanwhile, rage bubbles within Icarus.

She is enjoying this. If this is about justice, like Athena implied, it should not be gleefully enjoyed.

Icarus is frozen in her seat. There is no good option here. If she says something, the gods can literally smite her where she sits. Besides, does she even want to say anything? She doesn't have all the facts. What if *she* is the one who is wrong, and this is a different group than the one from their training exercise?

The knife rips, tearing through the back of the tunic the mortal woman is wearing. The thin material falls to the floor, and she quickly raises her arms to cover her pale breasts from view. The blonde hair hanging in her face clings to her skin from the moisture of tears and snot.

Athena snaps her fingers, and two of her acolytes come running to the table, and pull the woman's arms out to the side and holding her in place.

"Now..." Athena says, turning back to the line of mortals. Their expressions range from shock, fear, and rage, but none of them say a word. "Each and every one of you is going to do exactly as I tell you. You think you can strike us without consequences? Absolutely not. It is time to remind you who is in charge. You." She points to the man at the end of the line closest to her. "Come here."

The man hesitantly steps out of the line and moves to

Athena's side. She takes his hand and places the knife in it, clasping his fingers around the handle. Athena guides the man with the blade to the woman's ribs, just below her breast.

"Cut her. Right here," she orders.

Icarus fights to keep her expression neutral as her heart shatters. Despite the warning not to, she can't help but glance in Aphrodite's direction.

The corners of her mouth are upturned just the slightest, and it is difficult to tell if she is smiling. Icarus's heart sinks at the thought that Aphrodite could be enjoying this. But Aphrodite catches her watching and shakes her head. Realizing her glance at her is much more obvious than she intended, she turns her gaze back to the vicious display. She stifles a small gasp when she finds Athena's emerald eyes boring down on her.

The man shakes his head vigorously and tries to jerk her hand away, but the goddess is stronger. She squeezes her grip around his wrist until he cries out in pain. "Do it, or I will curse every single one of your bloodlines. Right now, this punishment is yours to bear alone. Do you want it to follow your children as well?"

Icarus can see it. The moment in his eyes when he knows he has no choice.

When Aphrodite arrives in her chambers after the feast, Icarus is waiting for her as planned, pacing in front of the full moon light in the open window. When Icarus hears Aphrodite, she spins on her heel, her face distorted in a fit of rage.

"How could you just sit there and watch that?" Icarus looks into Aphrodite's eyes searching for any kind of answer, but the goddess refuses to hang her head in shame.

"Do you think I would do anything to risk further scrutiny on us? I can't go through another half of a century without you." Aphrodite tucks a strand of Icarus's hair that hangs loose from her braid behind her ear.

Icarus shoves away from Aphrodite. "That isn't enough of a reason to stand back and do nothing when people are being mistreated."

She takes in her lover standing before her. Examines the look of determination, the outrage for the weak. Everything she loves about Icarus and has loved about her in every life before this are the same things that put them at risk and could jeopardize everything. This reckless passion is dangerous.

"What would you have me do?" Aphrodite implores. "Stand

up and declare my protection for these mortals? So I can be the next one to end up in a god cage and they die anyway? Besides..." Aphrodite's voice softens, and she closes the gap between them once more, gently placing her hand on Icarus's hip. "They were traitors to the realm. I may not always agree with how the other gods handle the traitors when they find them, but you cannot expect me to risk everything, to risk *you*, over people who would gladly watch me burn while pissing on my ashes."

Icarus drops her head onto Aphrodite's shoulder, leaning into her. "I thought everything would be so much more cut and dry. In Thessaly, when I dreamed of protecting the big cities, I never imagined that there would so many layers of gray to sift through."

Icarus lifts her head to look into the goddess's eyes.

"Tell me more about the rebels, please. I don't know much about them, and maybe if I did, it would make it easier for me to feel solid about the things I have to do."

Despite herself, irritation claws at Aphrodite. She should reassure her lover. Tell her all the pretty things she needs to hear to feel safe and secure in this world. But all she can muster is annoyance.

"Don't be ridiculous, Icarus." Aphrodite narrows her eyes. "I'm a fucking goddess. I am not going to sit here and give you a lesson on the bad guys. You are a soldier. You take orders. Your orders are that all of these rebel scum are traitors and they are to be wiped out. There is nothing else for you to know; it's above your pay grade."

A shocked look crosses Icarus's face, like Aphrodite punched her in the gut. Well, too bad. If Icarus is too petulant to handle the rebels, she does not belong here.

Would Aphrodite really be willing to spend this life, Icarus's last life, separated over this silliness? If the rebels get what they want, this world will cease to exist, and then it will not matter if they were together or not.

"Fuck you," Icarus spits out. "It's nice to see your true colors. Under that pretty exterior is a heartless bitch."

Icarus turns to leave, but Aphrodite grabs her by the wrist and yanks her toward her. "You've got a lot of nerve to say that to a goddess." Aphrodite pulls her tight against her body. "Especially a goddess who knows exactly where to touch you."

Running her free hand along the side of Icarus's body, she smirks in satisfaction when Icarus moans beneath her touch as she cups her rear.

Teeth grazing over the edges of Icarus's ear, Aphrodite says, "I'm sorry. I was tense from the feast. Being around those assholes always puts me on edge. Can we please talk more about this another time?"

Icarus brings her forehead to Aphrodite's and nods.

"Okay. Thank you," Aphrodite murmurs into Icarus's hair. "Now, we are going over to the bed, so you can tell me how much of a bitch I am again, and I can punish you properly."

Icarus pulls back, breaking free from the stupor of her desire. "I'm not in the mood. Can we just lay together? Please?"

"Of course." Aphrodite pulls Icarus back into an embrace, but not a sensual one. "I'm sorry."

They crawl into bed, sliding under the satiny sheets. Aphrodite opens her arms and Icarus folds into the goddess, putting her head on Aphrodite's chest, their arms and legs twining together. Aphrodite's long, slender fingers carefully remove the hair tie from the end of Icarus's braid and deftly loosen the plait until her golden tresses spill down over her back and shoulders.

"What was it like before?" Icarus asks softly.

"Before?" Aphrodite repeats.

"In our past lives."

"Oh." She smiles. "Which life do you wish to know about?"

"Hmm." Icarus turns her head up to face the goddess. "Where did we meet for the very first time, in my first life?"

Running her fingers through Icarus's soft locks, Aphrodite says, "When I was brought into existence by the Fates to be the Goddess of Love, I spent a lot of time out amongst the people. I wanted to know more about them and find out what was important to them."

Aphrodite can still remember it, clear as day. The smells of the food stalls and fragrance carts, and the clamor of city sounds.

"I was in the Olympic Markets outside of the Temple of Olympus with Hestia, my oldest and dearest friend." Aphrodite is uncertain, but she would swear she felt Icarus stiffen at the mention of the former goddess, but she continues. "I heard laughter from several stalls over that was heavenly, as if her voice were crafted by Thalia, the muse of comedy, specifically to call to me like a siren. I approached the source of the sound trepidatiously.

"My identity was not as easily known as it is now, and while an intimate confidence comes naturally with my domain, I found none of it was available to me as I neared the figure in the soft green cloak with her hood up."

The light from the sconces flickers back at her from inside of Icarus's fiery amber irises, and her enraptured silence pushes Aphrodite to continue.

"I tapped you on the shoulder and held my breath as you turned around. You looked me up and down with an assessing gaze that made me want to run back to my temple and hide, but I did not falter. Somehow, I found the words to ask you to join me for dinner that evening."

"Did I say yes?" Icarus asks curiously.

Aphrodite laughs. "No."

Icarus's jaw drops. "There is no way, in any lifetime, I would not have been madly in love with you from the moment I laid eyes on you. I call bullshit."

"It's true." Aphrodite tucks a strand of hair behind Icarus's ear. "You said your ship was set to depart soon and you would no longer be in Olympus."

"Well, what happened? Because clearly the story doesn't end there." Icarus nudges her.

"You told me you and your family were returning to Ithaca

and asked how much I really wanted to see you again." Aphrodite cups Icarus's face in her palm. "But my ships are much faster than those that can be charted by mortals. I had a lavish dinner laid out and waiting for you in the Solar Temple when you arrived in Ithaca."

At Icarus's shocked expression, Aphrodite feigns innocence. "What? It's good to be a god sometimes."

"So where does our story in that lifetime go from there?"

Aphrodite's expression clouds over, and she shakes her head to clear the noise that threatens to pour in if she allows it. "That's a story for another day, my love." She kisses Icarus on the forehead, cheeks, and lips. "Let's go to sleep. Tomorrow, I can tell you about another time we found each other."

"That sounds perfect. I'm sorry we fought earlier."

"As am I. No matter what, please never doubt my devotion for you. I would go toe to toe with the Fates for you."

It wouldn't be the first time.

1 7

ARACHNE

*W*aves crash against the rocks, and the salty spray of the water splashes Arachne as she skitters away from the damp mist.

Hera sits on one of the rocks at the edge, her feet dangling into the water below. She does not know why she followed the goddess out here; it is not like Hera will be able to escape their isolation any more than Arachne.

"Do spiders not like getting wet?" Hera wonders.

I cannot speak for all spiders, goddess, but this *spider does not.*

Hera chuckles but says, "Noted."

Gathering her coral skirts into her hands, Hera carefully stands on the rock, pausing to brace as a wave slaps against her.

Together, they walk back to the temple ruins they call home and linger for a moment in the overgrown gardens. The intoxicating scent of the blossoms fills the air, dancing around on the breeze.

"What is your favorite flower?" Hera asks Arachne.

That is easy, goddess. The bleeding heart is my favorite flower. My mother always called me one when I would rescue small creatures that got trapped in our home. Then when I found the flower, I was stunned by its beauty and the way the blooms cling so delicately

93

to the stalk. My mother made bleeding heart out to be a bad thing, but then I find this beautiful plant by the same name, and it is anything but.

"That story is both beautiful and sad."

Why sad?

"Your mother should have recognized that part of you is special. It should have been nurtured and encouraged to flourish. Hearts like yours are the ones that will set this world right again, I know it. And it's sad to me that you have been taught it is a bad thing."

Hera smiles, but the warmth of it does not reach Arachne. Remembering her mother, her past, has her off-center. The world is shaky beneath her feet.

No, it is much easier when Arachne can shove it down and forget about it. It changes nothing regarding her current situation.

I don't want to talk about this anymore.

"Alright."

What's yours?

"What's my what?"

Favorite flower.

"Hmm," Hera muses. "Lillies. They smell divine and come in so many types and colors. They are a good representation of people. They are beautiful, no matter which version you are looking at, but some are toxic."

That doesn't seem like a very trusting answer from the Queen of the Gods.

Hera frowns. "I never liked that title anyway. Besides, it is my position that has made it abundantly clear that more lilies are toxic than one would expect. If I hadn't been so trusting of my husband and the other gods around me, I would not be here with you right now.

"But I will say that my time getting to know you has been a gift. If we make it off this Fates forsaken island, you will always have a place at my side should you wish it."

Arachne is certain that every one of her arachnid eyes have bugged out of her head at that statement.

Thank you, goddess. Is there anyone you look forward to seeing if we ever leave?

Hera blushes, and Arachne wonders what is going through her mind.

Shouts carry up the hill from the water below, and Arachne cannot believe what she is seeing. A ship approaches the small harbor that sits on the end of the island, but it carries no Pantheon insignia or markings.

Every hair on Arachne's body stands on end. Are they here to take Hera? Have they hunted her down to appease the gods?

Over my dead body.

18

HESTIA

As the ship docks, Hestia looks up the hill of the island to the temple ruins. It is hard to imagine an important book being somewhere like this, so remote and run down, but who is she to question Cassandra's visions?

The small landing party gathers and goes ashore. Hestia, Alec, Medusa, Psyche, Cadmus, Dionysus, and Cyril trudge up the long walk.

Hestia pauses to catch her breath, wishing for a single cloud to cover the blinding sun as its rays mercilessly beat down on them. She is still learning the limits of this mortal body and curses herself every time her stamina fails her.

"What are we hoping to find again?" Dionysus asks.

Hestia pinches the bridge of her nose, rethinking her decision to ask him to come along. Thus far, he has depleted their mead stocks, complained about the food, and is responsible for multiple crew members returning to their ship posts late.

Stifling her irritation, Hestia takes a deep breath. By some miracle of the Fates, she has yet to let her brave face slip despite the almost constant worry.

"A book. I'm not sure what it looks like, so unless we find a library or something, just bring me any books you find," Hestia answers with a sigh.

As they get closer to the temple, the amount of spider silk across rocks and covering the trunks of trees increases. Hestia sends a prayer up to the Fates that the creator of those webs is long gone. The rumors of the island being overrun by spiders has always been considered a myth, but it looks like there is more truth to them by the minute.

Up ahead, Alec and Cadmus are murmuring between themselves, pointing in the direction of the webs, speaking too low for her to hear.

The scraping sound of metal on metal echoes off the rocks as swords are drawn.

Hestia steps back and lets the armed members of the party walk ahead. Dionysus does the same, and the god and former god exchange nervous glances.

The closer they get to the temple, the quieter everyone else becomes. The useless chatter has ceased entirely, and the tension in the silence is so thick, it would take a hydra to cut through it.

The tall walls of the temple are before them and blissfully cast the party in shadow, giving Hestia a blessed relief from the sweltering sun. Her cloak is rough beneath her fingers as she pulls a corner of it up to wipe the sweat from her neck and brow.

Next to her, Dionysus uncorks a container and hands it to Hestia. "Drink."

Hestia gives him a pointed look, narrowing her eyes.

Dionysus sighs. "It's water. Drink it," he urges.

The cool liquid soothes Hestia's dry throat, and she drinks half of the container, and wipes her mouth with the back of her hand when she is finished.

Up ahead, Cadmus puts his finger to his lips to tell everyone to be quiet, and the whispered conversations stop instantly.

Hestia's pulse thunders in her ears when they reach the entrance to the temple. Do they need to look for traps?

Frantically looking around the entrance, Hestia's breath stops when she sees the giant white spider above the doorway, descending from silken webs onto Cadmus and Alec too quickly for Hestia to warn them.

Someone else comes running out of the temple. Hera! Hestia's heart soars at the sight of her friend, but the moment is short-lived.

"Stop!" Despite Hera's shouts, the spider collides with the two men, and Hestia is surrounded by the sound of swords hitting stone and slicing through the air.

It all happens so fast. The spider, Cadmus and Alec, Hera. Clashing together in the blink of an eye.

Cadmus's sword slices a gash down Hera's arm.

The goddess cries out in pain, and Hestia's world stops.

19

MEDUSA

*H*estia, Psyche, and Dionysus rush forward to help Hera, while Cadmus and Alec keep their attention on the spider, swords drawn.

Medusa watches the spider carefully, taking in the stunningly beautiful creature. Its white exterior looks almost a bluish purple in the shadows as it cowers, shrinking into itself and backing away. Its arachnid eyes dart between the people, an escape, and Hera, lingering on the latter.

Is the spider... protecting Hera?

Hera cries out as Hestia gingerly wraps a piece of cloth around the gash in her arm. Alec and Cadmus turn back to the spider and move closer, as if the sound of Hera's pain makes them want something or someone to lash out at and blame.

The spider's gaze is fixated on Cadmus, the current source of Hera's suffering. He raises his sword at the creature as the tension mounts.

The spider backs away from Alec and Cadmus until it hits a stone wall. With nowhere to go, the spider skitters forward and sinks a fang into Cadmus's thigh. He grunts in pain, and Psyche is by his side in an instant assessing his wound.

No. This isn't right. She is only protecting herself and Hera.

Alec pulls his sword back as if he means to strike the creature, and Medusa steps in front of him.

"What the Fates do you think you're doing? Move," Alec says, anger swimming in his eyes as a muscle works in his jaw.

"What am *I* doing? What are *you* doing?" Medusa asks angrily. "We don't even know the full story about what is happening here, and you are going to kill this creature?"

Alec gives Medusa an incredulous look. "Don't you see what happened to Hera? To Cadmus? That thing is dangerous."

From behind them, Hera calls out, "That dangerous thing is my friend. If any harm comes to her at your hands, I promise it will be the last thing those hands ever do. You will go to Tartarus without them, and I will mount them over my mantle like a trophy."

A stunned silence falls over the group, and Medusa turns to Alec. "I thought you of all people would know better than to judge based on appearances. I thought better of you, Uncle."

When finished with the bandage, Psyche walks over to the spider and whispers. After a moment and some more hushed words from her, the goddess places her hand on the spider's head and closes her eyes. Wind gusts roll in as Psyche's hand glows, reflecting in the creature's multiple eyes. The light builds until it is blinding, and Medusa is forced to look away, using her arm to shield her vision.

Once it subsides and Medusa uncovers her eyes, a naked woman lies on the ground in the spider's place. She is pale and skinny, with long white hair that falls down to her mid-thigh. As the group watches in a stunned silence, Cyril pulls off his cloak and gently drapes it over her.

Medusa stands there, frozen. Jealousy claws at her soul as she stares at the woman.

Why didn't that work when Psyche did it for me? This curse is so tied to the fabric of my being that even Psyche's magic is no match.

Hera falls to her knees next to the woman. "Arachne, are you alright?"

At Hera's voice, the woman lifts her head and smiles at the goddess. "Quite well, goddess. Look!" She holds out her arms, stretching and wiggling her fingers.

Bringing her into a deep hug, Hera says, "I'm so glad." She looks up at the group of mostly strangers staring in shock and waves. "Hi. Welcome to Corcyra."

HESTIA

Hestia's leans into Hera's hug as shame sinks down into her bones. Hera thinks of her only as a dear friend. How can she hide these feelings?

"Hestia, I cannot believe you're here." Hera sobs but pulls back, looking into Hestia's eyes.

"Of course I'm here. I haven't stopped looking for you." Fates damnit, she's gorgeous. Hestia tears her gaze away before Hera can see right through her. How could a mortal's crush not be repulsive to such a goddess? Hera never asked for this.

Hera's eyes are full of concern. "What's wrong? Something is different."

"You didn't see the Fire Moon recently?" Hestia asks, affixing her gaze to the grass beneath their feet.

"Fire Moon? No. It can't be."

"It is. I am no longer the Keeper of the Flame. I'm just a mortal."

Hera scowls. "Do not start with that 'just a mortal' bullshit. You and I both know that the mortals are capable of so much greatness, just as we are. Probably more so if we stopped shoving them down into poverty."

A knot Hestia did not realize was twisting in her stomach

loosens. "Is this why Zeus sent you here? Because of your open-minded policies on mortals?" she asks.

At least if Hera attributes my awkwardness as my new mortality, she will be less likely to see that I have feelings for her. Now I must hide them from both Hera and Alec.

Hera nods, then grimaces. "Among other things."

Out of the corner of her eye, Hestia catches Dionysus lingering on the outskirts of the group, close enough to Hera but far enough away that she wouldn't notice him directly.

Jealousy bites at her, but Hestia points to Dionysus, directing Hera's attention. "I wasn't the only one who missed you, you know?"

Hestia watches as Hera walks over to Dionysus. His eyes light up when Hera speaks to him.

At least she will be with someone who is devoted to her and dotes on her like Zeus should have. I should have done it myself when she was right there in front of me.

This is all so confusing. How can her heart be hurting over Hera, but also be so full and protected with Alec? Hestia's love for him has not dimmed even with the direction of her heart's gaze slightly distracted right now.

Hestia never knew she could hold this much love for two people. So many of the gods have multiple partners, but she hardly thought she would have even *one* partner, let alone two.

Alec walks over, as if he senses the internal distress that Hestia thought she was hiding better. He pulls her into his strong arms, and his smell envelops her. She closes her eyes and breathes in deeply.

His voice is low in her ear as he says, "I know it's hard right now, but it will all get sorted."

Eyes still closed, she nods against his shoulder. "I love you, you know?"

His chest rumbles as he chuckles. "I never had any doubts, my goddess."

Bringing her lips to his, Hestia kisses Alec deeply, hoping that her love is pouring into the gesture.

Cadmus calls out to the group. "I hate to interrupt these lovely reunions, but I don't think we should tempt the Pantheon by staying here longer than necessary."

Hera crosses her arms. "You have a point. But who are you? I know Hestia, Psyche, and Dionysus which leads me to believe you should be trusted, but I know nothing of who you are and who you represent. I'm going to need a little more information before I get on a boat with you."

The group exchanges wary looks with one another, not wanting to piss off a goddess but unable to violate their oath.

Cadmus offers a polite smile. "My friend, I understand your hesitations. You are free to remain on this island once we depart, but I cannot tell you anything else until we are on the ship. I give you my word that no one on our ship will harm you."

Hera furrows her brow as she processes. "Fine. But if any of you betray me, you will find I have had a long time to myself and can get very creative with my punishments."

"Before we go," Hestia adds. "We came here in search of an old book, but I do not have a title or description. I was told I would know it when I saw it. Is there a library here I can browse?"

Hera nods. "There is, but I can't imagine any of the books there being special."

Arachne chimes in, her voice low and scratchy from years of disuse, "Actually, I know what book you mean. I'll be right back." She disappears into the temple on wobbly legs, and Cyril rushes after to her to help keep her upright.

When they return, Arachne pulls strand of spider silk off a book and Hestia can already tell is exactly what she was supposed to find. It calls to her like a missing part of her soul. Arachne hands it to Hestia, and it hums beneath her fingertips as she gently runs them over the soft brown leather.

"Alright, you've got your reading material, now let's get off of this island before Zeus shows up and chars us to a crisp," Cadmus says, and the group makes for the boat once more.

21

ICARUS

Icarus runs a brush over Amara's smooth champagne-colored coat, watching it shimmer under the light. Training has been intense the past couple days, and she has been steering clear of Athena and her short temper. Today alone the goddess sent five Heroes to the infirmary for things as silly as looking at her at the wrong time.

Ever since the feast, all the gods have been on edge, even Aphrodite. Is the rebel threat growing?

Placing the brush back on the shelf, she picks the saddle up off the rack and puts it away in the tack closet. The door sticks as the strips of leather from the reins keep getting stuck, and Icarus grunts in frustration as she tries to close it, but they keep falling out.

Giving up, Icarus turns and kicks a bucket. Flames come roaring from her hands, catching the nearby hay on fire, and she falls over backwards.

She hits the ground hard and stares at her hands in horror before she snaps out of it and scrambles for a bucket of water to douse the flaming hay. At least she was alone for that debacle.

"My, my, you've been hiding some talents from me, golden girl."

Apparently not alone. Icarus freezes as Athena comes around the corner.

"Well, don't just stand there looking like an idiot. Explain yourself, and I warn you, girl. I am in no mood to be trifled with." Athena narrows her eyes.

Shit. Aphrodite told me not to tell anyone about my Phoenix powers, but Athena will kill me if I don't tell her.

Icarus chews nervously on her bottom lip.

"This was the first time anything like this has happened to me. Truly."

Athena's stare bores down on Icarus as she awaits the goddess's judgement.

"Get your things from the barracks. You will no longer be housed there. A room will be waiting for you in my temple. Your training will be with myself or Telegonus, and you are to inform me of any new developments in your abilities. Is that understood?"

Double shit. "Yes, goddess." She nods.

Athena steps into Icarus's space, bringing their faces frighteningly close together. "Good. I knew as soon as I saw you that you were special. But be careful, golden girl, my favor can be lost in an instant. If I feel you are keeping secrets from me, our next chat will be much less comfortable."

Not waiting for an answer, Athena turns on her heel and leaves.

Icarus still stands right where Athena left her when Telegonus walks into the stables and heads straight for her. He barks, "You. Let's go. Saddle up."

"But I just finished cooling Amara down," Icarus replies warily.

"That was not a request." His deep voice carries all manner of threat within its gravelly depths.

"Yes, sir."

Icarus pulls the saddle, blanket, and bridle from the tack

room, slipping them back onto Amara with ease. To her credit, her steed puts up no protest to the additional work for the day.

Sticking her boot into the left stirrup, she swings her legs over the saddle and gets situated in the cushioned seat. She collects the reins and clicks her cheek, guiding Amara to start walking. Around the corner of the stables, they find Telegonus on his own mount, ready to go. He takes off without a word into the sky, and Icarus follows.

Once she is alongside him in the air, her voice is strained as she raises it to ask, "So what are we doing?"

Icarus can barely hear his reply over the wind as he says, "Found a group of rebels that we need to flush out of their hidey hole."

Anger rises in Icarus's chest at the thought of the rebels. The night of the feast was fucked up to be sure, but if the they overthrow Olympus's entire way of life, things would be so much worse for the realm. Why can't they see that?

She nods to Telegonus, and the rest of the flight is silent as Icarus lets the complicated emotions course through her.

The rebels want to threaten everything that matters because they are jealous of the power of the gods. So, what are they thinking? If they can't have that power, no one should? How does that logic play out? It doesn't seem like enough of a reason to be risking so many lives to go up against the Pantheon.

The story Castor told her about the encounter he and his brother had with the monster, Medusa, comes to mind. His stone hand and dead brother are all she can think about as Telegonus signals for them to land.

There is a long chain of unnamed, uninhabited islands to the east of the mainland in the Olympic Isles, and it is on the shores of one of them that Icarus and Telegonus touch down on the sandy beach. He dismounts and draws his sword silently, and she follows suit.

Holding a finger to his lips, Telegonus walks along the beach, his sword at the ready. She follows him around a bend, and a series of small caves comes into view. They walk into the first one, but it is only a few feet deep and completely empty. They have similar luck with second, but in the third, they find a small group of people huddled together as far back into the short cave as they can go. She counts four adults and two young children, a boy and a girl.

Telegonus turns to Icarus and chuckles darkly. "You see? They find little nooks and crannies to hide in, hoping to flag down a rebel ship to pick them up."

One of the men in the group protests, "No, we aren't rebels or anything like that."

Telegonus gives the man a withering glare. "Then what are you doing all the way out here?"

The man's wide eyes are pleading. "My kids always wanted to come visit the islands, so I figured why not bring the whole family."

The low laugh that comes from Telegonus is anything but amused. "Is that so?"

The man and his companions nod.

Dropping to one knee, Telegonus beckons one of the children to him. The boy shyly hides his face, but the girl is all smiles as she skips to the Hero, not sensing the threat before them all.

"Hello, little one. What is your name?" he asks.

If Icarus didn't know better, she would almost mistake that for genuine kindness in his voice.

"Mila," her little voice squeaks out proudly.

"Mila. That's a lovely name. Is that your brother?" Telegonus points to the little boy.

Mila nods enthusiastically. "Yes. That's my brother, Joshua."

"Mmhmm. And where were you off to?"

"We came to get Uncle Krys and bring him back to the secret place with us."

Icarus's heart skips. *Does this kid know where all the rebels are?*

A woman from the group calls to the little girl, "That's enough, Mila, please come back to Mama."

Telegonus's smile turns into a sneer as Mila tries to run back to her mother, but she yelps when Telegonus's hold tightens on her wrist. "Not so fast, little one. I think I have more questions for you."

He picks her up and carries her to the front of the cave. When Mila realizes her family is not following, she starts crying for her mother.

"No! You cannot take my child!" Mila's mother rushes forward to try and save her daughter, but Telegonus runs his sword through her as if she were nothing. Mila shrieks, and the men start to run after her, but Icarus holds her own weapon up to keep them at bay.

As he passes Icarus, Telegonus leans in. "Torch it. Let's see if you can put those flames to use."

Telegonus leaves the cave, and Mila's cries slowly fade until they no longer echo off the walls.

Icarus stands there, sword drawn, facing the small group of rebels for several seconds. She knows what she needs to do, but the reality of doing it is tougher than she thought it would be. When she envisioned the glory of joining the Heroes growing up, she never imagined having any difficulties claiming a life in the name of justice and the safety of the realm. So why is she hesitating now?

Tears well in her eyes, and she drops her sword. The men slump in relief, but only because they have no idea that she is pulling on her powers and will need her hands free to wield them.

As the flames form at her fingertips, Icarus repeatedly reminds herself what is at stake if the rebels win, all the atrocities they have committed in the name of their new world.

The cave erupts into a world of fire and ash as tears stream down Icarus's face.

This shall not break me.

22

ARACHNE

The world spins as Arachne leans over the side of the ship, again, and vomits. Years as a spider followed by a rapid transformation back to her mortal form has left Arachne struggling to cope with equilibrium regulation. And of course, their destination is as far away as it possibly can be.

She and Hera quickly took the oath once on board the ship, both agreeing to help knock the Pantheon down a few pegs. Each itching to get retribution for their time on that island.

A calloused hand strokes her back, and Arachne smiles despite the nausea. She does not have to look up to know it is Cyril. He has remained by her side the entire journey, quick to care for any need that might arise.

"How do you feel about letting Psyche help you with your nausea today?" Cyril asks gently.

Arachne wipes her mouth and stands up, using the railing to stabilize herself with her wobbly balance. The ship suddenly lurches, and her stomach heaves again. She is hesitant to trust a goddess, or anyone aside from Hera or Cyril, for that matter, but she doubts she can withstand much more sea sickness.

"Okay," she says weakly while hanging over the railing.

Arachne hears his footsteps retreat, and she breathes in deep, trying desperately to soothe her stomach.

The sun bounces off the glassy surface of the water, and Arachne leans over to try and get a look at herself. There aren't any mirrors on the ship, and none of the metal surfaces are shiny enough to see her reflection. How is her appearance now? The only thing she has been able to see so far is that her skin is still the pale ivory color it used to be, and that her long hair that was black is now snow white.

The ripples in the water prevent her from seeing a clearer image of herself, and leaning over to look is making her more nauseated.

A few minutes later, Cyril returns with Psyche in tow. They both help Arachne to a sitting position, and she immediately brings her hand to her mouth.

From the pocket of her dress, Psyche removes a stone the color of jade, along with a small pouch of ground herbs. She places it on Arachne's forehead and closes her eyes. The stone glows beneath the goddess's touch, and the nausea recedes with each passing second.

The goddess smiles. "There. That should take care of the immediate nausea. Drink this tea every day when you wake up and again if you feel any more nausea coming and I'm not around."

"What's in it?" Arachne asks shakily.

Psyche pats her shoulder comfortingly. "Valerian, Arnica, chamomile, and ginger."

Arachne grips the bag of herbs tightly, clinging to it like it is a lifeline. It is still so strange using her hands and fingers, not to mention walking upright.

When Psyche leaves, Cyril stays with her and with her nausea abated, she can finally enjoy walking around the ship. She finds the chaos and commotion that goes into sailing fascinating.

As her body settles down, Arachne remembers the stories she would make up as a kid about pirates and sea captains. How she longed to feel the sea mist on her face as she rushed from rigging to rigging, tying and loosening knots. Perhaps if the rebels do set this world right, one day she can spend her life at sea... if this sea sickness is not permanent. That part was never present in her fantasies.

Arachne looks out across the vast expanse of the sea before her. She has no idea what to do with her life if the Allegiance is successful. How long were they even on that island? Is her family still alive? Her heart sinks at the thought of them being gone.

It boggles her mind that the Allegiance would even allow Arachne to take their oath and join them. What does she have to offer? Perhaps in her spider form she could provided something worthwhile, but in this body, she is weak. She chuckles at the irony.

Every second on that island, she wished for her own body— her hair, her ability to speak. But now that she has those things again, she feels useless and fragile.

Cyril remains by her side, a silent comfort, as the sun sets on the horizon. Arachne may not have her spider strength anymore, or her webs, but in their place she latches onto something to drive her forward: making Athena pay.

23

HESTIA

*H*estia runs her fingers gently along the spine of the book collected from the island. The cover has a faded circular marking too worn from time to make out, and the text is faint. Sliding the lantern closer on the small table, she squints and tries to decipher the title.

The language is ancient, one Hestia would have certainly known if she were still the Keeper of the Flame. Chewing on her lip, she closes her eyes and shakes her head to clear her vision and thoughts before looking at the spine once more.

Now, the ancient script is legible to Hestia, plain as day.

Blinking rapidly, she is certain her eyes are playing tricks on her. *How is this possible?*

She smiles as she murmurs the title to herself. "The Book of Fates."

The lantern light flickers as soon as the words leave Hestia's lips, and she swears she feels a soft, cold breeze flutter through the room.

Inside the book, Hestia flips through the delicate pages. There are diagrams of ancient temple schematics, sketches of prominent flora, and several charts with no immediately apparent purpose. She is about to close the tome in frustration, deeming it a dead end, when a page in the very back catches her eye. At first, it is blank, but when under a closer look with the firelight of the lantern, script appears, along with a drawing of tall standing stones positioned in a circle.

The language in this page is not the same as the rest of the book, and this one Hestia cannot read at all. Her heart thumps heavily in her chest.

There is one single line of script that is in the same language as the rest:

This information has the potential to shift the balance of the universe. Do not let it fall into the wrong hands.

Goosebumps erupt along Hestia's skin, and the hair on the back of her neck stands on end.

This has to be the reason I was sent for this book. But what does it mean?

She moves her thumbs aimlessly over the inside of the back cover as she stares at the drawing, then her finger bumps on something sewn into the binding.

Hestia walks to Alec's bag sitting at the foot of the bed. A blush forms on her cheeks at the familiarity and intimacy they are building. She slips a small knife out of one of the pockets, grateful to know where Alec keeps spares.

As delicately as she is able, Hestia slices a thin line into the back cover of the book, sending up a silent prayer to the Fates to forgive her for marring their tome if this is all for nothing. A satisfied smile spreads across Hestia's lips as she slides a small brass key topped with a heart from the fabric.

Hestia leaps up to go show the key to the others, but her hand hovers over the doorknob. She swallows. There is not a single person on this ship that she does not trust, but something gnaws at her gut.

Hesitantly, she walks over to her bag, tucking the key into a small interior pocket. Until she can do more research on the book and talk to Cassandra, she will keep it safely in her possession.

It is the middle of the night when the ship sails through the Mysts. Clouds hide any light from the moon, as if it too wants to aid in the stealth of the Allegiance. Unlike the first time the Allegiance arrived in the Underworld, there is no greeting party, no bustle of activity. Other than the addition of the rebels, it is business as usual for the home of the dead.

Hestia and Alec part ways with their traveling companions and begin the long walk to their shared room in the temple. Weariness hangs on her like a soaking wet cloak, and she tries to fight the bitterness arising when she is reminded of her weakened state.

There is an ache in her bones that set in after mere days of being at sea. Her immortal body would have been mildly inconvenienced by the physical exertion of the trek, but in this mortal one, she wonders how she will possess the strength to continue this fight.

Hestia should be getting used to her fragile state by now and adjusting to it. Instead, she feels the effort of every single step.

When they arrive at their room, Alec goes straight into the bathing chamber, and Hestia is relieved to have a second to let her guard down. Hiding the toll everything takes on her body saps even more life out of her, but she knows he will just worry too much about her, and she cannot bear that thought.

Alec comes back into the room and extends his hand. She takes it without question and forces a burst of energy through her to stand and follow him.

In the bathing chamber, candles are lit all around the hot spring pool. He walks her over to the edge and gently takes off her clothes.

Hestia opens her mouth to tell him she could not possibly

engage in intimate relations right now, but he puts a finger to her lips, and the thought dies in her throat.

"I can see how much our journey affected you." The rasp of his voice pebbles her sensitive skin, but she kicks herself for not successfully concealing her exhaustion. If she isn't hiding her fatigue well, does that mean her secret thoughts about Hera are equally as transparent?

"I'm fine, my love," Hestia replies, but Alec shakes his head and guides her into the water.

He sits on the edge of the pool, out of the water, legs dangling in, and pulls Hestia over to sit on the seat in front of him. He leans her head back into his lap and deftly removes the pins holding her hair up. As her locks cascade down her shoulders, Alec slowly runs his fingers through them.

Hestia sighs. Tears of relief threaten to fall as her body finally has a break from its torment in the warm weightlessness of the water.

Beside the pool is a small bowl and glass bottles of soap and shampoo, their colorful containers casting multicolor speckles of light around the room from the candles.

Alec picks up the bowl and dips it into the water. Hestia closes her eyes as the warm liquid douses over her hair. He does this a few more times until all her hair is wet. Next, he opts for the blue bottle first, and the floral aroma hits her nostrils as he massages the substance into Hestia's locks.

As his fingers work their way through her thick tresses, her heart soars. She can feel the love that he has for her in every touch and gesture, each moment of care and tenderness. As his devotion pours into her, her woes about her body and the state of world fall away for a few blissful minutes.

The lioness does not stir from her spot this time when Aphrodite walks into the woman's lair. It seems silly to call it a cell since she does not see a door anywhere keeping her contained within.

"Hello, goddess. I knew you would return," the woman says from the corner of the room where she is grinding herbs with a mortar and pestle.

"What is your name? Will you tell me this time?" Aphrodite asks, trying to hide the eagerness in her voice. She does not like to reveal her vulnerabilities so easily.

The woman's dark lips curl into a thin smile. "My name is Circe."

Aphrodite crinkles her brow as she tries to place the name.

Circe chuckles. "No point in trying to remember who I am. The owl removed all knowledge of me from your history books. It's easier for her if people do not remember."

"But why?" she presses, eager for answers.

The woman tuts, "Ah, it is not time for that yet. I know you likely think me mad, but you know nothing of how delicately this must be done."

Aphrodite steps closer. "How delicately *what* must be done?"

"I've already likely said too much. Did you seek something from me besides my name?" Circe asks.

"That and what you are doing down here."

Circe gestures around the small room. "This is my home, of course. All my things are here."

Aphrodite sighs and pinches the bridge of her nose, causing Circe to laugh loudly.

"Oh goddess, if you think I am a cryptic pain in a minotaur's ass, you should try talking to the Fates."

More questions than answers hover over Aphrodite's head like a rain cloud. Each droplet containing either solutions or madness, and this unstable woman controls which ones fall.

The mortar and pestle clank on the counter as Circe abruptly sets them down and walks over to Aphrodite until they are face-to-face. "Did you find it?"

"No," Aphrodite bites out. That stupid object has been a source of incessant frustration and curiosity.

"I will tell you three things, goddess. And then you shall leave me be for today. One—the item is crucial to the outcome of this world. Two—through it, we can finally see the proper balances reflected in Olympus. Three—you will have a change of heart once you find it."

Aphrodite's jaw drops. "What the Fates is that supposed to mean?"

Circe's face is unreadable as she ignores the goddess before her and returns to her herbs.

Rolling her head back and sighing with frustration, Aphrodite leaves Circe's lair intent on returning to her island within the next few days.

Her quarters are dark and quiet when Aphrodite slips inside. A flicker of light from the guest suite catches her eye, and she hopes that it is Icarus. Her heartbeat quickens at the thought that it might be Oedipus. Is she going to have to fend him off today?

Aphrodite's lets out a sigh of relief at the long golden tresses spilling out onto her rose-pink sheets. She stands there, watching the glow from the lantern bouncing off Icarus's form.

The chaos of her thoughts must be unbearably loud, because Icarus stirs as if she can hear them.

"Why aren't you asleep?" Icarus asks, her voice husky from her slumber.

"I just have a lot on my mind. Nothing to worry about, my love." Aphrodite kisses Icarus on the forehead and runs her fingers through the golden tresses of her lover. "Did I wake you?"

Icarus shakes her head. "No, I had a dream."

"Tell me?" Aphrodite nudges.

As Icarus sits up in the bed, Aphrodite follows, pulling one of Icarus's hands into her lap and clasping it tightly.

"It was about the rebels."

Aphrodite stiffens at the mention of the agitators but gestures for Icarus to continue.

"In my dream…" Icarus swallows, as if she can barely say it aloud. "We found the entire rebel base—all of them. It was like I had no control over my own body. I was walking through their encampment with flames rolling off my skin. There were flaming bronze feathered wings on my back, and I killed them all. There were even children there. All while Athena watched from her pegasus with glee."

"But they were rebels?" Aphrodite asks, tilting her head. If they were the people responsible for the upheaval of their realm, she does not see what the issue is.

"I mean, yes! But they were people! And I just *killed* them because someone told me to." Icarus pulls her hair in frustration as Aphrodite gives her a cold stare.

"What do you think those same rebels would do to you if they got you alone and defenseless? Do you think they would spare you? Offer you a moment of reprieve because of your kind heart? They would eat you alive!" she scoffs.

Shock crosses Icarus's face, and Aphrodite knows she has gone too far; let her agitation over the rebels and the mystery woman spill into her time with Icarus, but she couldn't stop herself.

"It doesn't matter. It was only a dream. Why don't we try and go back to sleep?" Aphrodite offers, but the daggers in Icarus's eyes tell the goddess that will not be happening.

In a huff, Icarus gets out of the bed and paces around the room gathering her clothing and putting it on, muttering to herself angrily.

"Please don't leave. I didn't mean it." Aphrodite extends her hand. "Stay with me."

Icarus's chest visibly shakes as she takes a deep breath. "I'm going to my barracks. We'll talk tomorrow."

The silence following in the wake of Icarus's departure is maddening, leaving Aphrodite alone in her bed, regretting every word she said.

25

MEDUSA

The sheets stick to Medusa as she wakes up desperate to catch her breath. It takes several seconds in the dark to remember where she is: the Under Temple. Not the Sea Temple, and not with Poseidon or the Twins.

Yet the remnants of the nightmare cling to her, refusing to let go. On either side of her, Cadmus and Psyche still sleep soundly, a beacon in this dark abyss.

As she lays awake, her eyes adjust to the shadowy room. Waiting for her breathing to even, one word circles in her mind.

Justice.

It was always there, only drowned out by the cacophony of everything that she has experienced. But now, justice beats in her like a drum.

As gently as she is capable, Medusa slides out of the bed and throws on a simple pair of slacks and a tunic. She struggles to slip into the sandals in the blackness of the room, but after a second, they slide on perfectly.

Absentmindedly, she makes several turns and finds herself in a long hallway. Walking through it, she sees there are no doors as she is passing, just elaborate carvings she cannot decipher.

Padded footsteps sound behind her, and Medusa's heart blossoms when Cerberus runs up alongside her. She reaches down and threads her fingers through his thick dark fur, smiling into the three sets of green eyes staring at her.

Medusa has never seen his kind of canine before, and she wonders if that part of him is as unique to the Olympic Isles as his three heads.

At the end of the hallway, they come upon a ledge with a stone guardrail. Just below it is a river. The surface of it is smooth as glass, even though it sounds like it has a strong current.

Standing at the ledge, looking out, she finds Yiorgos in a black cloak with the hood down. She comes to a stop abruptly and turns to leave, not wanting to interrupt his train of thought or make him uncomfortable. He has kept his distance from her since day one and honestly, she cannot blame him. She still carried guilt for knocking him unconscious on his own ship.

But at least he is not a statue, right?

"There is no need to leave." Yiorgos does not turn around, his voice barely audible over the water.

She pauses. "I do not wish to bother you. I will find somewhere else to wander."

Yiorgos turns and when his eyes meet Medusa's, she finds none of the prior reservation and hesitation there, only warmth.

A smile spreads across her face. "Thank you. What is this place?"

Gesturing to the water, Yiorgos answers, "This is the River Styx. You saw it after coming through the Mysts, but did you know that it flows throughout the Underworld?"

Medusa's eyes widen, and she shakes her head.

"Accessing the different parts of the Underworld is a delicate game, and one that the river has a voice in. Even Hades himself must pay his coin and await the river's fate." Yiorgos points to the small boat tied to the edge of the riverbank. To the right of the balcony, Medusa can now see a set of narrow stone steps going down to the waterline.

"You sure seem to know a lot about all of this," Medusa remarks, raising an eyebrow.

Yiorgos waves a hand. "I get around. Besides,"—he gives her a pointed look—"I see much more than many would assume, and I learn from my observations."

Cerberus plops down on the stone floor and rolls onto his back with his feet in the air, a tongue hanging out of all three mouths.

Chuckling at the large canine, Yiorgos crouches down and scratches the beast's belly.

Medusa lowers and sits with the two of them while Yiorgos continues gently petting Cerberus.

"I am glad you are with us again," Yiorgos says after a moment, catching Medusa off guard. In this interaction, it has become clear that he does not resent her nor dislike her, but it still surprised her when people want her around.

"Th-Thank you," Medusa says, fighting the tear stinging in the corner of her eye.

Yiorgos continues, "This world has not been kind to you, yet you choose to still be kind to those around you. People like you are the true heart of this world, and the Pantheon knows that is a threat."

Standing up, Yiorgos walks over to the stairs, stopping at the top of them and turning back to face Medusa. "I can feel the stars moving, all turning their eyes on us, on our world. They know what is coming. I just hope we are ready."

He turns once more, and his figure shrinks as he retreats down the stairs, pulling his hood up over his head.

The room is silent when Medusa returns. She pulls the door gently to close it, but the old wood creaks loudly.

The sheets rustle, and the room fills with light from the small lantern on the bedside table next to Psyche.

"I'm sorry for waking you," Medusa whispers.

A loud yawn comes from under the sheets, and Cadmus says, "You didn't."

Psyche laughs and gestures for Medusa to join them again.

As she slides into bed between these two people who love her, Medusa decides she is done being held back by the past. She finally feels strong enough to take control of her own destiny. Reaching down and intertwining her fingers with Psyche's, she pulls Cadmus to her with her other hand.

He pauses, looking into her eyes. "Are you sure?"

Medusa has never been more sure of anything in her life. "Absolutely."

Cadmus brings his lips to hers, and the stubble of his chin brushes against her scaly skin. His hand comes up to the back of her head, the hood separating him and her serpents who seem calm beneath it.

Psyche slips her hand around Medusa's waist, pulling her back into Psyche's body while Cadmus deepens their kiss. His hands travel up Medusa's arms, over her collarbone, hovering just above her breasts.

He pauses as if waiting for any sign of distress, and when one does not come, he gently cups her breasts over her tunic.

Medusa gasps, the difference between his large hands and Psyche's small ones is quite noticeable. He breaks free from the kiss and guides her to a sitting position and removes her tunic.

Psyche positions herself sitting up at the head of the bed, back against the wall. When Medusa's pants fall to the floor and she is naked, Psyche pulls her backward against her. Psyche's nipples press into Medusa's lower shoulder blades, and the sensation sends heat straight to her core.

Cadmus watches Medusa, laid out before him, as he removes

his own clothes. She sucks in a deep breath when he is naked, taking in the impressiveness of his hard muscles. The firmness of his erection leaves little room for doubt that he loves her body.

He climbs into the bed, positioning himself between her thighs as he leans down and kisses her once more. She curls her fingers into his hair, and she moans into his mouth. Psyche's feather-light kisses pepper Medusa's back and shoulders until Cadmus breaks his kiss with Medusa and leans around to kiss Psyche.

His lips return to Medusa's, and as they travel down her neck, she can almost swear they are leaving fire in their path. Desire burns inside her, and she wants this more than anything.

Cupping her breasts in both hands, Cadmus runs his thumbs over her nipples. The sensation nearly causes Medusa to jump off the bed.

Psyche's voice is soft in her ear. "Does it feel good when he touches you?"

"Yes." Medusa's reply is so breathless it is almost inaudible.

Psyche kisses Medusa's neck again, while Cadmus's thumbs stroke her nipples. "Do you want him to touch you other places as well?" she asks.

Medusa moans, "Yes."

His hands roam wildly across her body as if he is worried there is not enough time to touch all of her. Psyche reaches around and cups Medusa's breasts, taking the space Cadmus no longer occupies as his own hands go higher and higher up her thighs, getting ever so close to her already wet center.

Cadmus and Medusa lock eyes, and heat floods through, her entire body flushing under the intensity of his gaze.

He does not look away as he slowly inserts a finger inside her. Medusa's eyes flutter closed, and she gasps, needing more. Cadmus slips another finger in, and the added pressure has her almost ready to explode from ecstasy.

Psyche lightly pinches Medusa's nipples while Cadmus gently

strokes her clit with his thumb while still driving her to the brink of destruction with his fingers.

"I think she's ready, don't you?" Psyche purrs, the heat of her breath tantalizingly close to Medusa's ear.

Cadmus quirks a grin. "More than ready."

Medusa's body trembles with anticipation as Cadmus centers himself in between her thighs.

"Are you certain? We can stop anytime, I promise." The sincerity in Cadmus's voice would melt away any remaining doubts if she had any, but Medusa *is* ready.

Not wanting to risk anything, she does another quick mental check with her serpents. To her delight, they are still as calm and docile as before, enjoying their slumber beneath her hood.

Medusa nods. "I'm positive."

With Psyche behind, cradling her, Medusa feels like this is exactly where she is supposed to be.

Cadmus brings the head of his manhood to her entrance, sliding it along her slickness before slowly entering her inch by glorious inch. Medusa moans, and Psyche's feather-light kisses on her back shoulders get more heated, her teeth scraping across Medusa's skin.

Once Cadmus fully inside, he stays there for a moment, pausing to visibly check in with Medusa. She nods her confirmation, and he withdraws almost entirely before thrusting his hips and plummeting into her.

Stars bloom in her vision as bliss washes over her with every thrust.

"Cadmus," Medusa cries out, his name spilling from her lips as her breath hitches. "I'm so close."

"Yes, that's it," Psyche's croons in her ear.

His pace increases as he drives Medusa toward the cliffs of her own oblivion. When she cannot withstand it any longer, she fully succumbs as her orgasm rocks through her.

Cadmus groans as he reaches his own climax, her walls clenching around him as they both shatter.

As he slides out of her, Cadmus leans forward and kisses Medusa, then Psyche. They get cleaned up, and return to the bed in an attempt to sleep.

The first to doze off is Cadmus, leaving Medusa and Psyche to chuckle over him tiring himself out. As her body still sings in every place he touched it, she is certainly grateful for his efforts. Psyche nods off next, and she knows she is not far behind.

Despite how wonderful it is to be intimate with the two people she loves, anger and vengeance still seep their way into her thoughts. Because of the Pantheon and gods such as Poseidon, Medusa came so close to never knowing what it feels like to be loved.

Now that she knows what if feels like, it makes her even more angry that they tried to steal it from her.

ICARUS

Rain pelts Icarus and Amara as they sail through the sky with a small group of the Rebel Taskforce. She rolled her eyes when Telegonus revealed the name he came up with for their unit, if you can even call it that.

Groups are sent out daily to hunt for rebels, and the rest times between missions is rapidly shrinking. Exhaustion weighs Icarus down along with the soaking wet rain.

What an abysmal day to be flying. Thank the Fates Zeus has all the Heroes warded from lightning, but you would think he could have thrown in some rain protection with it.

"Down there!" Telegonus calls out. At least Icarus thinks that's what he said.

With the wind in her ears, and the rain, she cannot comprehend how he expects anyone to know *what* he is saying.

This time, being the right hand of Athena's number one soldier has been interesting to say the least. Icarus does not like to let her pride reach boastful levels, but after several days in close proximity to him, it is clear why Athena was so excited by Icarus's performance in the arena.

Perhaps he is incredibly strong, or has a brilliant mind when necessary, but Icarus does not see it. His one tru talent, however, is hunting rebels. No matter how cleverly they are hiding, Telegonus roots them out every single time. The only thing he hasn't managed to find is their base.

Their group descends to the ground below, and Icarus hangs back observing the situation as Telegonus approaches the small campfire with five adults huddled around it, swords drawn.

"Afternoon, folks. What brings you out to the edges of the world on this fine, rainy day?" Telegonus asks. His teeth look almost canine through his grin, which is anything but friendly.

"We got stranded here. It was a shipwreck. Thank the gods, you found us!" A woman steps forward, tears streaming down her face. "Please help us."

Telegonus narrows his eyes and looks around the small beach. "I see no wreckage. No shattered cargo containers, ropes, nets."

She spots movement from the corner of her eye a good bit from the campfire. She can barely make out shadows moving along the rocky edge at the base of a shallow cliff. All eyes are still on the exchange with Telegonus, so she silently pulls Amara from the group. When she is out of sight, she kicks her heels and her pegasus takes off, flying around the outer rim of the tiny island until they reach the other side.

Amara lands on the rocky beach, and Icarus slides off. Her armored footsteps are heavy and sink into the sand as she walks. A small cave appears before her. It looks undisturbed, but her gut says to look inside. She pushes down the memories of the last time she was in a cave with rebels.

Inside is pitch black. Holding up her left palm, she calls forth a small flame to use for light. When she looks up, there is a man staring at her, hand on his sword, and several children.

"Please. They're just children," the man says. His eyes are kind, and his dark curly hair is damp from the rain.

Icarus wants to vomit as the illusion of what her life would be like as a Hero comes crashing down around her. This is not what she signed up for. All she ever wanted to do was help people and give back.

"Just tell me one thing," Icarus says, biting through every word as a war rages inside her. "Why are you doing this? Is it worth risking your children just because the gods have more power than you?"

The man tilts his head and drops his hand away from his sword. "Do you really think that is the reason we are fighting?"

Icarus narrows her eyes. "What other reason could you have? The gods provide everything we need, even down to the season to grow our crops."

"Your crops? Or their crops? How can *you* overlook everything they have done? And fight in their name? You think you are a hero, but tell me this. Do heroes kill children?"

He may as well have hit Icarus in the chest with a sledgehammer. She shakes her head.

"You listen to me, *hero*. You need to think long and hard about why so many people would rather *die* than continue to be oppressed under the Pantheon's heel." Icarus can see the man trying to remain calm so as not to scare the children, but the rage simmering in his eyes in unmistakable.

One of the children lets out a sob and that is the final straw for her heart. She does not know what this will mean for her future, but she will not allow Telegonus to hurt these innocents.

"I will try to direct them away from this cave if they go searching for others. I cannot do much about your friends on the beach."

The man hangs his head. "They knew their fates when they stayed there to be a decoy for the kids."

Icarus nods heavily and turns to walk out of the cave as the man says, "My name is Cyril."

He walks up behind her, and she stiffens at the threat but does not reach for her weapon. She feels a rustling at her hand and looks down as he slides a piece of paper into it.

"I can tell when someone's heart is on our side. Should you choose to follow it, you will find me here tomorrow."

Icarus unfolds the small piece of paper and discovers a crude map hastily drawn.

"The rest will have returned, but I will be there."

Icarus does not say a word as she walks out of the cave. Amara is still waiting for her several steps from the cave's entrance. As she is mounting, Telegonus and the rest of their group land beside her.

"We took care of the scum on the beach. Did you find anything else?"

Icarus swallows and steadies her breathing as her heart thunders in her ears. "No, all clear."

The pegasuses take to the air, and Icarus clutches the small map tightly against the reins until her knuckles are white.

As she walks through the room, lighting candles and sprinkling flower petals, Aphrodite's mind is not on the time she is about to spend with Icarus, but instead on Circe and her cursed riddles.

She hates how distracted she has been and regrets neglecting Icarus. Yet those regrets do nothing to keep Aphrodite's mind from wandering there anyway.

Why did it have to happen this way? After searching for Icarus for centuries, as soon as they are reunited, the world tilts off its axis? It isn't fair. Aphrodite's heart begs her, pleads with her, to focus on her rekindled love, but every part of her soul screams that this is bigger than the two of them.

She and Icarus have found each other in every single one of her lifetimes, so a slight distraction is harmless in the grand scheme of things. Right?

The door makes the faintest of clicks behind Aphrodite as Icarus slips inside the room. Forcing herself to be in the moment with her lover, Aphrodite smiles and turns to greet Icarus. Her smile falls when she sees the look on Icarus's face. Her lively, bright features are downcast, and her fiery amber eyes are distant.

Crossing the room, Aphrodite cups Icarus's face, looking

deeply into her eyes before pulling her into a tight embrace. "Are you alright?"

"I—no. I don't want to talk about it." The fog in her eyes lifts slightly, and Icarus presses her forehead to Aphrodite's. "Remind me that I'm alive."

Aphrodite hesitates. Icarus needs to talk about whatever is going on, but if she requires a few moments of oblivion first, that is something she will happily provide her.

As her slender fingers deftly undo the leather straps of Icarus's armor, Aphrodite gently walks Icarus to the bed. The series of clanking as each piece of armor drops to the floor is loud, but neither of them care.

Wearing only the tunic and breeches that go beneath her armor, Icarus sits on the edge of the bed and Aphrodite leans into her space, kissing her softly.

All of her previous distractions have dissipated from her mind. Seeing Icarus in this state is a gut punch she was not expecting. The goddess's touch is soft as she reaches for the hem of Icarus's tunic, raising it over her head. Aphrodite kisses her again, sliding an arm around her waist and scooting her further up onto the bed.

Lightly gripping Icarus's chin, Aphrodite looks her in the eye and asks, "Are you sure you want to do this right now, my love?"

Icarus nods, and her silky voice is low when she adds, "Please."

Aphrodite knows Icarus wants to do this. Knows exactly what she needs. The knowledge is second nature, her Fates-given instincts.

Everyone's thoughts about sex are so basic, assuming an orgasm—however achieved— is the primary purpose of sex. But the goddess knows it is so much more than that. The right sex can be freeing, healing, transformative.

It can be the one thing someone needs to move past something, it can allow them to see the beauty in themselves, and it can connect people on a spiritual level. Sex has so many different speeds, rhythms, and purposes.

Right now, its purpose is to bring Aphrodite's lover to oblivion so she can forget the world around them.

She grips Icarus's hips and flips her over onto her stomach. Icarus startles at the sudden movement but complies. Reaching up to the corners of the mattress, she grabs the delicate leather straps and fastens them around Icarus's wrists.

Icarus groans as she kisses her neck and then drags her teeth along her spine. Fingers pressing into the golden skin of Icarus's hips, she lifts them until Icarus is on her knees and elbows. Aphrodite does not hesitate before plunging her face into Icarus's center from behind, both of them moaning when her tongue slides over her lover's opening. It only takes a moment before Icarus is dripping wet, hips rocking as she silently pleads for more.

Reaching over into the bedside table, Aphrodite pulls out a harness and phallus, setting another one on the bed beside them. Once the straps are secure, she positions herself before Icarus's center and teases her lover's opening with the tip of the phallus, enjoying the whimpers leaving Icarus's slips in soft cresting waves.

Hands still gripping Icarus's hips, Aphrodite takes one of them and runs her nails along the same path her teeth previously ventured down her spine, only applying enough pressure to make Icarus arch her back and cry out.

Icarus's core is molten when she dips her fingers inside, slicking the phallus with Icarus's wetness. She presses into her, inch by inch, allowing Icarus to open for her and stretch to meet the larger phallus that Aphrodite selected. Once inside Icarus to the hilt, Aphrodite rocks her hips slowly at first, but she can sense what Icarus wants—more.

Aphrodite plunges into Icarus, until her lover's breathing is rapid and Aphrodite is certain climax is near. Abruptly, she pulls out of Icarus, ignoring the whimper of frustration.

It only takes a moment to situate the other phallus from the drawer, and Aphrodite once again dips her fingers into Icarus to lubricate the double phallus. Icarus sucks in a breath as the heads of the dildos are situated at both of her entrances. This time, Aphrodite enters her at an excruciatingly slow pace, to allow for more adjusting, but the sight of Icarus so full of her makes Aphrodite want to fuck her lover senseless.

Icarus cries out once both phalluses are fully inside her, taking deep gasping breaths. "Yes, goddess!"

"Do you like me inside of you?" Aphrodite asks, even though she already knows the answer.

"Mmhmm," Icarus whimpers, thrusting against the phallus. As her climax nears, Icarus's skin glows, a soft golden light as if the sunrise is there in their bed.

Aphrodite continues to drive into Icarus until she hears the familiar sound of her love's orgasm.

Gently sliding the dildos out of Icarus, Aphrodite sets them aside and unfastens the restraints. Icarus drops face-down onto the bed with a satisfied sigh and she lays next to her, untying Icarus's braid and running her fingers through the golden tresses.

The silence is peaceful at first as they lay together, intertwined, but after a while, Aphrodite has to ask, "Do you want to talk about it?"

Icarus hesitates before saying, "I had a run-in with some rebels while out with the task force."

When Icarus does not continue, Aphrodite says, "That does not seem too out of the ordinary. Did something happen?"

She notes the way Icarus pulls her bottom lips between her teeth and chews on it. She does that when she is not sure about what she wants to say. After so many lifetimes together, it should not surprise her that the tells are always the same.

"I did something I wasn't supposed to. But... I'm not so sure it was wrong."

"My love, you have to give me more to work with," Aphrodite presses gently.

Icarus heaves a sigh. "I let a rebel get away with some children today."

"You *what*?" Aphrodite throws her hands in the air.

"They were children!" Icarus exclaims, frustration tinging the edge of her voice.

Aphrodite pinches her brow, trying to keep her irritation down. This is what all of this was about? Rebel guilt? "Icarus, those children grow up, and when they do, they will come for you just as their parents did."

Icarus sits up, pulling the sheets up to her chest. "You can't believe that! If everyone is already guilty of whatever their parents did before the, what is the point in living life and making choices? Why bother having dreams and ambitions? What if one of them grows up disagreeing with the rebels and then is the key to ending this battle?"

How did the atmosphere in the room shift so rapidly? One minute they are two lovers in post coital bliss, and now they are bickering over the fundamental basics of the world?

"Icarus," Aphrodite says through gritted teeth, "you *cannot* possibly be this naïve."

Aphrodite watches the wall shutter over Icarus's eyes. Wishes she could not see the hard edge that is now pointed in her direction. She should not have called her that, but what did she expect? These claims are juvenile and show how little time she has spent in the real world making difficult choices.

"You're right, *goddess*." The term has no reverence now, no respect. Icarus spit it out like poison, and perhaps it is.

Aphrodite's heart screams at her to tell her to stop as she watches her put on her tunic and pants and collect her armor. But Aphrodite says nothing even as Icarus walks out the door, slamming it behind her.

The day has been tedious, and Aphrodite's heart is hanging on by a thread. She should have done more to prevent Icarus from leaving and to assuage her concerns about the rebels. It did not need to be a blow up like it did. Why did she let it go that far?

Icarus has been slipping through her fingers, and every opportunity to right the boat, Aphrodite watches helplessly as she makes choices that leave it capsized.

There have been a thousand things to do, meetings to attend, councils to oversee. Athena's island is bustling with gods and council members alike. It is odd for such a large volume of Pantheon business to be conducted here instead of the Temple of Olympus, and Aphrodite is very much out of the loop now that she no longer shares Zeus's bed.

Between the upheaval with Icarus and the extra Pantheon presence, Aphrodite is even more determined to return to her island for a few days.

Another thorough search for Circe's mystery object will be a good distraction. Her soul feels cleaved in two with the way things stand with Icarus, but there will be time to fix everything with her once this island is quiet again.

Returning to her rooms, she winces at the sting that comes when she walks inside and is confronted with the reminder of her relationship falling apart in this very space only a few hours ago. On her vanity, however, a scroll catches her eye. It does not have a seal; it is tied with long thick green ribbon that Aphrodite recognizes as one Icarus sometimes wears.

Despite her annoyance that Icarus would be so careless as to leave a letter unsealed, she can barely stop her hands from shaking as she unrolls it and scans the contents several times.

Aphrodite,
I do not know a lot about the intricacies covering our world and

*those that choose to disrupt it, but I don't think that should come
between us and our love. What we have
is so much more than the power balance between mortals and gods.
If you also think this is something worth fighting for, I will be in the
gardens at 11 p.m.
If you do not choose to meet me, I understand.
This time with you has been incredible. I did not know it was
possible to feel so alive.*

*Thank you, goddess,
Icarus*

The ink on the paper bleeds as a tear falls from Aphrodite's cheek. Out the window, the fading light tells her that the sun is setting.

There are still several hours between now and when she needs to meet Icarus. She has no idea what they will do or how they will move forward, but Aphrodite is determined that they will do it *together.*

The evening drags on at a never-ending dinner with the other gods that is full of forced smiles and fake conversation. Her eyes flit to the clock every few seconds. All Aphrodite can think about is her golden ray of sunshine that she has neglected far too much.

She can finally get away with only thirty minutes to spare. Her room is on the way, so she can stop and grab a few things in case they need to make a quick getaway.

Her blood freezes in her veins when she finds her door open. Is it Icarus? Surely, she would not have left it unlocked; she is not usually so careless.

Dread pools in her stomach, but Aphrodite pushes her shoulder back, lifts her chin, and walks into her room like the goddess that she is. The false bravado deflates in an instant when she finds Oedipus sitting at her vanity, reading the letter from Icarus with one hand and twirling the ribbon with the other.

"Oedipus. What are you doing here?" Aphrodite asks. She tries to keep her voice calm, but it comes out clipped, and she knows it belies her nerves.

"I was talking to Zeus," Oedipus drawls, a smirk spreading across his face. "It seems that the Goddess of Love has not been sharing too much of that love, and it got us to wondering whether you might have a secret lover."

Aphrodite opens her mouth to object, but he puts a hand up to stop her.

"I told him that was preposterous, but it turns out you've had an eye on a mortal all along?" He tsks, shaking his head, his eyes going dark. "You're too good for my bed, and you turn down the King of the Gods, but you let a *mortal* between your legs?"

"Get out," Aphrodite seethes, acutely aware that this is taking entirely too long.

Oedipus laughs but there is no humor in the icy sound. "Let me tell you how this is going to work, *Mother*."

He steps into her space, and Aphrodite stands her ground despite wanting to be as far away from her son as possible.

"You see," he continues, placing a hand on her throat but not squeezing, "I know that your little tryst is forbidden. So, unless you want me to inform Zeus what you have been up to, you will finally give me what you should have a long time ago."

"I am still your mother," Aphrodite bites out.

"Hm. That you are. And unless you want this little lover to share the same fate as the last one, you will spread your fucking legs for me."

A white-hot rage tears through Aphrodite. "The *last* one?"

High pitched ringing fills Aphrodite's ears as Oedipus says, "I didn't let you keep a mortal bitch for a pet then, and I won't stand by and let you do it now."

Five hundred years. For five hundred fucking years Aphrodite has been a ghost of herself, constantly searching for the love that she now knows was stolen from her. He has no idea that Icarus is a reincarnation of Andromeda, and she can be satisfied knowing he will never have that.

A cold calm washes over her, and she smiles at her son. "You're right, darling." Aphrodite flutters her lashes and flashes him her most alluring look.

His grip on her throat loosens, and he leans in to kiss her. She turns her head at the last second, cringing as his lips touch her throat. But while he is distracted with her false consent, her fingers slowly loosen the ribbon from his grasp. He does not notice when his head drops to the space between her breasts and she loosely circles the ribbon around his neck, not pulling it tight until it's perfectly in place.

When she is ready, she croons, "Oedipus."

He looks up at her from between her breasts, and when his eyes lock on hers, she pulls at either side of the ribbon until it tightens around his throat.

His eyes bug out, and his fingers fly to the ribbon, trying to get beneath the fabric, but his hands are too big. He swats at her grip, but she holds on tight; she is still a god after all.

His breathing slows, and as the life leaves his eyes she says, "This is for ever thinking you could touch me."

He collapses to the floor with a thud, and she allows herself one second to grieve the sweet little boy he used to be. It breaks her heart that her child could have turned out this way, but she did everything she could to help him.

A sob leaves her as she stares at his lifeless body on the ground.

A chiming sound snaps Aphrodite out of her grief as she realizes it is the sound of the clock... striking 11 p.m.

Aphrodite races to the gardens, not bothering with decorum or protocol, ignoring the confused looks on acolytes and Heroes alike as she tears down the corridors.

Her heart is hammering in her chest when she finally reaches the spot they were to meet.

On a rock, glistening in the moonlight, is Icarus's sunstone.

28

HESTIA

The familiar quiet of the empty library wraps around Hestia, cocooning her in safety as she pushes the cart through the stacks, putting books back in their places on the shelves. An acolyte usually does this here in the Under Temple Library, but she has taken over the duty.

She may no longer be the Goddess of Knowledge, but centuries spent amongst the ink and parchment have forever branded libraries as the place where her soul can truly rest.

Scouring the texts, however, has proven fruitless. There is nothing in them giving Hestia any hints regarding the key from the Book of Fates, nor anything even remotely helpful about the stone circle in the diagram.

A smile spreads across Hestia's lips when she hears footsteps walking down the aisle behind her. When Alec slides his arms around her waist, Hestia closes her eyes and leans her head against his.

His beard is rough against her skin as he peppers kisses along her neck, murmuring, "I missed you, my goddess."

Hestia spins around and brings her lips to his, and they back up against the bookshelves, thankfully carved out of the stone of the Under Temple itself and therefore sturdy as a mountain.

Books fall to the floor with resounding *thunks*, and pages flutter in the air as Alec presses Hestia against the shelf. She spends a mere second concerned about the state of the books, but Alec's hand travels up her skirt and finds her center, and Hestia cries out—the irony of her volume in the library not lost on her.

Alec grasps the back of Hestia's neck with his free hand, holding her tightly while his other hand drives her mad between her thighs.

He slows the pace of his fingers, leans in, and whispers, "Are we completely alone?"

Hestia fights off the fog of desire, trying to figure out what he is saying, what words are again. Finally, she nods. "Yes. I was closing up for the night."

He bites his bottom lip, and the gesture makes heat pool in her belly. A blush floods her cheeks when Alec drops to his knees and his head disappears beneath her skirts. Grabbing the closest shelves for support, Hestia herself disregards the books that go flying now as Alec's mouth dives straight for her clit.

A finger slides inside her, followed by another, while Alec continues the blissful torture with his tongue. The climax explodes out of Hestia before she even realized it was building, and her cries of pleasure echo off the marble floors and walls.

When he resurfaces and stands, the look on Alec's face tells Hestia he is not even close to done. He leans in to kiss her, and she can still taste herself on his tongue.

As he presses into her, Hestia can feel the rigid hardness of his lust for her. She runs her hand over his length above his trousers and the low, guttural groan that leaves him makes her knees weak.

Reaching down, he loosens the button of his pants, letting them fall to the floor. His hands grasp the back of her thighs, but before he can lift, she puts a hand on his shoulder to stop him.

Confusion crosses his face, and Hestia looks down at the floor. "I weigh too much. You will hurt yourself."

Alec gently cups Hestia's chin, pulling her gaze up to his. "Look at me."

Hestia's face flushes as she peers into his silvery gaze. He says nothing, however, only stares intently into her eyes as he reaches back down for her thighs.

Gripping them tightly, he lifts her off the ground, wrapping her legs around her waist. Alec never breaks the eye contact, allowing her to see how little effort is required of him.

In seconds, Alec slides into her and stars are shattering throughout her body every time he drives all the way inside her. She wraps her arms around his shoulders, clutching his hair into her fist in euphoric bliss.

In her ear, Hestia can hear Alec's breathing pick up its pace, and she knows he is nearing his climax as well. The most sensual supernova erupts in Hestia's soul as Alec moans and spills into her.

After a moment, he gently stands Hestia on her feet as they both try to get their breath back.

Looking around at the mess, laughter bubbles out of Hestia. She turns to Alec, who is examining his finger.

"What's the matter?" she asks, stepping forward to take a closer look.

Alec laughs and shows her the thin slice of blood on his finger. "Paper cut."

Hestia walks into a small lounge with the Book of Fates tucked beneath her arm and a steaming cup of tea in her hand. It is morning, but with the absence of daylight in the Underworld, Hestia's internal clock is off, and she yawns loudly.

It does not help that she needs more sleep these days, as well.

Do mortals always need this much rest? Or is it just while her body is still adjusting?

As Hestia sits on the dark velvet couch, Hera comes in, and a smile immediately blooms on Hestia's face.

"Hera, am I to be blessed with your company this morning?" she greets.

Hera chuckles, and the rich sound sings to Hestia's soul. She was not certain she would ever see her friend again. The relief she feels now that Hera is back will be enough for her, right?

It seems selfish to even continue to entertain the idea of more when she should just be grateful that her friend is safe. Hestia has the love of Alec, and the state of the world is a disaster. It feels like now is not the best time to push further with something so delicate.

"We haven't had much time together since my return. I have missed you terribly." Hera's eyes gleam as Hestia searches them for any deeper meaning, any subtext.

"I never gave up looking for you," Hestia says softly.

Hera nods and sits down next to her. She places her hands over Hestia's, sending a jolt of electricity through her body. "I know you did, and I am forever grateful."

Hestia can smell Hera's lily perfume as the Queen of the Gods leans over and kisses Hestia's cheek. She goes rigid. Did she really...

Hestia's hand flies to the spot Hera's lips vacate as her face reddens.

Glancing up at approaching footsteps, Hestia scoots a couple inches away from Hera as Dionysus walks into the room. Guilt courses through her like a tidal wave. Would Alec, or even Dionysus feel betrayed by such a thing?

Dio looks between Hestia and Hera, but his jovial expression never falters as he sits in one of the armchairs in the room. An acolyte comes in behind him carrying a tray of fruits and cheeses. He pulls a bottle of wine from his robes and sets it on the table.

Hestia raises an eyebrow. "It's ten o'clock in the morning, Dio."

Dionysus waves Hestia off and gestures to the tome on the table. "Tell us about this book," he says, changing the subject.

Hestia tells them what little she gleamed from the book on the ship back from Corcyra, pulling the key from her pocket. Hera and Dionysus thumb through the pages, looking at the various sketches and diagrams.

When they get to the back, Hestia grabs one of the candles sitting on the table and slides it closer to the book. Astonishment flashes on their faces when the sketch of the standing stones appears on the page.

"Have either of you ever seen anything like this?" Hestia asks, raising her eyes to glance at Hera and Dionysus.

The latter shakes his head. "Have you shown Cassandra or Isadora yet?"

"I haven't had a chance to tell her when she is alone. My gut tells me that this is not information that should be shared freely, not even amongst the Allegiance."

Hera seems worlds away as she says, "I think you're probably right."

The blank pages in the back of the book reveal nothing new, even with the presence of a flame, and Hestia thumbs through them mindlessly hoping something will come to her.

She gasps and stops when words spontaneously appear on one of the pages. Hestia reads them aloud as the glittering ink materializes.

"The Hearts of the Fates
are the keys to righting the realm.
Like the Fates,
there are three.
The first you have already found,
embedded in this tome.
The next two will require more.

Sacrifices must be made,
powers reclaimed.
First.
Shining brightly,
but not in the heavens,
a star has been hidden.
Only the worthy can ascend
to retrieve what it protects.
Lastly,
The true power of this realm
has been hidden from those
who should wield it.
One of the lost daughters of Rhea
will step into her strength,
bringing those that have wronged her
to their knees.
But only if she can look
without going mad.
Hurry now,
Make haste,
Before the tides have turned for good."

29

ARACHNE

"Your move," Psyche says with a grin, gesturing to the table before them.

Arachne studies the pesseia board before her and is delighted to see a move that will allow her to capture one of Psyche's pieces.

Since arriving in the Underworld, she has been devouring books and games. The absence of entertainment on Corcyra leaves her unable to get enough of it now. With the Allegiance based out of the Under Temple, there is an abundance of game partners and people to converse with. She feels alive again for the first time after being cursed by Athena.

A constant by Arachne's side has been Cyril, and she wishes he was here now. His presence makes her feel safe and grounded, which she finds odd since she hardly knows him. The only other people she feels truly trusting of are Psyche and Hera. Everyone is being so kind to her, but it is too risky to completely open up just yet.

Psyche studies the game board, reaching for one of her purple pieces when Cyril comes running into the room calling for the goddess. Arachne blinks hard, trying to assess if she is hallucinating him after wishing for his return only seconds prior.

He flashes Arachne a quick smile as he rushes over to Psyche. "Goddess, pardon the interruption, but your presence is urgently requested."

"What is the matter?" Psyche asks, all previous amusement gone from her expression.

"There's someone that needs to be oathed. I will explain on the way, but I must implore that we leave *immediately*. This person will be a huge asset to the Allegiance, but if we are not quick, she might change her mind or worse—the Pantheon could discover her intentions."

Psyche leaps up, abandoning the game, as she and Cyril make for the door. Sadness pokes at Arachne as she watches him walk away after only *just* being excited to see him again.

The thought of both Cyril and Psyche not being here, hardly having anyone she can comfortably talk to, makes her skin crawl.

"Wait!" Arachne calls out, running after them.

Cyril stops for Arachne, while Psyche continues on to prepare for the impromptu journey.

The idea of being back on the sea again makes Arachne's stomach turn, but she wants more time with Cyril. "Can I come with you? I promise I'll stay out of the way."

Cyril offers her a warm smile. "Did you miss me?"

Arachne nods, and he reaches out to take her hand. "Let's go."

Exhilaration and dread take turns being the dominant emotion as they get closer to the ship. As they walk up the ramp, Arachne sends up a hope to the Fates that Psyche will have more of her sea sickness tea.

Reaching into her pocket, she thumbs the stone within from the precious journey, thankful she always has it on her. Arachne does not need the stone's anti-nausea properties on land in the Underworld, but after the time at sea, she is accustomed to its presence and uses it to fidget.

Like the ship before, this one only holds enough room for a small crew and very few additional personnel.

In a matter of moments, they are pulling away from the docks and on their way to retrieve the mystery asset.

ICARUS

Waves slap against the rocks, and Icarus runs her hand through Amara's mane, trying to calm the pegasus. Can her steed sense the tension in the air, or is it simply that their bond is so strong that she can detect it?

Pulling the folded piece of parchment from her pocket, Icarus checks the crudely drawn map on it against her official Pantheon one. She is certain she got the small island correct, but as every second passes, her confidence shrinks.

The first parchment Cyril had given Icarus led her to a small cove near their initial run-in. After a brief discussion with him, he gave her a new map and said he would return shortly.

Icarus's mind drifts to Aphrodite, and the stabbing pain in her heart tells her she's following the wrong line of thinking right now. If the Pantheon discovers her betrayal, her lover will be the least of her concerns.

In the distance, a ship appears on the horizon, and Icarus's breath catches in her chest. In a few short moments, she will either be well on her way to helping the realm like she always wanted... or she will be dead.

As the ship draws closer, she could cry with relief when she sees it bears no official Pantheon markings. A lantern flashes on the deck, and she grabs the reins, slinging her leg over the saddle and taking to the sky on Amara.

The pegasus lands on the small deck of the ship with a loud *thunk*, and Cyril comes running over to greet them.

"Fates damnit, am I glad to see you and not Zeus," Icarus exclaims as she climbs down from Amara.

"And I'm equally glad you didn't have a legion of Heroes waiting here to betray me." Cyril claps his hand on Icarus's shoulder and turns to introduce her to the small crew.

Several sets of eyes look at Icarus with suspicion, and none say a word to greet her. Her Heroes armor may have been a mistake, but if she is going to rally against the Pantheon, it would be idiotic to leave behind protection of this quality.

A figure emerges from below deck, and her heart skips when she recognizes the goddess Psyche. Her unmistakable dark hair and beauty is intimidating, but a more concerning realization has Icarus questioning everything even further.

The rebels have a god on their side?

Everything Icarus knows of Psyche is her warmth and kindness. Most gods have at least a rumor or two floating around about hidden cruelties and proclivities, with only a rare few maintaining a genuinely good reputation.

Unlike the crew of the ship, Psyche greets Icarus with a friendly smile.

"Hello, Hero. What can we help you with?" Psyche asks.

Icarus looks around at the assembled personnel and can see the uncertainty on their faces. Someone needs to be the first to trust here, and the rebels have already taken a step toward that by bringing Psyche. The situation is precarious; the wrong word can too easily result in bloodshed.

Icarus's heart flutters rapidly as she takes a deep breath and says, "The Heroes are not what I thought they were. This was not what I anticipated when I signed up."

Psyche nods. "There are few who see the Pantheon for what it is. The story on the surface is easy to swallow, rather compelling. Why would most bother to look any further?"

Shame flushes Icarus's cheeks. "I know better now."

Psyche takes a step forward, putting a hand on Icarus's shoulder. "Almost everyone you will encounter amongst our movement believed in the cause of the Pantheon at one point. And virtually every story you hear about why they joined will be different and equally horrendous."

Icarus casts her gaze down at her boots. "I can only imagine after what I've already seen," she mumbles.

"Do you wish to join us then, Hero?" Psyche asks.

Thoughts race through her mind as Icarus weighs the decision, but the image that keeps repeating is that of the children in the cave, the fear in their eyes. "I do. I know it will take time to trust me, but I am willing to work toward earning that trust."

Psyche's dark lips quirk into a smile. "Then there is an oath you must take. Should your soul prove to be genuinely devoted to our cause, we will welcome you with open arms."

Icarus presses her lips together. "I will gladly take your oath. On my honor, I will not betray you."

The smile vanishes from Psyche's face, and her tone becomes serious as she says, "The consequences of betraying your oath go farther than punishment in this realm. Before you take this oath, I must caution you. The suffering that will befall you should not be taken lightly."

Icarus shakes her head and says, "Consequences be damned. My entire life, all I have ever wanted is to fight for the people, to protect the realm. Now I know it is the Pantheon the realm needs protection from."

Psyche smiles, taking Icarus's hand. "Then let's get you to the Oasis, Hero."

Icarus rolls over in the bed, sheets twisting around her body as she tosses and turns. It has to be almost midnight, and then she will be twenty-five years old.

Should she have left the Heroes the day before her birthday? Probably not, but she had to get away—away from the legion, the lies, being gaslit by her lover. Her chest feels hollow as she thinks about Aphrodite.

After all her grand speeches about their past lives and how they are destined to be together, it was callous and cruel of Aphrodite to brush Icarus aside like she for the last few weeks.

A hot flash surges through Icarus, and she flings the blankets off, allowing the cool air to caress her skin. The itching between her shoulder blades is almost unbearable. The dread of leaving and adrenaline of her defection was a temporary distraction from the torment, but it cannot be ignored any longer.

Icarus jumps out of bed and searches the room, looking for anything she can use to scratch her back. The only things she can find are her weapons, and she knows she really should not, but the itching is incessant. Finally, she decides on her dagger and tries to angle it to reach the torturous source of discomfort.

The clock on the wall chimes, and as the twelve gongs ring out, the itching fades. Icarus lowers the dagger with relief.

Without warning, searing pain erupts between her shoulder blades, and she screams, doubling over and dropping to her knees.

The door flies open, and several people come running in. Icarus knows their faces, but her brain is nowhere near capable of forming words or names as the pain rips through her body, pressure building from the spot of the initial itching.

"What the Fates is going on?" someone asks urgently, a man, but Icarus does not know who.

A bright light in the mirror catches her eye, and Icarus watches in stunned silence as bronze flaming wings sprout from her back in the reflection. They unfurl and spread out, feathers ruffling as they situate.

At last, the pain finally subsides, and Icarus can breathe again.

"Holy fucking shit," someone says, and Icarus finally recognizes the people who came into her room—Psyche, Cadmus, and Medusa.

It is a shock to see the gorgon, especially in Icarus's own chambers. Everyone here seems to trust Medusa, but Icarus still has her doubts. How can she sort through what was Pantheon lies, and what is fact?

She has seen for herself the aftermath of Castor's run-in with her, and she remembers the innocent nymphs that were harmed in Medusa's escaped attempt. Or were those lies, too?

Medusa mutters to Psyche but it is loud enough for Icarus to hear. "You weren't kidding when you said Phoenix, were you?"

Psyche shakes her head while looking at Icarus in equal parts awe and amazement. She told Psyche everything in the Oasis. About her past lives, the phoenix curse, her relationship with Aphrodite—all of it.

"Happy birthday," Psyche says gently.

"Thanks," Icarus responds in a whisper, staring at the wings that still glow in the mirror. "I guess I'm learning how to fly tomorrow."

31

MEDUSA

The warmth of the hot spring bubbles around Medusa as she leans her head back against the cool stone wall. Psyche steps into the water to join her.

After the chaos with Icarus, Cadmus left to go on watch duty. Neither Psyche nor Medusa could sleep, so they are both hopeful that the soothing warmth of the water will make them drowsy again.

Psyche's hair is twisted up into a bun, with a few simple pins holding it in place. The candlelight of the bathing room casts her ebony locks in a soft golden glow. A few tendrils hang loose from the rest, damp from the water and clinging to her neck.

All Medusa can think is that is where her lips should be.

Bringing her mouth to Psyche's skin, the goddess sighs when they connect, leaning into the gesture.

She pushes off the side of the bath and moves in front of Psyche, between her legs. The spark in Psyche's eye is all she needs to see to move in for a deep kiss, digging her fingers into the goddess's hair.

Gently pulling back, Psyche softly gasps when Medusa's lips return to her neck, flicking her tongue over the hollow of her throat.

Gripping Psyche's thighs, Medusa lifts her out of the water, setting Psyche on the edge of the bath without breaking their kiss. Medusa's thumbs find her already pebbled nipples and squeeze gently, eliciting a moan. Then her lips travel over Psyche's collarbone and down to her perky breasts, running her tongue over the goddess's small, dark nipples.

Psyche giggles as Medusa's kisses tickle her ribs, continuing her journey south until Psyche's center is before her. Spreading her legs wide to make plenty of room, she cups Medusa's cheek.

Closing her eyes, she leans into the touch, kissing Psyche's palm. Her lips brush against Psyche's opening, and Psyche's holds the back of Medusa's head. Her serpents slither around Psyche's fingers, and Psyche cries out as Medusa's tongue slowly circles her clit.

Psyche bucks her hips in a slow rhythm that matches Medusa's. Bringing her fingers to Psyche's slit, she's pleased to find it slick with arousal. The first finger slides inside of the goddess with ease, and Medusa adds a second and then third as her lips never leave Psyche's clit.

She brings her mouth a little lower to join her fingers, and with the goddess's wetness on her tongue, she swears she would happily drown in it. With every lap of her tongue, the way Psyche tastes is forever being etched onto her brain.

Psyche frowns when she stops abruptly, but understanding crosses her expression when she realizes Medusa is leading them back to the bed.

They fall into the sheets together, with no regard for the dampness from the baths. Their lips meet in a frenzy, and they kiss as if it is more vital than oxygen. Briefly, Medusa makes to return to the paradise between Psyche's thighs, and Psyche guides Medusa on her side, her own core now inches from Psyche's lips.

As Medusa's tongue dives back into the divine pools of Psyche's center, Psyche's does the same. Medusa pauses to moan into Psyche's core as the goddess's tongue or fingers hit the right spot.

Together, they bring each other to the brink of bliss, falling into the waves of climax crest and crash.

Gasping for breath after, they lie in bed together, limbs tangled in the darkness.

The corridor is dark and cold, the usual state of things here in the Underworld. It is two in the morning, but it would be no brighter even if it was noontime on a sunny, cloudless day.

Cerberus's soft footfalls sound beside her as they walk together. He always knows when Medusa is wandering aimlessly and never fails to accompany her.

Psyche fell back asleep quickly, but slumber continued to elude Medusa. As usual.

After several turns without paying attention, Medusa realizes she is not quite sure where she is. She has covered a lot of ground during her walks when she wants to think, but there is still more than enough left undiscovered and she could really get lost here.

She is uncertain what motivates her to pick the directions she takes, but after a little while, she realizes the floor is slanted and that she is getting deeper underground. Yet turn after turn, she keeps going.

Her thoughts are a million miles away, and she wishes they were on the good things she has to focus on, but it shames her that they are focused on revenge.

Every day Medusa's confidence builds along with her defenses. She always imagined with that would come peace, but it is the opposite. The tougher her armor, the angrier Medusa gets over everything stolen from her. It makes her furious that instead of focusing on the two people who would go to the ends of the earth for her, all she can think about is watching the life leave Poseidon's eyes.

The slanted floor soon turns into stone steps, and Medusa continues without noticing, visions of vindication glimmering in her mind.

Cerberus barks, and it pulls Medusa from her distracted thoughts.

Her jaw drops when she looks around. She is no longer in a corridor but in a massive cavern. She squints and peers up to see how high it goes, only to be nearly blinded by a glowing light.

The brightness nearly makes Medusa's heart stop, forcing her to shield her eyes as the words from the Book of Fates return to her.

Shining brightly, but not in the heavens.

This is it. The star.

Cerberus is fast on Medusa's heels as she races back up the stairs to go find the others.

"What do you mean you don't know where she is? You're the fucking oracle for Fates' sake!" Aphrodite sighs. An hour of talking in cryptic circles and getting nowhere is testing every ounce of patience she possesses.

"Goddess, even the Fates cannot tell you what is hidden from them." The oracle's gravelly voice is almost swallowed by the darkness of the room.

"This was a waste of time." Aphrodite stands abruptly, knocking her chair to the ground as the lights in the room turn on.

Brushing past the acolytes and their endless swarm of questions, Aphrodite pulls the hood of her cloak over her head and storms out onto the streets of Olympus.

Useless oracle. She could not even tell Aphrodite a cardinal direction in which to begin her search.

Yet the pain in her heart is too much to bear.

I cannot believe she is really gone.

This is it. Icarus's last life. Five hundred years yearning for the missing piece of her soul, and she callously tossed it aside when the universe brought it back to her.

The cobblestone street is uneven beneath Aphrodite's

sandaled feet, and the congestion of the crowd is stifling, but the goddess is grateful for the anonymity it provides as she makes her way back to her ship.

As she gets closer to the harbor, the cluster of people thins, and Aphrodite pulls her hood down farther, praying to the pointless Fates that no one recognizes her.

Sunlight reflects brightly off a set of armor. Athena and Ares walk down to the marina in front of her. Aphrodite almost ducks into a narrow alley to hide, but then she stops. What do the other gods talk about when she's not around?

Heart pounding, Aphrodite picks up speed until she is close enough to hear their conversation.

"Some Goddess of War," Ares growls. "If you cannot even keep your trainees in line, perhaps you are past your prime."

"You are not without defectors yourself. Now is not the time to turn on each other. Believe me, I am livid. Icarus is a true Hero, not like these buffoons with inflated egos."

Ares scoffs. "The Heroes are an elite fighting force, trained by you and me. Maybe your ability to recognize greatness is not what it used to be. I knew that girl would prove to be a disappointment."

Rage bubbles in Aphrodite's chest, and she fights the urge to defend Icarus's honor. It won't do, though; better to continue listening.

"It matters little now. Telegonus will find her, and then she will regret betraying the Pantheon," Athena snaps.

With nothing else to focus on, Aphrodite tears through the storage rooms of her temple, wracking her brain for any clue in Circe's words.

The artifact room glitters as she steps into it. Jewels, precious metals, and important items from the Temple of Love fill the shelves, and she tenderly runs a finger over them.

It cannot be somewhere as obvious as this, right?

There is a small, jeweled box covered with sparkly flowers—the same ones from the painting with the forgotten name. The short green stems curve at the top, allowing the white petals to hang. They remind Aphrodite of those first days of Spring when Winter is still clinging to the earth.

Aphrodite sets the box back on the shelf and notices a silver hand mirror propped against the wall behind it. A serpentine dragon swallowing its own tail frames the circular mirror, similar to the full-size ones that hang in the temples.

As she gazes into the silver reflection, even when nothing happens, Aphrodite knows this is the item she was supposed to find.

33

HESTIA

"Huh," Alec mutters as the collected group stares up at the mysterious star in the cavern beneath the Under Temple.

"This has to be the star the Book Fates was talking about," Hestia insists, squinting against the glaring brightness of the underground celestial body.

She does not want to get her hopes up, but it feels like something is finally going right for the Allegiance. What are the odds of one of things they need the most being beneath their feet? It seems too easy.

"Only the worthy can ascend. Is that what it said?" Isadora asks.

"Yes," Hestia answers with a nod. "To retrieve what it protects."

"All right. So the second key, or heart, is in that star. So how do we get it out?" Isadora raises an eyebrow and looks at the stumped group for any ideas.

"Can we shoot it?" Dionysus wonders, pursing his lips.

Everyone turns to him, brows crinkled as they try to determine if he is serious.

Shrugging his shoulders, the God of Partying continues, "I

don't see anyone stepping up with better ideas. Worst-case scenario, we lose an arrow, right?"

Hestia is certain that is *not* the worst-case scenario, but they need that key.

When no one responds, Dionysus gestures to Alec. "I am useless with a bow, but why don't you give it a try?"

Alec looks to Isadora who rolls her eyes but says, "Do it. Go grab a bow from one of the nearest archers on watch."

Hera puts her hand on Dionysus's shoulder. "It isn't a completely terrible idea." She chuckles, and Dionysus blushes beneath her attention.

Hestia cannot describe the emotion that fills her while watching the two of them. Is it jealousy? She does not think so. She genuinely wants Hera to be happy, even if that means never sharing her feelings.

A realization dawns over her then, and her stomach feels as if the floor has fallen out beneath her feet; she is not jealous that Dionysus is touching Hera, Hestia is merely envious that *she* is not.

Dionysus looks up and catches her watching them. Glancing away quickly, Hestia walks over to where Isadora, Medusa, and Cassandra are deep in conversation as they brainstorm thoughts about the star.

The chatter between them flows freely, and Hestia nods along as if she is listening, using it as cover to let her thoughts float back to Hera.

Does Hestia wish she was with Hera and not Alec? No, that doesn't feel right either. Her mind frantically tries to grasp a scenario that makes sense, but centuries alone in a library has given her little knowledge on how to navigate a situation as precarious as this.

If she is not careful, Hestia will lose both Hera and Alec, as well as her newfound friendship with Dionysus. Are these feelings worth blowing up everything she *does* have?

Footsteps sound on the steps behind them, and Alec appears with a bow and a quiver of several arrows.

Conversations comes to a stop, and everyone watches in silence as Alec hands the bow to Medusa.

At the surprised faces, Alec laughs and says, "Assumptions will get you nowhere." He winks at Medusa. "Show 'em what you can do, kiddo."

Medusa takes a steadying breath and nocks an arrow onto the bow, pulling the it back tightly and bringing her fingers holding the string to the corner of her lips.

Bracing against the bright light, Medusa raises the bow and aims the best she can before loosing the arrow. It disappears into the brightness of the star.

For a moment, nothing happens and the disappointment is palpable.

Then the ground rumbles suddenly, and Hestia struggles to remain standing as rocks come crashing down. The group scrambles up the steps, tripping onto them as the debris blocks off the entrance to the cavern behind them.

Brushing off the dust from the collapse, Isadora narrows her eyes at Dionysus. "Worst-case we lose an arrow, my ass."

"Hey, no fault of mine that you chose to listen to *me* of all people." He laughs and the sound echoes loudly, especially since no one else joins in. Dionysus rolls his eyes. "I'll go grab some people and get the clean-up started."

Isadora's fierceness does not relent as she says, "Make it quick, please." The leader of the Allegiance then addresses the rest of the group. "I guess we will reconvene once we have access to the cavern again. In the meantime, I guess carry on as usual."

Irritation radiates from Isadora's retreating form as she ascends the steps without saying goodbye to the group.

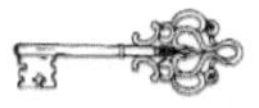

The small sitting area near the room Hestia shares with Alec is chilly, and she pulls her cloak around her tightly. She doesn't think she will ever get used to the frigid cold of the Underworld as a mortal.

Noticing the gesture, Alec wraps his arm around Hestia, pulling her closely to his warm body. She sighs, leaning into him and breathing him in, his woody cedar scent grounding her.

"Supervising clean-up was exhausting," Dionysus sighs as he plops down onto the same sofa as Hestia, leaving a gap between them. Hestia's heart could rival a hummingbird's as Hera sits in the space.

An acolyte enters next with a tray of bottles and the usual plates of cheeses, breads, and fruits that always follow Dionysus wherever he goes.

As the acolyte places the bottles of wine and mead on the table, Alec laughs. "Are you expecting more people, Dio? There's enough alcohol here for an entire Legion of Heroes."

"One can never be too prepared when it comes to the imbibing of spirits. Better to have entirely too much than run out early and ruin a party." His smirk is almost hidden by his flaxen mustache and beard.

"Oh, so this is a party now, is it?" Hestia asks.

Dionysus raises his goblet in a toast. "It is always a party when I am present."

Hera purrs, leaning into the God of Wine. "It certainly is."

Hestia squirms in her seat, looking away from what should possibly be a private moment between them. An unfamiliar feeling tugs at her consciousness.

Am I jealous?

She dismisses the thought almost instantaneously.

Alec picks up a cup and reads the labels on the bottles before uncorking one and pouring it. When he leans back with it in his hand, Hestia's eyes widen when he places the goblet in her grasp. He nods in encouragement, and she brings the rim to her lip, letting the cold metal ground her. Perhaps this is precisely what Hestia needs to move past her silly hangups.

The bubbles tickle Hestia's nose as she sips the honeysuckle sparkling wine. Its sweetness sends an energetic spark through her body, and she takes a deeper drink, welcoming the loosening of her inhibitions.

Hestia remembers the berries from her first time being at one of Dionysus's events, but she does not care if he has them with him here. She wants this. Wants to let go of the blocks in her mind that are holding her back from confessing her truth.

Her eyes flit to Hera, and wine almost dribbles out of her mouth when she finds the goddess watching her with a gleam in her eye.

Oh Fates, is there even a chance this could be real? Is this a cruel trick to force me back into my loneliness? Have I betrayed your plan of solitude for me?

As the wine swims through Hestia, her brain takes on a fuzzy edge she finds incredibly pleasing. Her anxieties are notably absent. She gulps another long drink, closing her eyes and letting the delicious nectar work its magic.

After a while of chatting, laughing, and increasing levels of inebriation, Dionysus clears his throat. "I may not be the God of Love and Sex, but I can spot tension anywhere. It is past time that we had a discussion, and now I believe everyone is ready for it."

A giggle spills out of Hestia, and she clamps a hand over her mouth, thoroughly enjoying the buzz filling her body.

"Definitely ready, then," Alec says, nowhere near as tipsy as Hestia, but he is not the one who will have to bare his soul.

"What are you talking about, Dio?" Hera asks, a loose laugh lingering on her lips as she sips her own wine.

"You and Hestia have feelings for each other. I know it. Alec knows it. The only people who don't seem to know it are the two of you." Dionysus levels a look at her that finds it mark, even through her buzz.

Hestia looks to Alec, searching for any signs of betrayal or understanding in his eyes. Did he and Dionysus just ruin everything?

Alec's face is unreadable, and Hera says, "Dio, perhaps now isn't—"

"It is true," Hestia says, taking another sip of her wine for liquid fortitude. There is no point in denying it now that it is out in the open. She can only hope Alec will forgive her.

Hand moving to her chest, Hera says, voice low in almost a whisper, "Hestia?"

Hestia looks into Hera's eyes, and the world moves in slow-motion when she finds hope in them. Is this her chance?

"I wish I had known my true feelings for you before you were taken. Perhaps then, I could have prevented it. If I hadn't been such a cowardly hermit, if I had experienced the world the way it was meant to be experienced, perhaps I would have been aware so much sooner."

Hera takes Hestia's hand into hers, interlacing their fingers together, and her heart skips a beat at the contact. How could Hestia have never noticed the electricity in their touch in the past?

Looking around, Hestia realizes Alec and Dionysus have stepped out of the room to allow them this moment in private. Hestia's stomach drops at the thought of him being angry with her. But one problem at a time...

With the absence of an audience, Hestia feels emboldened as she reaches out and cups Hera's cheek.

She is unsure who moves first. Their faces draw closer until she can feel the warmth of Hera's breath on her skin. The world falls away as Hera's soft lips brush against hers.

A tear rolls down her cheek then, and Hera reaches up to wipe it away with her thumb before gently grasping Hestia's neck and pulling her in for a deeper kiss, their lips parting for each other as their tongues meet. Hera sighs into Hestia's embrace, and the sound ignites the inferno of desire within her.

She is unsure if it is the wine causing her increased boldness, but as the heat pools between her thighs, a thought occurs to Hestia that she cannot ignore.

Breaking free from their kiss, Hestia takes Hera's hands. "I have an idea, but if it is beyond insanity, we can chalk it up to the spirits and never speak of it again."

Hera's mischievous smirk is the only encouragement Hestia needs as she continues, "It seems a shame that Alec and Dio aren't here, after all they were ones to orchestrate everything."

"I think I know where you are going with this, if it is what I hope," Hera says.

"I can only pray to the Fates that that is the case." Hestia laughs.

"The chambers he and I share have a bed that is *quite* spacious." Hera's voice is laced with desire, and Hestia cannot believe this is happening.

"Let's go find our men, shall we?" Hestia proposes.

"Yes. Let's," Hera answers, but her mood dims. What state will Alec be in when they find them?

34

ICARUS

"Are you sure?" Cyril asks, his voice full of uncertainty.

Icarus digs her heels into the sand of the training ring, nodding as she focuses on fortifying the armor-like magma coating every inch of her body.

All her time these last few days has been spent learning the extent of her newfound powers. Were she still with Aphrodite, Icarus could have asked questions about her abilities in her past lives. The fresh loss of her lover stabs in her heart, but she cannot get lost in that pain if she wants to make a difference.

Cyril shakes his head but pulls his arm back and hurtles a spear in Icarus's direction.

Icarus grits her teeth and cries out for joy when the spear incinerates as it comes into contact with her molten casing.

Thus far, in addition to the wings that sprouted on her birthday, Icarus's abilities include lava armor, accelerated healing, and increased speed and strength. The latter was discovered in the weight room of the exercise facilities. Icarus desperately misses having Lysander as a training partner, but Cyril has proven to be a wonderful friend.

Fortunately, neither he nor anyone else had been present for her failed attempts to take to the skies with her new wings.

The aforementioned boost to her body's healing hid the evidence of her clumsiness, and Icarus kicked herself for not realizing her wings would need to build up strength before she could use them.

"Do you want to call it for the day?" Cyril asks, catching his breath.

Icarus ponders for a moment. "Yeah. I still need to get some training in with Amara today."

"Start again tomorrow morning?"

"See you then." Icarus waves him off with a nod.

Icarus encounters few people on the way to the stables, and she hates how her mind wanders to Aphrodite in quiet moments like this.

There is no magma armor surrounding the tender part of her soul, and each thought of the goddess pierces like an arrow. With every brave smile and conversation used for distraction, a cork plugs up the leak, but the relief is temporary. How long before there are too many cracks to repair?

Amara lets out a whinny of delight when Icarus walks into the stables, and the sound immediately soothes her. As she runs her hand over the silken coat of her steed, she revels in her connection with Amara, stronger than ever despite not being in the Pegasus Legion anymore.

"I know you miss the sunshine on your wings, but this is the safest place for us right now," Icarus whispers, pressing her forehead against Amara's muzzle.

The weight of the saddle is familiar as Icarus pulls it from the tack room, and in a few short minutes the breeze flutters through her golden tresses.

Darkness surrounds them, and on a hunch, Icarus channels the power within her, delighted when a soft glow radiates out from her body, casting enough light to keep them from colliding with one of the many mountains and rock formations that make up the Underworld landscape.

Spotting a cliffside overlooking the well-lit harbor, Icarus guides Amara to land and slips out of the saddle.

At the cliff's edge, Icarus looks down to the water she knows is below, though nothing but blackness stares back at her.

This was not how her life was supposed to go.

She got everything she ever dreamed of, but how was she supposed to know those dreams were based on lies and propaganda?

How many other people have signed their life over to the Heroes to protect the realm and genuinely do some good, only to be forced to commit atrocities that will haunt them for eternity?

The anger seething inside Icarus burns brightly, and she looks into the dark expanse below once more.

Pebbles crunching under her feet, she takes several steps back before giving her wings a flap, running to the edge of the cliff, and leaping off.

Air whooshes past, and she flexes her shoulder blades to fan out her wings, but the motion is jerky and only slightly slows her descent.

As Icarus continues to flex to no avail and the ground or water below rapidly approaches, a fleeting thought of the stupidity of this moment flits into her mind.

Amara whinnies, and the proximity indicates her steed took flight with her and is possibly attempting to catch her.

The crashing of waves against rocks informs Icarus she is very close to learning which element will greet her body as it falls from the sky.

With a scream of effort, just as sea mist splashes her face, Icarus's wings completely fan out, igniting into flames, carrying her safely into the air.

Clutching her chest, trying to catch her breath, Icarus cries out in victory.

3 5

ARACHNE

Cyril walks into the library, and Arachne blushes into the book she is reading. Still not used to be perceived so regularly, she finds it both terrifying and thrilling.

With little to do to be of use to the Allegiance, she spends most of her time in the library, devouring each story she can get her hands on. Every day she and Hestia would smile politely to each other and then go about their reading, but before long the two found themselves reading together in silence at the same table —Hestia with her Book of Fates, and Arachne with one adventure after the next.

Watching Cyril cross the room to her, Arachne cannot help but notice the alluring way his dark curls fall into his face, or the warmth of his lopsided smile.

She was turned into a spider at such a young age; she has had little experience with love. Little flirtations, sure, but *love*? If she has any experience with it, it was so long ago that Arachne cannot even be certain her memories of it would be accurate.

"I'm famished. Would you care to accompany me for some food?" Cyril asks, his eyes eagerly awaiting Arachne's answer.

She nods, dropping her gaze to her hands in her lap where she wrings the fabric of her skirts. Wearing clothing still feels odd, but this dress is so beautiful, and Arachne enjoys the way the soft pink of it looks against her pale skin.

Cyril extends his elbow to Arachne as she stands from the table. She loops her arm through his, tucking a strand of her long white hair that has come loose behind her ear.

As they walk together to the dining hall, Cyril talks excitedly about his training with Icarus. His excitement sparks a jealousy in Arachne, but not over Cyril's attention. She would give anything to have the powers and strength of Icarus so she could bring that bitch Athena to her knees.

If Arachne were a Phoenix, she would show those gods *exactly* what it feels like to live in fear of their tyranny.

"Where did you go?" Cyril asks, bringing Arachne back to the present.

Deciding on honesty, she replies, "I wish I could do some of things Icarus can. I want to help you in your fight against the Pantheon, and I just feel useless."

"Hey, don't say that." Cyril stops and puts his hands on her shoulders. "Besides, one of the things that makes leaving the safety of the Allegiance to go on these runs so much easier is the knowledge that when I return, I will be able to continue getting to know you."

Arachne's stomach fills with butterflies at the sincerity in his voice and expression. How can this man look at her with stars in his eyes when she has no clue who she is anymore?

She cannot remember the girl she was before her curse, and desperately wants to figure it out outside of her spider form.

Although, moments like this when the emotions are overwhelming, she almost wishes she could return to her arachnid state and skitter away to hide from being perceived. Perhaps it is not so bad though, when it comes with such a pleasing smile.

They resume walking as Cyril twines his fingers between Arachne's, and despite her nonchalant reaction, her heart thumps a mile a minute.

"I have to leave again after dinner," Cyril says after a moment.

Arachne sighs sadly, but she knows how important his missions are. Arachne will never forget the haunted looks in the eyes of the many children Cyril has brought safely into the folds of the Allegiance and won't ask him to risk the lives of those simply for selfish reasons.

When they are almost to the dining hall, Cyril comes to a stop once more, turning to Arachne.

"I am really going to miss you while I am gone." Cyril shifts his weight between his feet nervously. "I would to, erm, would it be all right if I kissed you? If not, that will not change my warm feelings for you. Please do not feel pressured. I promise I—"

Arachne puts a finger gently over his lips to silence him. "I would like that very much," she murmurs.

The anxiety eases from his expression, and he grins at her. "Are you sure?"

Smiling shyly, Arachne steps into his space and says, "Most definitely."

Cyril lowers his face, and his lips hover just inches from hers, allowing her that final moment of consent as she steps onto her tiptoes and kisses him.

Arachne's heart surges as their lips stay softly pressed together, before she parts hers for him and his tongue slides into her mouth. A restrained groan escapes him, and his desire for her is intoxicating. With this newfound confidence and headiness, Arachne laces her fingers around his neck, digging them into his thick dark curls.

She swears she sees stars when they finally part and walk into the dining hall together with broad, silly grins plastered across their faces.

After dinner and seeing Cyril off, Arachne wanders around a small harbor of the Underworld. There is heavy daily Pantheon traffic at the main marina as shipments of food and supplies come and go. As a result, Allegiance operations must be conducted from a peripheral location so the hustle and bustle are absent.

Not ready for bed yet but also not in mood to read, Arachne decides to go for a warm soak in one of the bath houses.

While a lot of the rooms have their own private bathing pools, the public ones are still a common gathering place for relaxing conversation and socialization. This time of night, it will not be too crowded, but she will also not likely be alone with her thoughts.

Her assumptions are confirmed when there is only a handful of people in the humid space.

Scanning the room, Arachne spots Icarus waving her over to one of the pools along the far wall with open windows over-looking the dark mountainside.

Arachne is grateful for a friendly face and undresses, then steps into the warm water.

"I'm surprised you're not on the mission with Cyril," Arachne says softly. Her voice still so timid as she gets used to using it again.

Icarus sags her shoulders. "I wish. The Allegiance says I am too valuable of an asset to send out on everyday missions. Especially while we are still learning the full extent of my abilities."

"You don't sound like you agree with them."

"I don't. I joined the Heroes because I wanted to help people. When I saw the truth of who they were, I joined the Allegiance. I just want to protect the innocent and make my time here mean something." She presses her lips together.

Arachne nods. "I completely understand. I do not even know who I am, much less what I bring to the table. But I want to help."

"Can I ask you a question?" Icarus removes the tie from the

end of her braid, loosening the plait until her hair falls freely around her shoulders.

"I suppose," Arachne answers hesitantly.

"How did you end up as a spider?"

"Oh, that." Her expression sours. "Athena."

Icarus's eyes go wide. "As in the Goddess of Wisdom and War *Athena? That* Athena?" she asks.

"The one and only," Arachne replies with a wry chuckle.

"Tell me everything," Icarus implores, before adding, "Please, if you can."

"I grew up in a small village near the Temple of the Hunt. My family lived in the foothills of Mount Eurymanthus and raised sheep. My sisters and I were in charge of spinning the wool into thread to take to market.

"When I was very little, my mother showed me how to take some of the wool that was not suitable to sell and weave it in the beautiful loom we had in our family room. Every single night, Mama and I would weave at the loom while my sisters sat in front of the hearth and Papa told us stories."

Arachne takes a breath, continuing when Icarus says nothing.

"Over the years, I got quite good at weaving. There was one other girl in our village who could weave almost as well as me, Lyantha. I was fifteen and headstrong, and I let my emotions get the better of me one day when I found her flirting with Tynias, the boy I loved.

"In my years of reflection since, I see the likelihood that Tynias lied to both of us to string us along. Back then, however, I believed he loved me and that she was a threat."

Arachne's cheeks flush with shame.

She goes on, "Lyantha boasted to Tynias that she could best me at anything, even weaving. Me, being the stupid teenager I was, responded that not even the mighty Athena could best me at weaving, even if she had the loom of Daedalus."

"Oh, dear." Icarus covers her mouth in shock.

"I know now how idiotic that was, to challenge a god so

brazenly, but I don't think children really believe the stories of how fragile the gods egos are. We chalk it up as an exaggeration to teach us the importance of a humble ego, not that they will literally materialize out of thin air and turn us into monsters for insulting them."

Icarus shakes her head. "You couldn't have known."

"There was never even a contest. She turned me into a spider for having the audacity to even make the claim in the first place. Part of the curse was losing the memory of my name."

Icarus is silent for a moment, then says, "I have never seen that side of Athena before."

"Had you not heard the rumors of her nasty temper?" Arachne asks.

She makes a face. "When you are in her favor, I imagine she hides that part of herself. What a manipulative bitch!"

Arachne laughs at Icarus's indignation on her behalf, and it soothes some of the lingering trauma.

"Thank you," Icarus says softly. "For sharing your story with me."

36

MEDUSA

*C*admus and Psyche watch Medusa intently as the three of them stand in a circle in the Oasis.

With Psyche now able to reverse the effects of her serpents, Medusa has fewer hesitations about training with Cadmus. So far there have not been any more accidents, and her communication with the snakes gets stronger each time. It takes less and less concentrated thought to keep them at bay.

They are part of her, and the more Medusa sees them as a tool, a layer of protection, the more ownership she possesses of her narrative.

Emboldened by the thought, Medusa pulls her hood back.

Psyche smiles brightly when Cadmus has no reaction. "I think we can take this training out of the Oasis soon,"

All the blood drains from Medusa's face at the thought, but Cadmus says, "I agree. We will begin somewhere isolated, but then we need to start incorporating new people."

"No. Nobody else." Dread laces Medusa's voice. "It's bad enough to put *you* at risk."

Psyche shakes her head. "He is right, my love. We have to make sure you are the one in control of that ability so you can become stronger and safer. If something happens and you are once again out in the world or, Fates forbid it, in the hands of the Pantheon, I would feel so much better knowing you can protect yourself without having to worry about the risk to innocents."

Medusa opens her mouth to speak, but Psyche continues.

"No. There have been too many times where you could not use the power that could protect you because you were too concerned about the people who might unjustly fall victim to it."

"You're right." Swallowing and looking down, Medusa says, "If you are certain you can reverse it, we can start tomorrow."

"I am."

Psyche laces her fingers between Medusa's, in a blink they are no longer in the Oasis and back in their chilly room in the Under Temple. Cadmus walks across, crouching down to light the hearth.

Psyche glances at the clock on the wall, then looks back to Medusa with a smirk. "We have some time before we meet up with Isa and Cass."

Desire floods through Medusa, and she croons, "So we do. Whatever shall we occupy our time with?"

Backing Medusa onto the bed, Psyche crawls to her as they scoot back toward the headboard. Their lips meet, and it is full of heat and passion, tongues colliding and intermingling. Medusa slides her hands up Psyche's thighs and hips, pulling the goddess's dress up and breaking their kiss to lift it over her head.

The bed shifts with the weight of Cadmus climbing in behind Psyche, who leans up to twist and kiss him deeply.

Medusa sits up enough to remove her tunic, tossing it to the floor as Psyche focuses on her once more with a delicious grin on her face. Fingers deftly unfastening the buckle of her belt, she slides off Medusa's pants.

Laying against the pillows, Medusa closes her eyes, gasping as Psyche's kisses create a scorched trail across her reptilian skin, working their way down until the goddess situates herself between Medusa's thighs. Behind Psyche, Cadmus runs his hand up and down Psyche's spine, and she arches against his touch, sighing into Medusa's skin.

Watching him touch Psyche and seeing her respond sends shockwaves of need through Medusa. A desperate wish for both of them to consume her and claim her.

It is difficult to recall the loneliness of her isolation with two stunningly attractive people in her bed now. Cadmus's masculine strength and hard edges contrast against the soft sensual felinity of Psyche, and together they have brought Medusa back to life.

Medusa's head swims with lust, and she cries out as Psyche dips two fingers inside of her.

Psyche moans again, and Medusa opens her eyes to Cadmus mirroring what she is doing to Medusa, his fingers deep inside of the goddess.

Despite the pleasure Cadmus is bringing her, Psyche does not lose focus on Medusa, and her tongue flits over Medusa's clit before plunging inside of her core. The heavens explode behind her eyelids, and an immediate climax crashes through her.

Sliding her fingers out of Medusa, Psyche moves as Cadmus takes her place, and Medusa crooks her finger to bring him closer. She guides his hips in front of her face, propping up onto her elbows as his hardness is right before her mouth.

"Are you sure?" he asks, voice so husky with desire that it is almost a growl. Yet it does not escape Medusa that he still takes the time to check in with her.

"Definitely." Medusa smirks and licks her lips before running her tongue in a circle around the head of his cock.

He groans, and Psyche curls her fingers tightly in his hair, whispering, "Do you like that?"

Before he can answer the goddess, Medusa takes him into her mouth, eliciting a guttural, "Mmhmm," from him.

After a moment, Medusa removes her lips from his cock, leaning back onto the pillow once more and guiding himself to her entrance. Cadmus presses the tip of his length into her and slowly enters her to the hilt.

Medusa's soft whimpers sound throughout the room as he fills her, and she adjusts to him accordingly.

Taking Psyche's hand, Medusa pulls the goddess to her, positioning her pelvis to be hovering inches from Medusa's mouth, but facing Cadmus. As he leans in to kiss the goddess, Medusa brings her lips to Psyche's center, finding the goddess already dripping wet. Psyche moans into Cadmus's kiss as Medusa's tongue drives her to madness.

It must be their connectedness or perhaps the strength of their bond, but it does not take long before all three of them are basking in climactic bliss.

The meeting room smells like damp stone, as does the rest of the Under Temple. With the entire complex carved into the mountainside, every space feels like a cave, reminding Medusa of the island Poseidon forced her to call home. That feels like lifetimes ago.

"How long do you think we have before the Pantheon figures out the Allegiance is here in the Underworld?" Isadora's voice brings the chatter around the table to a halt.

All eyes turn to Hades and Persephone, eager to know their thoughts about Isadora's question.

Meanwhile, Medusa's pulse races. Poseidon could show up here at any given moment. Would the Pantheon be less likely to attack the Allegiance if he were no longer after her?

I need to eliminate Poseidon from the equation before *he is here and everyone I love is at risk of being caught in the middle.*

There are so many innocent people here, and Medusa is determined to see this through.

"Communications between my three sisters and I gives no indication that the Pantheon has figured it out yet, but that is not something we can rely on. We must assume that they will find us at any time and be fully prepared for a rapid evacuation if necessary." Persephone's soft voice is firm as she speaks.

Isadora nods her agreement. "We will begin assessing the logistics of that immediately. When all of the cards are on the table, will your sisters side with us?"

Persephone presses her lips together. "I believe so. I know Artemis and our half-brother Apollo will certainly be on our side. Despoina, too. Demeter is the main toss-up, but I cannot see her choosing cruelty."

"Hopefully it won't come to that." Hades puts a soothing hand on Persephone's shoulder, and she leans into his touch.

"Hestia, have you learned anything new about the star or other keys?" Isadora asks.

Before Hestia can answer, Cassandra speaks up, but her voice is that of the Fates.

"The first heart
you have found.
And the star,
hidden below ground.
On the wings of Fate,
must a sacrifice be made.
For key three,
patient you need to be.
Icy beauty for all to see,
shall bring the final key of the three."

When Cassandra returns to normal, Hestia wraps her arms around the oracle's shoulders as Isadora says, "Fucking riddles. Let's get to work."

Medusa closes her eyes. *What does it all mean?*

From the moment Psyche, Alec, and Yiorgos arrived on her shores, it has felt like Medusa is being pulled forward by destiny, a crucial part of the Fates' plan. But why won't the Fates tell them what her role is supposed to be?

How can she prepare for something when she has no idea what to expect?

As Aphrodite makes her way to see Circe, she continuously checks over her shoulder. She does not think anyone saw her arrive on this island, but with all the uncertainty in the air right now, she cannot be too sure.

The mirror is cold against her skin as she grips it tightly in her pocket.

It is time for answers. The oracle was of little use in tracking Icarus's location, but Circe has an ancient power brimming in her veins, Aphrodite can sense it. It feels like a predator lurking in the bushes, keen eyes homed in on its prey, waiting for the perfect moment to strike. Surely, she of all people can find Icarus.

Aphrodite rushes into the room, catching the witch at her dinnertime apparently as she lifts a spoon from a bowl to her lips. Circe rolls her eyes when she sees Aphrodite but beckons for the goddess forward, dropping the utensils with a clatter.

"I can tell you where she is," Circe says bluntly, and Aphrodite's jaw drops. "What?" she asks. "You think I am prophetic enough to find her, but not enough to anticipate the question?"

Aphrodite blinks. "I found it. The mirror."

"I know," Circe replies, tone clipped and lacking any patience.

"What do I do with it? Why won't you give me any answers? How far does this world have to fall apart before you and the Fates decide you can share your secrets with us?" Anger rises in Aphrodite's chest as it feels like she will just be talked in circles once more.

Circe's voice is low, almost a raspy whisper. "You will know what to do with it when the time is right, and you are in luck because its journey follows the same path as yours to find your lover."

"And where does that path lead? Where is she?" Aphrodite's heart hammers in her chest at the thought of finding Icarus.

"While the mirror's route is a crucial one, to access it and find the girl, the universe requires a price. What are you willing to pay?"

Price? What price?

Circe points to a mirror hanging on the wall. "Take a good, long look, my dear. The Fates will weigh what it is you seek and what they deem a fair price to be. If that risk is an acceptable one, step forward and offer yourself up to the three sisters."

Without an ounce of hesitation, Aphrodite briskly walks to the mirror. If she were not so desperate to right things with Icarus, she might have stopped to think about what the Fates might ask of her. In her frantic mind, there is nothing she would not give.

For a moment, nothing happens, and Aphrodite's reflection alone stares back at her. She is about to turn ask Circe if she is certain it is working when the surface of the mirror begins to swirl as if the reflective silver morphed into a liquid.

The motion suddenly stops, and instead of her reflection, Aphrodite sees the stars in the heavens, as if she is in a room floating amongst them, looking out the window.

A flash of light forces Aphrodite to glance away, and when she looks back there are three women looking at her, sitting in thrones made of stardust.

"Hello, goddess." All three women speak in unison, and the effect is haunting.

"You're the Fates," Aphrodite says. "I did not expect to actually speak with you. Thank you for honoring me with your time."

"Do not waste your niceties on us, goddess. We know you are eager to hear our price," the trio of women hiss.

"Yes, please. I have to find her again. I can't have messed it up this colossally." Aphrodite can hear the desperation in her voice, but she does not care.

"You have spread much pain, goddess. Many innocents have fallen at your behest. We have devised a cost that will also serve as a reminder that while your beauty may hide your misdeeds, it is not a guarantee."

Aphrodite looks between the three sisters, their features hidden behind the glimmering cosmos. The only thing she can see are their cold eyes staring hard at her. Do they mean to take her beauty? Make her ugly?

Panic gnaws at Aphrodite's heart.

Will Icarus still love me if I lose my beauty? What if the price keeps her from wanting me?

"Well, goddess, what will it be?" the Fates ask.

Images of Icarus flutter through Aphrodite's mind on golden wings. A tear rolls down her cheek as she pictures Icarus's bright smile, her laughter. "Do it."

"Yes, goddess." The heavens swirl until the mirror is silver once more, and Aphrodite's reflection looks back at her.

Aphrodite stares in disbelief as she examines herself. Essentially, she still looks the same, but leaning in she sees that her facial features are sharper, harsher. A shriek bubbles out of Aphrodite as she notices the fine lines around the edges of her eyes and faint wrinkles in her forehead.

Circe rushes over. "What's wrong? What is the matter?"

"What do you mean? Look at me!" Aphrodite lashes out at the witch.

"I *am* looking at you. Nothing has changed," Circe scolds.

"Look!" Aphrodite points to the mirror. "Don't you see it? My hideousness?"

"Goddess," Circe says firmly, "your appearance has not changed. It must just be your reflection."

The horrifying reality seals into Aphrodite. She is immortal, and this will be her reflection forever. She will never look upon her true self ever again, never see her beauty with her own eyes. It feels as if the floor has opened beneath her and threatens to swallow her whole, like a part of her is now missing.

But it *is* missing. The part of Aphrodite that brought her down into the catacombs in the first place.

Taking a steadying breath, Aphrodite turns from the mirror and looks at Circe. "Now tell me where she is."

38

ICARUS

The cool air of the Underworld flutters through Icarus's feathers as she and Amara gracefully fly through the skies. Flying *with* Amara instead of *on* is exhilarating, and Icarus finds herself doing it frequently when she wants to get out of her head.

Her wings are getting stronger with each flight, and soon they will be ready for what she needs them for.

Down in the harbor, a ship approaches, and she recognizes it as the one Cyril left on. Banking on Arachne being there waiting for him and wanting to spend time with her friend, she descends with Amara right behind her.

Arachne's long bright white hair catches her eye, and Icarus lands next to her on the ground. She smiles excitedly and throws her arm around Icarus's shoulders. "Hi! Did you come to see Cyril with me?"

"I did, if that is alright with you? I can leave you alone if you prefer?" Icarus asks.

"Don't be ridiculous! Of course I want you here." Arachne loops her arm through Icarus's, and the pair turns to watch as the small vessel pulls into the slip.

The smiles fall from their faces at the sight of the somber

expressions the crew carry. Arachne's grip on Icarus's arm tightens.

Icarus leans in and whispers, "I'm sure everything is all right."

But dread clings to her as her gut tells her something is really wrong here.

The crew disembarks, and Arachne watches eagerly, waiting for Cyril. Iris is the last one to leave the ship, and Arachne rushes over to them.

"Where is Cyril?" Arachne asks frantically.

Iris drops their gaze down to their boots as they answer, "It was an ambush. The Pantheon is getting smarter. If it wasn't for Cyril, none of us would have made it."

Iris continues, but Icarus does not hear them as Arachne wails and drops to her knees.

"I'm so sorry," Iris says to Icarus as they squeeze her arm and leave her to attend to Arachne.

Icarus lowers to ground and pulls Arachne into an embrace. "Shh. Shh. Come here,"

"He can't be gone," Arachne sobs while Icarus gently strokes her hair.

A flame burns brightly inside of Icarus, brighter than her wings or her glow. The Pantheon must be stopped. At any cost.

How could she have ever believed that these people were the ones in the wrong? It genuinely baffles her that she fell for the indoctrination so easily. Now that the veil has been lifted, she sees things so clearly for what they are, and it sickens her to know that she bought into it.

Icarus has no idea how many life cycles she has remaining, but with every new cruelty she witnesses from the Pantheon, the less she cares. Even if this is her last, she will gladly sacrifice it for a better world—like she wanted to achieve all along.

It takes hours for Icarus to soothe Arachne enough to allow her to sleep, thanks to the additional help from Psyche. The shockwaves of Cyril's death are rippling through the Allegiance, and the mood in the Under Temple is somber.

As she walks through the corridors, she catches moments of conversation when she passes groups of people. Everyone is sharing stories about Cyril, and she wishes he could hear all of the oral epitaphs in his honor and know how loved he is.

Lost in her thoughts, Icarus finds herself making her way down the long set of steps. The debris from the cave-in was cleaned so thoroughly, one almost would not know it ever happened.

The bright glare of the star does not bother Icarus as she finds a large boulder and takes a seat on it.

Looking up at the celestial orb, she pulls out two pieces of parchment and a quill.

39

HESTIA

Key Allegiance members sit around a large circular table trying to decipher the text in the Book of Fates. The diagrams of the stones have been under the most scrutiny for the past few hours as everything in Hestia's gut screams that they should be their focus.

The mood has been heavy as they throw their energy into defeating the Pantheon. The loss of Cyril ripples through every conversation, every action.

Hestia's mind is also plagued by the situation with Alec. She hasn't had a chance to talk to him about her relationship with Hera. Is it really urgent Allegiance matters that have him tied up and busy? Or is that the excuse he is using to avoid her? The tumultuous emotions make it hard for Hestia to concentrate, but she closes her eyes and searches for anywhere she might have seen the illustrations before.

The drawing feels like something she should know, but Hestia is certain she has never read about it in any of the books in the Library of Olympus.

"Do you think those stones are the site of something important that we need to find? Like a source of magic maybe?" Hades asks the group.

"Hmm," Hestia muses. "I can feel their importance, but I feel like we are still missing something big."

"I hope it isn't a weapon," Isadora says, her voice low. "Anything that has enough power to give us an edge on the Pantheon has the potential to be used against us, and I don't like the idea of that."

"That's very true, Isa," Hestia says, then turns to Persephone and Hades. "Do you think the Pantheon has any idea about these?"

Hades shrugs, and Persephone shakes her head. "Other than my sisters, I do not have much contact with *those* gods."

The door to the meeting room opens, and one of the Muses, Epiphany, comes flitting inside. Her black twists that fall to her shoulders mirror the almost obsidian tone to her skin. Hestia fights a sigh. Epiphany is a sweet soul, but her chaotic energy crashes in like a wrecking ball.

"What are you all up to?" Epiphany asks, her unending optimism oozing out of every word.

"We are really busy, so now might not be the best time, Epiphany," Isadora says gently.

Epiphany waves a dismissive hand. "Nonsense, I am here to help."

"Not now, Epiphany," Hades chides.

With a pout, Epiphany looks at Hades. "I go where the universe directs me, and I am supposed to be here."

Hestia pinches her brow, but she notices that Cassandra is fighting back laughter. "What do you say, Cass? Do we let her stay?" she asks.

Cassandra laughs out loud then. "I think it is a lesson in madness to try and argue with a Muse."

Hestia chuckles softly. Of course there is value in having a Muse around.

Shame creeps in as the laughter subsides. Hestia drops her head. They shouldn't be jovial so soon after Cyril's death. It feels like dancing on his grave.

Epiphany leans over the table and looks at the book in the middle, squinting at the faded illustration. "Hey! What's that doing in there?"

Hestia's breathing stops. "What do you mean?"

Epiphany pulls the book closer and studies it. "Yep! Don't you recognize that symbol there?" Her ebony finger points to a small emblem drawn onto each of the stones. "You can find these symbols on some of the stones in every single temple in Olympus, of course."

Cassandra practically jumps out of her seat. "She's right! I remember seeing that exact image carved into some of the stones in the Solar Temple. I always wondered why some had them and some did not."

Is the answer truly so simple? How can she never have noticed the symbols before in any of the temples? As someone who prides herself on her attention to detail, she cannot help but feel like she let everyone down.

Would Cyril still be alive if this was discovered sooner?

"Sebastian!" Hades calls out, and an acolyte comes rushing into the room.

Hades beckons him over to the book, grabbing a piece of paper and a pencil. After a quick sketch, he hands the page to Sebastian.

"Make a few copies of this, please," the god orders. "Any acolytes who do not have urgent duties to attend to must scour the Under Temple for these markings on any of the stones. Write down where you found them, and how many there are."

Isadora looks around the table. "Do we want to go assist in the search?"

As the group agrees, they disperse and make their separate ways to go symbol hunting.

Deciding to begin with the library, Hestia makes the short walk to her familiar space. At the doors, she finds Icarus standing there waiting for her.

"Hello, Icarus. How are you?" Hestia asks.

"I'm alright. I have a lot on my mind, but that's nothing new." Icarus chuckles, but it doesn't have her usual pep.

"Can you do me a favor?" Icarus digs into her pockets and pulls out two sealed scrolls.

"Of course," Hestia says, eyeing the papers.

Icarus hands her the scrolls. One has her name on it and Aphrodite's on the other.

"Please don't open it now. In the ever-cryptic tone of the times—you'll know when it's time."

Hestia laughs, but is conflicted. She is eager to find the symbols, but Icarus seems to need a shoulder.

"Do you want to talk about the stuff on your mind?" Hestia hopes her interest comes off as sincere and not nosy.

Icarus shakes her head. "You have things to do. Thank you for this."

As Icarus turns and walks down the hallway, Hestia makes a mental reminder to have a serious check-in with that girl once this upheaval with the symbols settles.

40

MEDUSA

A few steps ahead of Medusa, Psyche and Cadmus chatter amongst themselves while the group searches the Under Temple for more symbols. Seven have been found so far, and if the drawing is any indication, there will be thirteen in total.

Medusa should be more present, but she is still stuck deep beneath the waves in the Sea Temple. Yet her thoughts are no longer ones of despair or sadness; they are full of rage. A tempest of fury that has been building for millennia with every woman who has been wronged at the hands of callous men who act on a whim, with no regard for the trauma they spew in their wake.

The regret that churns in Medusa's gut is no longer for Poseidon's actions, only that she did not possess the strength to punish him then and there.

It is all too easy in Medusa's mind to replace the decapitated head of Perseus in her memories with that of Poseidon. How she yearns to feel *his* blood running down between her fingers, or to watch the horror cross his face as it turns to stone.

"Hey." Cadmus's voice is low and gentle as he gently grips Medusa's elbow. "Your serpents..."

They slither around, poking out from beneath the hood, and their chaotic emotions are palpable. Looking into his amber eyes

196

and warm smile slowly brings Medusa back to this reality as her anger dissipates.

Medusa places her hand on his upper arm and says, "Sorry about that. Did either of you see anything of note while I was distracted?"

Psyche and Cadmus exchange a quick look, but Medusa spots it immediately.

Her brows furrow in concern. "What?"

Psyche steps forward, biting her lip. "You've been up in your head a lot lately. We are just worried about you," she admits.

Medusa's hackles raise. "I think if anyone has reason to be locked in their mind, it is me."

"Of course, no one is saying you don't have reason, my love." Psyche's tone is soft and gentle, meant to calm Medusa, but it is only stoking the flames of her ire.

"Don't take that condescending tone with me. I am not made of glass. I am allowed to be angry. I didn't ask for any of this!" Medusa hisses, her serpents quietly joining.

Cadmus raises an eyebrow. "The anger is a good step in the right direction. It means you are getting stronger."

He tries to put his arm around Medusa's shoulders, but she shrugs it off, stepping away. The corridor feels entirely too small, their presence too close.

"I know I am getting stronger. And that is my point. Cadmus, I am so fucking angry, and I have nowhere to direct it. How many innocents are harmed every second that I still allow Poseidon to live?" she challenges.

"Sitting and waiting is difficult, but sometimes that is the best way to look for the right opportunity to strike. We cannot focus solely on Poseidon, no matter how much I want to slit his throat myself," Psyche bites back.

Medusa's blinks, shock filling her face at the level of violence from the goddess who is normally so patient.

"We love every part of you. Even the dark ones, my darling," Psyche says, so low it is almost a whisper.

Does she really want to push away the two people who at least *try* to see her? There is nothing she wants less, but they do not understand. They patiently wait for her to heal, but what if Medusa needs something more to fix this wound? To move on?

An acolyte comes running up to them, wheezing for breath after ascending the long row of stairs leading up to where the trio was searching. "The." *Wheeze.* "Star." *Huff.*

Cadmus holds up a hand. "Deep breaths."

The acolyte nods, taking short, heaving breaths. "Star. Cavern. Icarus. Now." The blood drains from the acolyte's face as he crumbles to the floor, fainting.

Sighing, Cadmus collects the limp acolyte, tossing him over his shoulder as if he weighs nothing. "I guess we need to go see what got this fella so worked up."

*A*phrodite hands the Ferryman a coin, and he silently gestures for her to board his vessel as she pulls her cloak tightly over her face.

The small island just on the other side of the Mysts is only known to the gods of the Pantheon, and passage is always guaranteed with proper payment. It cannot be simply any coin; it has to have significant meaning and be something the offeree will truly miss. Otherwise, is it really a worthy enough fare?

As soon as the coin leaves her hand, Aphrodite's heart cleaves in two. But with this being Icarus's last life cycle, what use will it be to Aphrodite?

The thick fog of the Mysts coats Aphrodite's skin even through her heavy cloak, and she shivers against the uncomfortable sensation.

Just as Aphrodite was hoping, the small dock is empty and silent when she disembarks. Before she can demand the ferryman to keep his mouth shut about her presence, he is already gone, fading back into the fog.

Facing the landscape before her, she takes a staggering breath. Where to go first to look for her lost lover? The stables?

Having been to the Underworld several times, she easily navigates to where the horses are kept. She encounters next to no one along the way, and instead of finding that suspicious, she praises her luck for not being discovered so far.

A loud thunking from inside the building has she pushing the door open in a hurry. There she is—Amara, stomping the ground and kicking the walls of her stall. She rushes over to her lover's steed and gently strokes the creature's neck.

Amara's eyes flare when she sees Aphrodite, and she nuzzles the goddess but continues to stomp agitatedly.

"What's wrong, girl?" Her stomach turns to a ball of hot lead as dread rises.

Amara stomps again and swings her head down, huffing.

"You want me to get on?" she asks, brows furrowing as she tries to understand.

Amara swings her head again, and she sends a prayer to the Fates that this is not the dumbest thing she has ever done in her very long life. She leaves the stall door open and uses an overturned bucket to climb onto the pegasus. There is no time to bother with a saddle, plus she hardly knows how to use one.

Threading her fingers through the flaxen mane of Amara, Aphrodite clenches her teeth as the pegasus trots out of the stable, then builds to a gallop before taking to the skies.

The rush of the wind flapping against Aphrodite's cloak is exhilarating, but she can hardly enjoy it as she drowns in worry for Icarus.

Amara lands next to a large doorway, and Aphrodite dismounts. "I'm sorry, I don't think I can bring you in here with me. I'll find her, all right?"

Aphrodite strokes the mare's neck before slipping into the doorway and getting her bearings.

The occasional person comes by quickly, paying her no mind. They all seem to be heading in the same direction, so she decides to follow them.

She winds down corridors and stairways until the air begins to chill around her. They must be getting pretty far underground by now.

Two acolytes come rushing by, and Aphrodite picks up her pace, hoping to pick up snippets of their conversation.

"I think she's going for it!"

"She can't be. It's too dangerous!"

"She's a phoenix, *you idiot. She can handle it."*

Aphrodite's blood runs cold. They are definitely talking about Icarus. Every step down the staircase feels like the tick of a clock, getting closer and closer, tick-tock.

At the base of an enormous set of stairs, a crowd is gathered, looking up to the top of the cavern. The bright light of a star is blinding, but Aphrodite squints against it. There, nearing the celestial orb, she can just make out wings.

As she struggles to breathe, Icarus and the star collide. She is forced to look away from the solar rays that burst out.

The brightness fades, and Aphrodite looks up again just in time to watch Icarus's lifeless form free falling, hitting the ground with a thud.

No. No. No. No.

Someone shrieks as Aphrodite scrambles over to Icarus, still and crumpled on the ground, and she realizes the sound is coming from her, along with heaving sobs.

Seeing Icarus's broken form sends Aphrodite over the edge as she pulls Icarus close to her, ignoring the blood and her mangled limbs.

Aphrodite's own hands now covered with Icarus's blood leave a macabre trail of handprints as she grasps her face, her shoulders, shaking her, anything to bring her back.

Hands land on Aphrodite's shoulders, but she shakes them off, unleashing a guttural howl that sends whoever approached backing away.

Aphrodite cradles Icarus's hand to her face. Her other hand is closed in a fist, clutching something. She pries her fingers open, and a small metal key clatters to the floor.

Aphrodite stares at the key, twirling it between her fingers. Was this really worth Icarus's last life?

Someone lowers to their knees before her, and the goddess locks her face with Hestia's. There is no anger or animosity, only kindness and understanding in her former rival's eyes. She cannot be bothered to care about whatever petty thing they fought over in the past.

With Icarus gone, the world feels hopeless, worthless.

Without a second thought, Aphrodite hands the key to Hestia, watching as her jaw drops.

"I don't know what she was doing, or why this was worth her life, but she clearly meant for you to have it." Aphrodite's throat is raw as she speaks.

Fresh sobs well in the goddess's chest and she throws herself over Icarus's body.

"You can't be gone," she wails. "We were supposed to have forever this time."

"She left you a letter," Hestia says softly, placing the scroll in Aphrodite's hand.

Aphrodite grasps it tightly as if it is a lifeline.

A gruff voice interrupts, "Come with me."

Aphrodite looks up. Hades is standing before her, extending a hand.

"I cannot leave her." Aphrodite clings to Icarus even tighter.

Hades kneels down and takes Aphrodite's bloody hand. "This is merely her vessel. She is no longer there. Come with me and let them prepare her body for rites."

Aphrodite is numb, an empty husk, as Hades and Hestia help her to her feet.

Acolytes in long, dark hooded robes come out and tenderly collect Icarus's body, draping it in white cloths and carrying it out of the cavern on a ceremonial litter that Aphrodite knows is usually reserved for those receiving the highest honors in death.

42

HESTIA

Moved by Aphrodite's pain, Hestia takes the goddess's hand as they walk with Hades, surprised when she does not reject the gesture.

The letter from Icarus is crumpled in Aphrodite's other hand. She had read its contents and dropped to her knees sobbing. The rest of the walk has been silent, with Aphrodite re-reading the parchment over and over.

When the trio reaches the floor-to-ceiling cast iron doors to the King of the Underworld's study, Aphrodite finally looks up from the crinkled parchment. Hestia has never seen her look so lost and fragile. It is heartbreaking.

She tries to picture having to endure the loss of Alec repeatedly. Hard to say what she would do in that madness.

The tears in Aphrodite's violet irises glisten, and Hestia gives the goddess a hug. It may not be welcomed, but she would not be herself if she did not extend the gesture, nonetheless. Her eyes widen with shock when Aphrodite returns the hug and continues sobbing on her shoulder.

"I destroy everything I touch. I'm supposed to be the epitome of beauty, but I make everything ugly. And it finally cost me everything that matters," she cries.

Hestia looks at the shattered goddess, her former friend. It is easy to see the connection they once had, even if it is doubtful they ever could be again. She wishes they still had the kind of friendship that would allow her to properly comfort her, but there is a bigger problem to be addressed: Aphrodite knows where the rebels are. She cannot be allowed to return to the Pantheon and expose the Allegiance, putting everyone at risk.

Hestia squares Aphrodite's shoulders, "You are the Goddess of Love and Beauty. So don't you think it's time you helped us remind the realm that it is supposed to be lovely and welcoming?"

She hates to take advantage of Aphrodite's emotionally fragile state, but this is necessary, not to mention the potential of having a goddess as powerful as Aphrodite on the side of the Allegiance.

"Don't you think it's what Icarus would want you to do?" Hestia presses.

Aphrodite narrows her eyes, but her shoulders sag, and she sobs again.

Hestia shoots Hades a look requesting his assistance in persuading Aphrodite, hoping he can read her intentions, but his stony features were made to be unreadable. As he gestures for Aphrodite to go inside his study, Hestia says, "Think about it. You could really do some good in her name. If you want someone to talk to, or a friend, come find me."

As she walks away, Hestia hopes the goddess will come over to the side of the Allegiance. But more importantly, if she doesn't, Hades will certainly not allow Aphrodite to return to the Pantheon.

In her pocket, gently wrapped with the letter Icarus has also written for Hestia is the key—the second Heart of the Fates. That leaves one remaining.

Reciting the prophecy as she walks, Hestia wracks her brain for anything to do with the daughters of Rhea. Who is Rhea? Why is she so important?

Her usual path to the library is a comfort with the coziness of routine. As soon as the smell of the parchment from the pages hits her nostrils, Hestia sighs contentedly.

The rows of shelves stare at her. Where should she start to climb this mountain? She desperately wishes there was magic or a spell that would summon the books related to her subject.

A small flutter of nausea makes Hestia stumble, but it passes quickly, and she returns to her pursuit of knowledge.

43

APHRODITE

Aphrodite walks through the empty corridors of the Under Temple. She has been walking in circles for hours. Perhaps everyone is intentionally avoiding her ire, but she couldn't care less right now. The few minutes Hades granted her in the Mirror of Remembrance were far too short.

Aphrodite should be grateful she had a precious few fleeting moments to say goodbye, but it also ripped her apart all over again.

The price for those few minutes was steep to be sure, but what is an oath in the face of final moments with your soulmate? Aphrodite will swear a thousand more oaths even for the smaller glimpse of her love.

What is she even supposed to do? Where is she to go? She spent so much time focusing on Circe and mysteries and now her actual reason for existing has been ripped out from under her, replaced with a desperate desire to follow her lover into oblivion.

It whispers in her ears that this is all her fault, that nothing in this world would be wrong if Aphrodite were not in it.

Ahead in the corridor, she spots Medusa sitting on a bench, petting that big three-headed beast. Aphrodite curls a lip when one of the giant tongues slurps across Medusa's face.

Medusa startles when she sees Aphrodite but laughs at her horrified expression. "What? Have you never pet a dog before?"

Aphrodite crinkles her nose. "Absolutely not. I cannot for the life of me see the appeal."

Raising an eyebrow, Medusa says, "I find it surprising that the Goddess of Beauty cannot see the beauty in all living things."

Aphrodite blinks as she realizes Medusa is right. "I never thought of it that way, I suppose."

Medusa pats the bench beside her, and Aphrodite cautiously takes a seat, eying the serpents that are currently slithering around unobscured.

"Don't worry. Despite that pile of gryphon dung cursing me, I have full control of them—most of the time. They are part of me, and accepting them allowed me to see all the ways they also protect me. And they will also help me destroy the one who cursed me."

Not believing what she is hearing, Aphrodite exclaims, "You are going after Poseidon?"

Medusa shakes her head. "Not yet. But I will. I cannot allow him to retain his life when he has harmed so many."

As Medusa's words run through Aphrodite's mind, she can feel the gears in her brain and heart turning. She's inspired by the bravery of a person who has been hunted by gods and mortals alike, yet still wants to see this world righted.

It stirs something in Aphrodite as she thumbs over the mirror in her pocket.

"Are you just going after Poseidon? Or does your path of justice carry you all the way to the end of whatever war we have brewing?" Aphrodite asks.

"I've seen enough of this world to know that innocents are being harmed in every corner and crevice. If you don't see it at first, look a little harder and you will find famines, families separated, the nymphs you and your friends callously sold into slavery, and more." Medusa's serpents softly hiss as her voice takes on a bold edge that makes Aphrodite shift nervously.

"If I had something that would help you, would you accept it from me? I have wasted centuries doing everything wrong, so I am going to try this Icarus's way." Aphrodite pulls the mirror from her pocket and hands it to Medusa. "I was told I would know when to give this to someone, and she was right. Everything in me is screaming that this needs to be yours. Use it, and bring them down, all of them. Even if that ends up including me."

Ignoring the shocked look on Medusa's face, Aphrodite gets up.

"Where are you going? What is this?" Medusa asks, visibly confused.

"I think you need to look into it when you are alone. Be warned though, I have a feeling in its depths you will be tested like never before. After speaking with you, I have no doubts you are the one to unlock its mysteries."

"And you?" Medusa tilts her head.

"I'm going to try and make up for all the years of bad." She leaves Medusa and the dog, immediately making mental plans to return to Circe. That witch knew Aphrodite would end up on this side of things, so it is time to see how Circe will shake up this battlefield.

44

MEDUSA

The mirror is a lead weight in Medusa's hand, her fingers curling around it in her pocket as she briskly walks back to her room.

She does not dare to glance at the object or pull it out until she is certain she is completely alone. Her fingers caress the scales of the dragon encircling the mirror, so similar to the ones on her own body.

Medusa closes the door behind her and walks over to the sofa, taking a seat as she slips the mirror out.

For such a small item, the detailing is exquisite. Each and every one of the dragon's scales have been rendered to perfection, and the teeth that protrude from its mouth are razor sharp to the touch. As she stares into the moonstone eyes of the dragon, the eyelids close, and Medusa startles as it begins to blink.

A clicking sound precedes the long serpentine body of the dragon beginning to move in a circle, continuing to feed into its mouth.

"Daughter of Rhea."

Medusa jerks her head, looking around for the source of the raspy voice, but she remains alone.

"Look at me, child."

209

When Medusa brings the mirror up to her face, her own surprised expression greets her, but the surface of her reflection swirls, and three faces appear. Their features are obscured, like a fuzzy memory.

"You are mistaken. I know no one by that name."

"*You do not know her name, but you are her daughter nonetheless.*"

Emotion wells in Medusa's chest. She has never known her mother's name. Rhea...

"*Your legacy has been kept from you by a charlatan, thinking she can control Fate herself.*"

"Who?" Medusa asks, forehead creasing as she surveys the mirror.

"*We cannot say, but you will know very soon—as long as you possess the strength to unlock this mirror. As a daughter of Rhea, granddaughter of Ola, this should be of little challenge to you.*"

"Ola? Who is that?"

"*We ask the questions,*" the voice hisses.

Medusa rolls her eyes but nods.

"*Do you consent to an examination?*"

"Do I have a choice?" Medusa raises an eyebrow. There is no turning back. If she is going to help the Allegiance and rid the world of Poseidon, now is the time to shoot for the moon.

"*Not if you want a chance at victory.*"

"Fair enough. I consent. What next?" The vagueness of the statement does not escape Medusa. What would a mirror deem victory to be?

"*Prick your finger on the dragon's tooth, then allow five drops to fall into the dragon's mouth. We will do the rest.*"

Medusa looks at the sharp fang skeptically but brings her thumb up to its point. After the briefest sting of pressure, the tooth pierces her skin. She counts as the drops fall, then sticks the tip of her finger into her mouth to stop the bleeding.

The rooms suddenly spins, and Medusa can barely feel herself slumping against the arm of the sofa.

When she next opens her eyes, she is no longer in her room, the Under Temple, or well... anywhere. There is nothing around her, no floor, no windows. Is this what the Oasis would be like if someone other than Psyche were to be the one orchestrating it?

"Yes, that is exactly what it would be like." Medusa whips around and finds Psyche approaching.

"How are you here with me?" Medusa asks, bewildered.

"I am not. You will be guided through this journey by three people of significance to you, but I am not them. We merely take their form, partially for your comfort and partially because it helps the subject open up."

Every one of Psyche's physical and vocal mannerisms is perfectly displayed on this artificial version of Medusa's lover, and the experience messes with her head.

"All right," Medusa takes a steadying breath. "Let's get this over with."

Psyche/Not-Psyche chuckles. "Your eagerness will not make this easier, but we shall begin. Together, you and I will revisit important moments in your past that have lingered and left a mark, good or bad. Do you want to start in the beginning, or go in reverse through your timeline?"

A mirror appears before her, a larger version of the handheld one.

"Uh, go backwards, I suppose." Medusa shrugs her shoulders, but the decision was an easy one. To her thinking, the worst of Medusa's experiences have been in the more recent years. Perhaps getting the hard part over first will be preferable?

As if they are watching it happen before their eyes, a scene appears in front of them. Medusa's heart rate kicks up when she sees they are in the Sea Temple, back in her cell as the Twins walk in.

"Can they see me?" Medusa asks, taking a few steps backward into the blackness.

"They cannot."

She breathes in relief. "Thank the fucking Fates." Fake Psyche shoots her a scathing look, and Medusa throws her hand over her mouth. "Apologies."

Fake Psyche nods, and they return their attention to the scene.

It is hard not to look away as Medusa is forced to watch the assault that resulted in one of the Twins' deaths and a permanent maiming of the other.

The space before them fades back to black once the scene concludes, and Fake Psyche turns to Medusa. "This was quite a violent ordeal for you. It is clear they were the aggressors, but are you happy about the outcome? Would you wish for the same one if given the chance?"

Medusa chews on her bottom lip, trying to really think before she answers. Impulsivity does not seem ideal for this situation. "I am not angry with myself for what I had to do to keep myself safe. However, I do not enjoy inflicting harm or ending a life."

Fake Psyche nods, saying nothing, and turns back to the vast emptiness before them.

In a blink they are back in the bath house on the Isle of Mysts. Medusa can almost feel the warm humid air.

Again, Medusa must watch as lives are claimed in her wake.

Again, Fake Psyche asks the same question.

"Do men like that have to answer questions like this when they die? You can clearly see the monstrous acts they will commit on a whim, but yet it is me that you ask to justify their deaths?" Medusa's serpents hiss loudly as she throws her hands up in frustration.

"It is not for you to know what those men experience, daughter of Rhea. Those men are not trying to unlock a great power that *we* must assess if you are capable of handling." Fake Psyche's tone is hard, cold.

"Fine. Would I wish for the same outcome in this specific situation? Yes. Those men violated me without a second thought. They will not be doing that to anyone else ever again." Medusa crosses her arms.

Fake Psyche continues to walk Medusa through her past, until the imposter's face swirls and morphs into Fake Alec. It is he who guides Medusa back into the garden with Poseidon.

Medusa sobs when she sees herself, the version of her before her curse. She almost does not recognize her. Her cheeks burn with shame as she watches the god look at her as if she is a meal. She has to remember that it is not really Alec watching this with her, and this is not real at all. It is in the past.

Fake Alec wanders through her days as an acolyte, and watching the old times in the Temple of Wisdom is like looking at an entirely different life. Perhaps, in a way, it was.

"There is one last memory to go through, but we can only share part of it. It has been tampered with by the charlatan, but rest assured all will be known soon. The test is almost over, daughter of Rhea."

Medusa turns abruptly, brow crinkling in confusion when no one there.

Faints voices sound throughout the void, and Medusa strains to hear them.

"No! You don't get to do all of them. That's not fair!"

"Oh, be quiet, sister!

"Clotho, Atropos, and I want turns with the memories, too."

An ancient voice sighs. *"Fine."*

"Hello, Lyra," a feminine voice pulls Medusa's gaze to her right as a woman approaches.

Medusa drops to her knees. She does not need to know this woman's name. She recognizes her own hair, eyes, skin. "Mama?" Her voice cracks.

"I am in her form, yes. But I am not your mother."

Medusa takes heaving breaths, calming herself. "What memory do you have to show me?"

The scene that unfolds before them is blurry, but Medusa can make out herself as a very small child, clinging to her mother's skirt, along with two little girls who look so much alike that they must be sisters—triplets?

"Do I have sisters?" A sob bubbles up to the surface. Cool

scales brush against her cheek, and Medusa leans into the contact from her serpent.

Fake Rhea nods. "Indeed. Kore and Della."

"Where are they?" Medusa holds her breath, scared to know the answer.

"Watch."

Rhea and her daughters stand in front of a swirling vortex, faintly surrounded by large standing stones. The shadow of someone approaching appears on the ground, but the identity of the stranger is obscured.

Rhea clutches her daughters tightly to her when she sees the new arrival. Words are exchanged between them, but Medusa cannot hear anything they are saying.

"Why can't I hear them?" Medusa asks.

"That is one of the tampered parts of the memory."

Before them, Rhea suddenly shoves her daughters into the vortex, and Medusa cries out in real time, watching as her tiny self breaks free from her sisters and runs back to cling to her mother.

"Lyra, no! Please go!" Rhea shouts.

"No Mama, I'm not leaving you!" Little Lyra wails.

Medusa watches in horror as the obscured figure jerks her younger self away from Rhea, who drops to her knees.

The stranger opens a giant hole in the ground, and a man is marched into the scene by Zeus.

"Kronos!" Rhea calls from the ground, and he rushes to her side, dropping to his knees.

After another heated exchange that she cannot hear, Medusa must watch her mother and Kronos jump into the pit.

"No!" Medusa cries out.

Fake Rhea turns toward an obviously wrecked Medusa as the image before them fades. "You never knew what became of your parents. Whether you are aware of it or not, you have blamed them for abandoning you your entire life. It clings to your soul no matter how many happy moments come your way. You felt discarded, but do you still hold them responsible?"

Medusa shakes her head as tears silently stream down her face. "Did I fail the test because I blamed them all this time without realizing?"

"That depends."

"On what?" Medusa swallows nervously.

"While we have been on our journey here, your soul has been placed on the scales of Fate by my sisters."

"Your sisters? Are you one of the Fates?" Medusa shoots off the questions rapid-fire, throwing her hands over her mouth to stop herself when Fake Rhea raises an eyebrow.

"Yes, dear. Whom else would you expect to be in charge of something like this? One of those idiot gods?" Fake Rhea scoffs.

"So how long do we have to wait on the outcome?" Medusa asks.

Fake Alec and Fake Psyche return, and Fake Psyche says, "Not long at all. My sisters and I have measured your merit, daughter of Rhea. Are you prepared for your judgement?"

Medusa shifts her weight, "Uh, what happens if I say yes and fail?"

"You will return to your room, and the mirror will go back to being a mirror. The war will be lost. Many innocents will be killed," Fake Alec answers.

"Ah. So low stakes then." Medusa chuckles anxiously.

All three Fates stare back at her with stony expressions, and Medusa purses her lips. "Guess I won't be traveling the realm as a bard."

Fake Alec pinches their brow, turning to Fake Psyche. "So much of her mother in this one."

The statement causes pride to swell along with a cascade of emotion that she resembles her mother in any way.

She is not granted much time to enjoy it, however, as Fake Rhea clears her throat. The illusions dissipate from the sisters, and in their place are three silhouettes of stardust. In turn, they each say their names.

The being of pink stardust steps forward and says, "I am Clotho."

"Lachesis," says the green figure.

Lastly, the purple sister raises a hand. "I am Atropos."

"Thank you," Medusa replies. "It is lovely to know your names and see your true forms."

"The honor is ours," Clotho says softly. "We have been waiting for a very long time for the ouroboros to be activated by a daughter of Rhea."

"This curse has been hard, and you have suffered greatly at the hands of others," Lachesis says. "Would you like to be relieved of your serpentine burden? You can look like your mother again."

Is this what I want? How many times have I stared in my reflection, desperately wishing for my long red hair, and soft skin devoid of scales?

The cool touch of a serpent brushes against her cheek once more, and it reminds Medusa of each time she has killed because of the deadly gaze of her snakes. But they were in self-defense. Every single one of those people wished her harm, and for what? Because a god got his ego bruised?

She raises her hand to her cheek and smiles as a serpent coils around her fingers. They saved her life countless times. While Poseidon may have intended for this to be a curse, Medusa has grown to appreciate her serpents.

They are part of her. So much so that Psyche can't separate them from Medusa's soul.

"No." Medusa steadies her voice. "Thank you for the kind offer, but that won't be necessary. Please tell me how to help the Allegiance."

"The realm is ready to know the truth. It is time for the tides of change to shift and for the oppressed to rise up against the Pantheon," Atropos says, their tone stressing the seriousness of their statement.

"Your soul has been weighed and judged. We find you to be a more than worthy wielder of the power that lurks in your veins. It cannot be fully yours just yet, but you will not have to wait long," Clotho adds.

An energy surges inside of Medusa, and it feels like the final lock holding her back from mastering her serpents fully finally shatters and breaks away. She can completely sense each and every one of them distinctly.

They feel strong—strong enough to take on a god.

"Why me?" Medusa asks. It is one of the parts of this that does not make sense to her.

"The day you were taken from your mother and father made the world wrong." Lachesis's tone is sober as they continue, "That was the day the balance of the scales was skewed. A daughter of Rhea was necessary to undo the curse, and you are the only daughter of Rhea in this realm."

Medusa shakes her head. "No, I have sisters. You saw them."

Clotho nods and responds, "But they are not in *this* realm."

Blinking back the confusion, Medusa asks, "What do you mean? This is the only realm. Don't you think we would know of others if they existed?"

Lachesis laughs. "Obviously not, because there are, and you don't."

The world feels like it is spinning, and Medusa wishes there was something in the darkness to hold on to to steady herself.

"How do we get to the other realms?" Medusa asks after taking a deep breath.

"Watch," Clotho says, pointing back to the void before them.

When an image appears, this time it is Medusa sitting in her room in the Under Temple with the mirror in her hand. She steps forward, squinting to get a better look at the mirror's reflection.

Inside the mirror, images flash at lightning speed. Glances of worlds flit into view and disappear just as quickly: columns and wisteria, castles and vines, a mind-boggling world clearly in the future, world after world.

The images finally slow, and she watches herself in the scene as she leaves the room and finds an ornate box. It is made of mixed metals and covered in swirls and gems, and vines that wrap all the way around the box keeping it closed. There is an open circular space on the top of the box, and she intently observes as the mirror is placed in the opening and turned clockwise until it makes a series of clicks.

The scene fades once more, and Medusa gapes at the Fates. "That's it? Where do I find that box? Does *it* open the other worlds?" she fires off questions.

Clotho chuckles. "So inquisitive, but I would expect no less. Your companions will know where to seek the box. As for the rest, it will make sense when it is time."

Medusa grunts in frustration and is ready to tear into the Fates, but before she can they are already fading, their stardust twinkling out. Blinking, she opens her eyes and finds herself back in her room, being shaken awake by Psyche—actual Psyche.

"I have to tell you everything," Medusa blurts.

45

HESTIA

The chaos and cacophony of the deconstruction of the Under Temple has been a persistent nuisance, and Hestia massages her throbbing temples.

With all thirteen symbols accounted for, Hades instructed that the stones containing the symbols be extracted from the surrounding rock and architecture. Hestia is skeptical of his plans to reconstruct the circles of standing stones in the diagrams, but it certainly cannot hurt to try.

Even in the sanctity of the library, the noise is continuous, but Hestia trudges on. She *knows* she has seen the box Medusa described. Was it in a book?

It sounds similar to one she has seen in Aphrodite's possession but not exactly the same. If only Aphrodite had not rushed back to Olympus, but she is at least grateful to know that her former friend is now an oathed member of the Allegiance.

Having Aphrodite deeply entrenched in Pantheon business will be an unbelievably advantage for the rebels—as long as she doesn't double cross them, that is. With how easily Nicodemus managed to evade his oath, Hestia cannot help but worry this will all backfire on them.

The library bustles with activity as others help Hestia research the box. Medusa sketched a crude drawing of her memory of it, but they have not seen her for a while now.

Hestia tries to stamp down her irritation when Epiphany comes whisking up the aisle, but she cannot help but roll her eyes when she sees the Muse is reading a children's book, for Fates' sake.

"Epiphany, dear, your time might be more useful going over the history texts," Hestia says, trying to keep her voice level.

The Muse laughs brightly. "But then how would I have found this?" Epiphany presents the open book to Hestia.

Reading the title of the fable out loud, Hestia exclaims, "Pandora's Box! Epiphany, you're a genius!"

"You're welcome!" Epiphany calls out cheerfully as she is already walking away.

Hestia scans the page, muttering out loud to herself. Of course! Countless fables for children are rooted in history and facts. It is truly shocking that she never considered that during all her research.

But what does a story about not letting curiosity get the best of you have to do with Medusa? Nobody really even knows if Pandora is or was a real person. At this point, her legitimacy is as much debated as her merit.

"Everyone, meet me at the center tables!" Hestia calls out and walks briskly to the spot, book of fables in hand.

Hestia is surprised Hades was assisting in the research, but it should not have been unexpected at this point. Since arriving in the Underworld, she has constantly been impressed by how hands-on the King of the Dead is.

The row of shocked faces when Hestia tells the group about Pandora would be humorous if the state of the world were not so precariously hinging on a fable.

Hades is the only person who does not look surprised. He merely sighs, "I wish we did not have to disturb her, but we do not need to look far for Pandora. Getting her box from her, however, might prove to be more difficult."

"Just tell her how important it is," Alec says, growing impatient.

Hestia glances Alec's direction, and he greets her with a tight smile. There has been no time to talk to him about their relationship and things with Hera lately. Allegiance missions have increased in frequency, and Alec is away more than he is here.

Hestia tries not to take it personally. The Allegiance is all that matters right now. She can only hope he knows she loves him, and she prays to the Fates that they get a moment to talk soon.

Shaking his head, Hades says, "It's not that simple. She has been driven mad for centuries. I do not know what was actually placed inside that box, or by whom, they torment her endlessly to keep its secret contained. Despite the fable's declaration otherwise, it has never been opened. Hestia, Cassandra, come with Persephone and me.

"Perhaps if only the three of us go and speak with her, it will not be as intimidating, and we will have some luck. This problem will require patience, not brute force."

Hestia glances around the cozy, dimly lit room. They are in a wing of the Under Temple she has not seen before, one reserved for Hades's personal one. On the walk over, he explained to her how he found Pandora centuries ago and someone got her here safely. He, and eventually Persephone, have been caring for her ever since.

"No. No. No. No. I can't. No. No. No. No!" Pandora shrieks, covering her ears and squeezing her eyes shut as she sits in a dark corner of the room on a lush velvet chaise. Hestia examines the frail being before her. She was likely otherworldly beautiful at one point, but now she is a husk. Her long, straight white hair looks so much like Arachne's, except Pandora's is stringy and lifeless. Her skin stretches over her body like it is two sizes too small for even her dainty frame. Hestia imagines that when healthy, her complexion is a rich olive, not the pasty ash-like flaxen skin she sees now.

"Who gave you the box, sweetheart?" Persephone asks, her voice sweet like honey, warm and inviting.

"No. No. Please. No. She will kill me," Pandora whispers the last words, and Hestia's heart breaks for her.

Hades raises his brows and looks at Persephone. He mutters to them, "That's more than she has ever said before."

Persephone nods, and places her arm on his bicep.

Cassandra clears her throat softly, and Pandora looks up at Cass for the first time. She tilts her head and asks, "Who are you?" Her voice is so strained it sounds like a whisper.

Is it merely from disuse, or is there that much fear in her right now?

"I am Cassandra. I see your pain and know it well. The Fates would like to speak to you through me. Will you allow them a message?" Cass asks gently.

Pandora looks to Hades, uncertain. He nods, his lips pressed together.

"Oh. Alright," Pandora says meekly, giving in.

Hestia is familiar with Cass's appearance when the Fates speak through her by now, but it still makes her skin pebble when her friend's eyes go white and her voice is no longer her own. "Pandora. You have been deceived. It is time for your story to be righted, as well as the realm's. It is time to relinquish the box."

"No! I cannot!" Pandora cries out as if she has been struck. Who did this to her?

"Do you doubt us, child?" the Fates ask, and Cass tilts her head.

"No!" Pandora shakes her head aggressively as tears run down her face.

"Do you wish to be free of your torment?"

"Yes. Please!" Pandora wails.

"Give them the box, child."

Pandora is despondent as she hands the box over to Hades. As soon as it is out of her possession, she slumps in exhaustion, passing out. He catches her quickly and gently places her in her bed.

"Let's get everyone together and crack this thing open, shall we?" Hades asks.

"My love, are you angry with me?" Hestia asks Alec once they are finally alone in her quarters.

Alec tilts his head. "Why would I be angry with you? I know the Allegiance has taken up my time, but it has nothing to do with you," he assures her.

His large hand cups Hestia's cheek, and embers of hope spark within her heart.

"You aren't upset about... my feelings for Hera?" Hestia picks at the fabric of her dress, avoiding his gaze while she awaits his answer.

He chuckles. "You think I couldn't tell? I have known the entire time you were searching for her so earnestly. You love her."

"That doesn't bother you?"

"You said you love me, right?" His voice is soft.

"Yes."

"Then why would it?"

Hestia lifts her head and looks at him. His steely gray eyes burn with the same love and devotion she always finds there, and the knot that was twisting in her stomach loosens.

46

MEDUSA

The warm sun is a welcome relief from the cold water as Medusa and the hippocamp splash to the surface. Guilt tugs at her over going against the wishes of Psyche and Cadmus, but rage and newfound power course through her veins with one purpose—to make Poseidon pay for everything he has done to her.

As she climbs onto the rocks of the small island, she leans down to the hippocamp, scratching the underside of her chin, and says, "Go tell him where to find me."

Sea mist stings Medusa's eyes as she watches the hippocamp disappear below the surface of the water.

Turning, she makes her way to a large flat rock and lays down, letting the warm rays of the sun dry her damp skin and clothing. She is uncertain how long it will take for him to reach her, so Medusa gets comfortable to prepare for the wait.

Her serpents slither happily in the sunshine, grateful to no longer be confined to the hood; Medusa did not even bring it with her.

She will have to tell the others about her new powers, but in the wake of fully gaining control over her serpents, the only though she could think of was her revenge. Medusa does not know what this strength and new abilities mean, but one thing is clear—there is more to her story than she has been told.

Will she ever truly know her past? Her history? Or will it merely be one lie after another? Do the people telling the lies even know that they *are* lies? Questions swirl in her mind like a cyclone.

Her eyelids are drooping and heavy as she watches the seagulls flying overhead, and she is close to nodding off when she hears a ship approaching. Jerking up to a sitting position, Medusa puts her hand over her eyes to block the sun as she scans the vast sea before her.

Her serpents hiss when she spots a small ship on the horizon. She smirks at his arrogance.

He assumed I will not be much trouble and did not bring his Legion as backup.

As the ship nears, Medusa sees the meager crew covering their eyes when they see that their target is the infamous gorgon.

When the boat is alongside the rocks, Medusa calls out, "As long as none of you leave the ship, aside from Poseidon, you shall not be harmed. Set one foot on this island to help your god, and I swear to the Fates one of my serpents will see it and it will be the last step you make before landing in Tartarus."

They nod frantically, but none of them brave uncovering their eyes.

Poseidon walks out onto the deck, and the crew members drop to their knees, bowing to him as if he is worthy of the gesture. A snarl curls on Medusa's lip, and Poseidon's monstrous smile that meets her is almost enough to waver her courage, but her new power will have none of that.

"Hello, Poseidon. Come to rein me in, have you?" Medusa asks with a playful lilt to her voice that does little to mask her fury.

Stepping onto the rocks, Poseidon says, "It is long past due, don't you think?"

Shrugging her shoulders, she bolsters her nerve. "I would say that is a matter of opinion, but it matters not. Only one of us will be leaving this little island—and it will not be you, in case that wasn't obvious."

He scoffs, and Medusa looks around the little island.

She smirks. "This seems like a pitiful place for a god to die, but I guess it'll have to do."

The amusement on his face falters, and the simmering anger underneath pokes out. "You need to learn your place. How dare you speak to a god with such insolence?"

"Your immortality is not reason alone to grant you respect. That is something that must be earned, mortal or immortal, and you have not come close to earning it."

He grunts an objection, but Medusa continues, "You cast harm and pain about wherever you go. You do not recognize the sanctity of life. Your expansive lifespan has made you forget, but I will make you remember, and it will be the last thing on your mind as the life leaves your body. Mark my words."

Shouting from the ship catches Medusa's attention, as well as the crew scrambling to get below deck. She turns around to see an enormous wave building behind her.

Using the distraction, Poseidon grabs Medusa by the neck and pulls her to the ground, kneeling over her as his face reddens with anger.

The wave comes crashing down on them, and Poseidon holds her still as the forceful waters plunge over her before she has a chance to suck in a large breath. Her chest burns as it begs for any scrap of air it can cling to. In an instant, mentally Medusa is back in the Sea Temple, as the Twins repeatedly bring her to the brink of drowning, only sparing her at the last second.

Instead of triggering her trauma, this time it is Medusa's power that responds to the memory. The injustices play in her mind as if she is watching it before her eyes.

She grunts in effort as she brings her knee up to Poseidon's groin as he leans over her. Her new strength ensures that when it connects, it sends him doubling over in pain. Medusa shoves him off her, a laugh bubbling up in her chest. A god is on the ground before her, and all she had to do was kick his cock. He may be immortal, but in this regard, he is no different from a mortal man.

While he is on the ground, Medusa pulls his sword from the scabbard, leveling it at him with a satisfied smile.

He is still clutching his groin, and Medusa raises the sword in the air over his neck. She cannot believe it was *this* easy.

She brings the sword down, and it whooshes through the air. Poseidon twists and raises a hand to stop the blade from beheading him, and he yells out in pain as it connects with his palm, cutting into his leather glove and slicing a deep gash.

"You fucking bitch," he growls as blood runs down his arm and Medusa pulls the sword back to her.

"Better to be a bitch than a god with no soul," Medusa laughs, even though it burns her throat.

Swinging in a circular motion, Medusa attempts to strike him again, but this time he raises his arm instead of his hand and it glances off of his armor. The reverberation of the blade makes Medusa's arms shake, and Poseidon rears back, bringing his fist to her face.

Stars explode as his blow lands on her cheekbone. Did she feel it crack?

The force knocks her from her feet, and Medusa grabs one of the rocks beneath her hands. She stands quickly, slamming the rock into his ear hard enough for blood to erupt from the spot.

Her cheek swells, and the upper part of it is visible in her periphery. Medusa squints against the pain, but watching Poseidon clutch his ear as blood gushes takes some of the sting out of it.

When he looks at her again, his face is red with rage. He raises his arms to his sides, and the winds pick up, gaining speed until they rival the force of a hurricane. Medusa clings to a boulder as trees uproot and smaller rocks fly into the air.

Poseidon takes forceful steps to close the distance between them, having to fight against the gale himself. When he reaches her, his hands encircle her throat, and Medusa gasps as it gets harder and harder to breathe.

A small rock hurtling through the air slams into Medusa's temple, and her knees go weak as she curses against the pain.

Looking into Poseidon's bloody face, she is delighted to see the assumed victory painted across his expression—just as planned.

His crimson smile drips with blood as he says, "It sure is a shame those serpents of yours work on everyone but me." He chuckles, and she lets him sit in the assumption for a moment longer despite the lightheadedness that threatens to overtake her.

"Sometimes, what we don't know is the source of our demise," Medusa croaks out against the strain of his fingers.

His brow furrows. Digging deep into the well of power that now resides in her soul, Medusa looks into Poseidon's eyes and with every ounce of her being expresses her will to her serpents.

Poseidon's fingertips turn to stone, and he pulls his hands away, staring at them in horror as the petrification slowly creeps its way up his his arms.

Medusa's smile is victorious as she walks over to Poseidon. "In these last seconds of your pathetic use of a life, I want you to remember every person you killed, harmed, and put under your heel just because you could. This is for them, and the days of callous, worthless gods like you are numbered. Even if I have to turn every one of them to stone myself."

47

ARACHNE

*E*verything is numb as Arachne walks aimlessly through the corridors. The others have moved on and resumed their research and planning, but she cannot. All she can think about is Cyril's last moments.

Did he suffer? Was it quick? Does he wish she was there with him to say goodbye? The last thought is somewhat selfish, but she allows herself to feel it anyway.

The hallways thin and narrow. Before too long, Arachne finds herself in the catacombs of the Under Temple. The air here feels ancient and powerful, and she breathes it in deeply. Spiderwebs drape across the corners and hang from sconces, the firelight illuminating their opalescent quality.

The presence of the webs brings Arachne back to Corcyra in a heartbeat.

Her path stops abruptly as this tunnel dead ends, and Arachne's shoulders slump. She does not want to turn around and walk back the way she came, but there is nothing left for her down here.

A breeze blows through, and Arachne freezes in place. How did wind reach her all the way down here?

An iridescent green spider skitters out from a large crack in the wall. Depending on how the torch light hits it, flecks of blues, pinks, and purples shine along its body.

Arachne puts out her hand and lets the palm-sized spider crawl onto it. She raises her arm and gazes into the many eyes of the creature.

"Hey there," Arachne says in wonder, then frowns. "This is absurd. Is this what Hera felt like when she was talking to me?" She continues, "Well, if it is madness, so be it. I used to be like you, you know?"

The spider tilts its head in question, and Arachne goes on.

"I was cursed by the petty, vengeful goddess Athena to be a spider. I wasn't a vibrant green like you, though. My body was the color of the most radiant pearl, with blush pinks and oranges tinging the edges in the sunlight."

Arachne shakes her head,

"I hated myself then. But perhaps I was too impulsive in my hate. Perhaps if my spidery state were not the result of a curse, I might have had a chance to appreciate it more," she muses sadly.

A tear runs a trail down Arachne's cheek, and she wipes it away with her shoulder.

"All I wanted was to be off that island. Then I met Cyril and thought the universe was finally giving me a break. How could the Fates rip him away from me so cruelly? Is this what everyone in the realm goes through day in and day out?

"I sometimes wish I still had my webs and strength. Without them, I am ill equipped to exact the justice that my soul burns for. I want to make all of them pay for everything they have done to Olympus."

The spider looks at Arachne, as if judging her. Then, without warning, it bites her, pincers digging into her delicate flesh.

"Ow!" She exclaims, and the spider drops to the ground and scrambles away.

The bite is red and swollen, and Arachne can feel it throbbing.

Great.

Tearing off a small strip of cloth from her robes, Arachne begins the long trek back to the upper levels of the temple to go see a healer.

APHRODITE

When Aphrodite walks into Circe's lair, she is fuming and ready for blood. How dare that witch not tell her this would be the outcome? How could she not put a stop to it?

When Aphrodite lays eyes on Circe, she snaps. "You absolutely fucking bitch! You *knew* and you didn't warn me!"

A large paw strongly swipes at Aphrodite, sending the goddess hurtling to the floor.

"Good girl," Circe says hoarsely to her lioness, walking over and stroking behind her ears as the massive cat purrs.

Aphrodite's eyes shoot daggers at the witch. "You *knew*."

"I did not." Circe puts her hands up innocently. "Truly. But even if I had, that does not mean the Fates would have allowed me to tell you. If you think you are the one steering this chariot, you're as delusional as the gods we now need to unseat."

"So you want to fight the Pantheon, too?" Aphrodite challenges.

"Of course I do," Circe says through gritted teeth. "You are not the only one who has suffered loss at their callous hands."

Aphrodite runs a hand through her pale blonde hair. "We need to figure out which other gods are on our side already, and who we think will join. Another important question—do we trust the rebels?"

Circe nods. "Most of them, yes. But they have a few more rats to root out before we can rely on them."

Raising an eyebrow, Aphrodite asks, "What do you know?"

"So much more than anyone on this Fates forsaken rock realizes."

49

HESTIA

Pandora's box is heavy in Hestia's hands despite the actual lightness of the metals. Can they really be about to open the fabled box of horrors?

"Well, let's open it," Hera says tentatively.

The gathered group glances between each other nervously, standing in the center of the newly erected stone circle. Dust still lingers in the air from the workers cutting into the rock.

Isadora holds up a hand. "No. We should wait for Medusa. I want to be certain we are doing it the way she witnessed in the mirror. We likely only have one shot at this; let's not toss it into Tartarus because we are being impetuous."

"No need to wait!" a voice calls, and Hestia breathes a sigh of relief when Medusa comes running to join them, catching her breath. "I'm here."

The bruise blooming on Medusa's cheekbone catches Hestia by surprise.

Cadmus steps away from the group and places a hand on her shoulder. Hestia can barely hear him as he leans in to ask, "Where were you?"

Medusa shakes her head and waves him off. "That is not important right now. We can discuss it after."

Cadmus nods and steps aside, but the tight line of his lips shows his frustration.

Medusa's voice is hushed and reverent. "This is really it? Pandora's box?"

"Isn't it neat?" Dionysus asks excitedly, and Hera shoots him a scolding look that makes Hestia chuckle silently.

Isadora extends a hand to Medusa, offering her the Ouroboros and two keys.

Medusa plucks the first key from Isa's hand and carefully inserts it into the lock on the left side of the box, letting go when it clicks into place. She repeats the steps with the other key on the right.

Hestia sucks in a breath when Medusa grabs the mirror. The tension in the air is palpable, but no one says a word as she delicately places it in the open circular space on the top of the box, closing her eyes and turning it clockwise until it clicks into place like the two keys.

Everyone collectively holds their breath as Medusa lifts the lid. The ground rumbles and shakes, causing the crowd to move away from the circle of large stones that could crush any of them if it toppled over.

Alec's strong arm encircles Hestia's waist as he helps to get her clear of any falling rock and debris.

Suddenly, he cries out and drops to his knees, clutching his neck.

Hestia is frantic. "Alec! What is wrong?" she gasps.

Cassandra and Cadmus also fall to the ground in pain. Cadmus holds his inner right thigh while Cassandra rubs her lower back. Medusa rubs her wrist but does not appear to be in the same level of agony as the others.

Wait. Hestia remembers that being where Medusa and Alec's birthmarks are. She has never seen whether Cass or Cadmus have one, but she is willing to bet they do.

The space fills with a blinding light, and Hestia hides her eyes in the crook of her arm. When it dissipates, she feels disoriented.

Memories that were not there before come flooding in, too many to keep track of.

Everything comes back, the *real* history of Olympus. Hestia's breath falters as she tries to reconcile the new flood of memories with her operating knowledge of the realm. It is staggering.

The Titans. How could everyone simply forget they existed? Their faces flash in her mind, and Hestia recognizes all of them.

She turns to look at Alec with awe and reverence. Her voice is swimming with admiration when she says to him, "Welcome back, Iapetus."

His expression is one of disbelief, but he pulls Hestia into a tight hug.

Remembering the others, Hestia turns to check on Cassandra and Cadmus, but the ground rumbles again.

"Oh no. What now?" Isadora asks.

The quake is much stronger this time, and Hestia genuinely worries that the ground is going to open up and swallow them whole. After several seconds of clutching to each other for stability, it eases off into gentle aftershocks.

As the chaos settles, Cassandra shouts, "Look!" She is pointing into the stone circle, and everyone turns to follow her direction.

In the middle of the circle, covered in dust, an unconscious figure is splayed out on the ground. Her raven locks halo around her. Her dress is tattered but does not look like anything made by any tailor found in Olympus, and Hestia cocks her head in confusion.

The mysterious woman does not appear to be injured, but she has yet to wake up.

"Well, I'm going to say it," Dio speaks up. "What the fuck?"

50

MEDUSA

Medusa steps out into the fresh air and walks to the harbor. She had walked away from the confusion of the group while their focus was on getting the mystery woman set up with Psyche in the medical ward. Now she sits on the edge of the pier with her legs dangling in the water, her favorite spot to clear her mind.

There will be so much to process, and Medusa is not ready for that yet. She has a new history of Olympus to learn.

Cadmus being a titan was a shock, but it does not come as a surprise to her. She always sensed there was more to him beneath the surface, and she could not have been more correct.

What does Alec's titan status mean for her? If he is her uncle, is her father, Kronos, was also a titan? For the others, they may have gained bright new insight, but for Medusa more questions sprout from this information than answers.

Between this and her confrontation with Poseidon, Medusa needs to step away and breathe before she can face this mind-boggling new world. The one thing she did notice, however, is that the Titans do not seem to have regained any powers they might possess, and that is definitely a curiosity.

237

Footsteps sound behind her, and she turns to find Cadmus. All she wanted was a few minutes to peacefully watch the ships come and go before having to deal with any of this.

"Where did you go?" Cadmus asks curiously.

"Does it matter? There is too much going on right now for you to be so focused on my comings and goings." She doesn't want to be cruel to him, but every second without the space she needs makes her snippy and on edge.

"Of course it matters. What if something happened to you and none of us were there to help you?" He runs a hand through his curls in frustration.

"I am more than capable of taking care of myself." How can he still think her so weak?

"I know you are." Some of the frustration leaves his tone. "But it is difficult when you love someone, and we are at war. Can you not see the difference?"

Medusa bites the inside of her cheek, casting her gaze down to her feet. "I suppose."

"So, talk to me," he says gently.

At the desperate look in his eyes, she says, "You are going to be angry with me. Maybe I am not ready to have that fight right now."

He furrows his brow in confusion, but then his eyes go wide with understanding. "You didn't."

Medusa's cheeks burn. "I needed to do it to move on. It was eating away at me. I want to heal. I cannot do that if he still lurks in the shadows, always waiting to find me. I don't want to spend my entire existence looking over my shoulder for him."

"You could have been killed!" he shouts.

"Don't you understand? I felt like I already had been!" Frustration claws at her. How can he not see her point? Deflated, she adds, "It doesn't matter, though. What's done is done."

Cadmus's face fills with shock. "He's dead. Seriously?"

Medusa nods, and Cadmus runs his hands through his hair.

"I can't say I'm not glad for there to be one less Pantheon asshole, but you are also not seeing my side of this. If the outcome were reversed, what do you think that would do to me? To Psyche? Alec?" He puts his hands on Medusa's shoulders, but she shrugs them off.

"I know. It was not a decision I made lightly…"

"It's not one you should have been making alone."

"But," Medusa continues stiffly, "what's done is done."

With a nod, Cadmus seems content to drop it, but everything about his demeanor adds a *for now* to the end of that statement.

"Am I interrupting anything?" a jovial voice asks.

Medusa startles and finds Hermes standing next to them.

"We didn't hear you approach," Medusa says.

Hermes chuckles and points to his shoes. "They are not as good as the pair you still have of mine—I will want those back by the way—but they get the job done."

"What are you doing here?" Cadmus asks.

Hermes pulls a sealed scroll from inside of his robes. "I'm afraid this is an official declaration of war from the Pantheon."

Medusa takes the message from Hermes. "Do they know where we are?"

Hermes shakes his head. "No. With my role as Messenger of Olympus, I can always find my recipient."

"Well, if you know where we are, I imagine they will know soon, no?" Medusa raises an eyebrow.

"Excellent question. I, and some of the other gods, have been sitting back and watching, assessing. We abhor the atrocious behavior of the other members of the Pantheon. Now that war has been declared, we are prepared to stand with you."

"How many of you does that include?" Medusa does not dare to be hopeful, but she can't fight the glimmer rising in her chest with Hermes's words.

"I will return to you with names. Deliver this message to Hades and the others."

Medusa and Cadmus nod, exchanging nervous glances.

They watch Hermes take to the sky and leave.

Cadmus turns to Medusa and says, "We have a war to strategize."

BONUS SCENES

Prior to release of this book, there was a pre-order reward campaign. There were enough pre-orders to unlock three additional bonus scenes! Thank you so much!

I have put those scenes here at the end of the book as opposed to sending them out through BookFunnel. I felt like this was the best way for the most people to actually see the content they earned with the pre-orders.

In the next few pages, please find the following:

Bonus Icarus Scene

Bonus Aphrodite Scene

Bonus SPICY Hestia Scene

BONUS ICARUS SCENE

Icarus knows what she is doing will destroy Aphrodite, but this is too important.

Her hands shake as she secures the tie at the end of her braid.

Amara whinnies and nips at her shoulder. Through blurry eyes, she takes a final look at her steed. Tears stream from her face down onto Amara's, creating dark rivulets in the mare's fur. "I know you must feel like I'm abandoning you, but you're in good hands here. I have to do what's right."

Avoiding everyone in the Allegiance as she makes her way to the cavern, Icarus sends a prayer up to the Fates that this is actually her destiny.

Please don't let this be for nothing.

She drops her cloak on the stone floor as her feet leave the bottom step. The star shines brightly, casting the entire cavern in a harsh light. Icarus stares at it for a minute, in awe of the draw she feels.

The golden feathers of her wings unfurl and she takes a steadying breath.

This shall not break me.

She flaps her wings and lifts off the ground, climbing higher and higher toward the star. The closer she gets, the more she can feel the heat emanating from the orb. There is still so far to go but in her peripheral, feathers comes loose from her wings, drifting the ground which is farther than she realized.

Grunting through the effort, she grits her teeth and climbs.

This shall not break me.

The temperature goes from mildly warm to scorching as she continues her ascent. Her goal is still so far away and her energy wanes, making her worry she will not be able to see this task through.

If I run out of steam, the fall will kill me and this will have been in vain.

This shall not break me.

Thinking of her family in Thessaly, the goddess who holds her heart, and the mortals who will die if she fails, Icarus musters the last of her strength for a final push.

Feathers fall from her wings in clusters as the heat sears her skin.

Just a bit farther.

She extends her fingertips, screaming from the pain caused by her proximity to the star.

Peace washes over her as her fingers close around a metal object. The star explodes into a supernova of light, and Icarus falls with one final thought.

This shall not break me.

BONUS APHRODITE SCENE

Aphrodite's silvery reflection stares back at her in the mirror. The door clicks closed as Hades leaves the room. He gave little instruction on what she is to do, so she waits.

His study is vast, with rows of shelves lining the walls, each one filled with books.

The pain of losing Icarus is too much to bear. She should just leave.

As Aphrodite turns to give up on this preposterous task, the reflection blurs and there she is. *Icarus.*

She looks exactly the same, just less corporeal. Sadness envelops Aphrodite as she takes in the lack of radiance, no longer sunshine personified.

"Aphrodite!" Her eyes light up, but the sparkle that used to rival the heavens is missing. "How is this possible?"

With a shrug of her shoulders, Aphrodite says, "I'm not sure, but I'm so glad to see you! Where are you? Asphodel? Elysian?"

Icarus shakes her head, "You know I can't answer that."

Despite the dullness to Icarus's once bursting with life demeanor, Aphrodite's heart still soars at the sight of her lover.

"I never had the chance to ask you," Icarus toys with her braid. "How many lives do I have left?"

Her heart falls at that questions.

This is it. The moment Icarus realizes she will hate me for eternity.

"This was your last one. There won't be another life cycle. I'm so sorry." Aphrodite wishes she could reach out and hold Icarus. Would this blow be so bad if they could at least be in each other's arms?

"What?" Icarus blinks and betrayal flashes in her eyes. "How could you not tell me?"

"I didn't want it to taint our time together. It was the wrong choice, I know." A tear streams down Aphrodite's cheek.

Icarus shakes her head. "It doesn't matter. I made my sacrifice knowing that it might be my final life. I would still make the same choice with that knowledge. You have to know the Pantheon is wrong."

Her cheeks burn as shame floods her veins. "It was too easy to get lost in the power in the centuries I had to spend without you. I tried anything and everything to numb the pain and I worry that it just numbed *me* instead."

"What are you going to do about it, then? Please don't let my sacrifice have been for nothing. If you really love me, truly, you will do what's right. Whether I am by your side or not."

It is easy for Aphrodite to agree with her, as she had already reached this conclusion on her own. She nods as the saltiness of her tears stings her cold skin.

"I have to go, time's up, my love." Icarus says.

"I'm going to fix this. I'll make it right." Aphrodite insists before Icarus can go.

"Me or the war?" Icarus asks. She fades away, the reflection in the mirror returning to Aphrodite's own once more, before she can answer.

"Everything." Aphrodite answers softly. She promptly exits the room where she finds Hades waiting outside in the corridor.

"Good. You're here. I know you rebels have an oath that you take —don't ask me how I know. I'm taking your oath and joining you."

Hades furrows his brow in confusion, but he simply says, "We would be fortunate to have you on our side."

BONUS SPICY HESTIA SCENE

Hestia sighs into Hera's kiss as they walk over to the bed where Alec and Dionysus wait for them. They both sit at the head of the bed, leaning back against the headboard. The soft glow of the candles on the deep purple bedding give the appearance that the only thing in this room is the four of them.

She cannot believe Hera suggested this but everything about it feels natural.

Breaking their kiss, Hera climbs into Dio's lap, while Hestia does the same to Alec. The two men are close enough together that is easy for Hera to pull Hestia back into a kiss. Alec's hands roam over her body as she slowly rocks her hips over his hardness.

Hera's tongues intertwines with Hestia's and the sweetness of her taste is intoxicating. Dio unclasps the broach holding Hera's dress together and the fabric falls, pooling around her waist.

Without an ounce of hesitation, as Alec's thumb rolls over her clit through her skirts, Hestia trails her lips down, taking Hera's large perky nipple into her mouth. Hera groans and digs her fingers into Hestia's hair.

When she looks back at Alec and Dionysus, Hestia finds a hunger in their gazes that thrills her.

She straightens, pulling her dress up over her head, the cool air on her skin leaving a trail of goosebumps in its wake.

"Fates, Hestia, you are so beautiful." Hera's voice is filled with an awe that Hestia has never heard from her friend.

And it's directed at me?

Desire and warmth spread through Hestia's body, all the way to her toes. "If I had known you looked like that beneath your dress, I might have worked up the nerve to leave the library and join you in your bed decades ago."

Alec sits up and slides his trousers off, and Dionysus does the same. Hera caresses the soft honey hair on his chest as she lifts up slightly for him to guide his erection inside her.

Hestia watches as it disappears inside of Hera, her own nipples growing harder at the sight. She lowers her hand between her legs finding herself dripping wet and Alec already hard as stone for her.

With a quick motion, he is inside of her and the world spins around her as she slowly slides down his erection.

Hera reaches out, interlacing her fingers with Hestia's. They lock eyes as Hestia whimpers in ecstasy.

"Are you close?" Hera asks her.

Hestia nods, unable to form words.

Hera chuckles and sighs. "Me too."

She leans in and kisses Hestia once more as their collective orgasm builds.

The power the gods who share her bed possess is unmistakable as the room fills with a blissful chaotic energy. Her climax rips through Hestia, setting every cell in her body ablaze with bliss.

Laying in the bed together after, Hestia drifts off to sleep. Her mind floats on a sea of thoughts. She never dreamed of having any kind of relationship with someone as incredible as Alec. But now, she has Hera and Dionysus to share this domesticity with? It shouldn't work, but all she can think about is right it feels.

ACKNOWLEDGMENTS

I always want to thank my family first. Without Shannon and Jess, I wouldn't have the support needed to write not only one book, but multiple. They are the first ones to hear my new ideas, and the first ones to feel my absence when I'm in my writing hole.

Ophelia, there is no part of my writing journey that would be happening without you. Thank you for inspiring me to write and wanting to be my co-author. I think our planned projects are going to be so much fun!

Renae, Taylor, and Shawna thank you for always encouraging me to keep going! Thank you for understanding that sometimes I disappear for weeks haha.

Tay and Lacey, thank you for always hyping me up and being amongst the first to read my stories and bouncing ideas around with me.

No acknowledgements would be complete without thanking my incredible trio of beta readers. JK, Rikke, and Jan you three are the readers every author dreams of finding. Thank you for loving my stories as much as I do and truly FEELING the worlds that I create. I'll be your Charlie for as long as you'll have me! May every author find their Angels.

I would lastly like to thank my sweet lab, Chloe. Thank you for being the best girl for 12 years. My time with you is almost up, and I'm going to miss you every day.

ABOUT THE AUTHOR

River Bennet is a romantic fantasy writer with a focus on queer Greek Mythology stories.She lives in New England with her partner, teenage daughter, two dogs, and three cats.

From the rural farm where she grew up in Texas, to the bustling city life of Manhattan, and now the serenity of the Berkshire Mountains, River has always had an obsession with mythology, a love of nature and animals, and can often be found savoring a cup of green tea.

www.ingramcontent.com/pod-product-compliance
Lightning Source LLC
Chambersburg PA
CBHW022122310726
48972CB00007B/2148